bignightout

bignightout

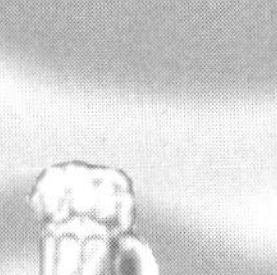

Lorraine Freeney
and Tara McCarthy

St. Martin's Griffin *New York*

Book design by Bonni Leon Berman

Library of Congress Cataloging-in-Publication Data

McCarthy, Tara.

Big night out / Tara McCarthy & Lorraine Freeney.—1st St. Martin's Griffin ed.

p. cm.

ISBN 0-312-19834-5

I. Freeney, Lorraine. II. Title.

PS3563.C25919B54 1999

813'.54—dc21 98-37532

First St. Martin's Griffin Edition: April 1999

10 9 8 7 6 5 4 3 2 1

Acknowledgments

The authors would like to thank their agent, Daniel Greenberg, at James Levine Communications; their editor, Marc Resnick; and their family and friends—especially Carina, Flix, and Steven.

warning!!!

Do not read this book from beginning to end! Contained in these pages are many different adventures you can have in the big, bad city. Along the way, as you read, you will be asked to make decisions. The path you choose may lead to success and jubilation or failure and (sometimes extreme) mortification.

The adventure you have is a result of your choices. You are responsible for your own behavior at every turn. Think hard before making a decision. In this lascivious tale of drunkeness and debauchery, any choice might be your last.

Will you get laid or end up passed out in a bar bathroom? It all depends on you.

Good luck!

prologue

Get your ass out of the bathroom!"

She screams in frustration and kicks the door, takes a swig of the beer she's holding, and debates whether or not to kick the door again. Better not; these are new boots.

Inside, he's assessing his gaze in the mirror, trying to decide whether it appears nonchalant or simply vacant. There's a small cluster of hairs in between his eyebrows that makes him look, close up, like an aspiring Gallagher brother. "Hello, Sadie," he whispers to the mirror. "I'm Dicknik, the Gallagher brother that not even Liam and Noel wanted to hang out with." This will not do. "Where are your tweezers?" he yells.

"Try the cabinet under the sink, in the basket with the hair bleach and the depilatory cream and . . ."

"You can stop there; I found them."

"Will you hurry the fuck up? I've got ten minutes to get out of here."

"Hold on a minute. Jesus Christ." Sharing a bathroom with a woman you're not even sleeping with. That was one of the inner circles of hell Dante lacked the imagination to describe.

Tweezing the hairs out one by one, he realizes his hand is shaking. Can he really be nervous about possibly seeing Sadie again? She's gorgeous, true, but is she that gorgeous? He drops the tweezers, picturing her hair and imagining that deep throaty laugh. The half bag of pretzels he ate two hours ago has just formed itself into a ball and is playing squash with his left ventricle.

"Oh god. She is that gorgeous."

He opens the bathroom door and his roommate rushes past him, playfully nudging him in the ribs. He leans against the door frame and watches as she opens the mirrored cabinet and takes out a lip pencil, slipping it into her bag. "Okay, I'm ready," she says, turning to him. "I *am* ready, aren't I?"

"Except for the beer bottle, which sort of ruins the lines of your outfit, I think so."

"You look good, too." She nods. "That raw red patch of skin over your nose is very in, very now."

"Where are you going anyway? Personally, I'm hoping to crash a party I'm not invited to."

"Funny, me too!" She laughs. "Well, that's not the first destination, but it's where I have to end up," she says, putting her beer down to spritz a little perfume on her wrists.

"Because of Mark?"

"Because of Mark. He'll be there, and with some deft planning, a little cunning, and the careful application of a few stiff drinks so I can build up my courage, so will I."

"We think alike."

"God, I have to see him," she groans. "Three months I've been waiting for this party. He just split up with someone. He's single, vulnerable, and very likely to be drunk out of his mind. This is it."

"This, indeed, is the night we've been waiting for," he agrees.

Ten minutes later they're both standing on the street outside their apartment. "Well, first thing I have to do is meet Dave at the Pub. Guess I'll see you later."

"God, I hope not," she says.

"Me too. You going over to Suzy's house?"

"Yeah, after that we'll see what happens. Good luck."

To go to Suzy's house, turn to page 6.

To go to the Pub, turn to page 3.

big night out 3

The Pub, a small divey bar you adore mostly for its proximity, is a short walk from your apartment, and Dave isn't there yet; there's not really anybody there yet, actually. Just a few of the neighborhood regulars. You take a seat, one that might as well have a Reserved sign on it. You've probably spent more hours sitting on that bar stool than Jewel has practicing that constipated lovelorn look of hers.

"Hey," you say to the bartender, Kate.

"Hey," she replies.

"The usual," you say.

Her mouth spreads into a smug smile. "Let's be clear here. Are you saying you want all nine shots of Jim Beam up front, or are you going to have them one at a time?"

"Just one tonight," you say quite seriously. "I've got big plans."

"Ooooh." Kate grins, reaches for a bottle behind her, and pours your drink. "You mean you're going to throw a Long Island Iced Tea in tonight? A Kamikaze maybe?"

"Very funny," you say, and reach for your wallet. What you don't say: "Tonight, whether I get lucky or not, I will not—repeat not—end up back here getting drunk."

You turn when you hear the door and see Dave coming in. He's wearing his obligatory baseball cap—backward—and you cringe inwardly. Tonight, of all nights, you need to project a manly-men vibe.

"Hey," Dave says, taking a stool beside you.

"Hey," you reply, watching Kate move to the other end of the bar. That tight black dress certainly does her body justice.

Dave nudges you and gestures toward the object of your gaze. "She still playing it really cool?" It starts like this every time.

"She's not 'playing it cool,' Dave. She can't stand you."

"Oh come on! You're not buying this 'I'm too good for you' aloof crap?"

"I sure as hell am." You take a swig of your drink. "I've been on the receiving end of it enough times to recognize the genuine article when I see it. And that"—Kate bends over to retrieve an obscure liqueur, sticking her rather fine butt out in your direction in the process—"is the genuine article."

"Uh-oh." Dave puts his elbows on the bar and ducks his head down so he can adjust his cap. "You're not in a feeling-sorry-for-yourself mood, are you? I'm not going to have to convince you to skip school and then sing in a parade and trash your father's car, am I?" Dave relates everything in his life to a movie plot.

"*Au contraire,* my friend. Tonight, the only person I'm feeling sorry for is the woman who dares to try and resist my charms."

"You might want to send a little pity my way, in that case," Kate cuts in. "What's it going to be, Dave?"

"Sex on the beach." Dave nudges you—he likes to nudge—and smirks. "Oh"—he turns back to Kate—"you mean to *drink*?" He fakes a laugh.

"I know it's hard for you to decide," Kate says, pouring a pint for another customer. "I mean it's not like we have lukewarm Coors Light in a keg in the corner. But I can give you whatever you want in a bright red plastic cup and try to find 'Push It' on the jukebox if it'll make you feel more at home."

"A pint of Bass will do," Dave says. He's visibly humbled—as he usually is by Kate's acerbic wit. Still, he'll give it another shot next time. He always does. "Speaking of keg parties," he says, recovering quickly and turning to you.

You're confused. "I thought we were going to the Lunar Lounge to see your friend's band. I told Mike and some of those guys I'd meet them there for a martini beforehand—like in an hour or so. Mike's invited to a party Sadie's going to be at, and I'm going if it kills me."

"Who are 'some of those guys'? And whose party is it anyway?"

You explain: Mike is going to be out with Lisa, the vivacious blonde he went to school with, and Will and Tracy, who you think are kind of an odd couple. (Tracy is generally a bit of a loudmouth, and Will, who hardly says a word, is basically her yes-man, except he's always disagreeing with her.) Dave knows this. He's met them before. He also likens going out with Mike to *Groundhog Day* because Mike introduces you to whomever he's out with regardless of how many times you may have met them before. The important thing, however, is that Tracy works with both Sadie and the woman having the party—somebody named Kelly. "I'm *going* to that party," you say. Your tone indicates you mean business.

"Calm down. We'll meet them at the Lunar Lounge." Dave takes a hearty gulp of his Bass. "But first, we're going to my college buddy Joe's kegger. We don't have to stay long, I swear. Or I could just meet you at the Lunar later. Hey, that's fun to say—Lunar later, lunar later. . . . Anyway, it's up to you . . ."

To go straight to the Lunar Lounge by yourself, go to page 8.

To go to Joe's keg party with Dave, go to page 16.

If you think you can trick Dave into skipping the keg party, go to page 10.

Suzy lives four blocks away, in a cramped apartment that a real estate agent might euphemistically describe as bijou. The two of you have been friends ever since you moved into the neighborhood and bonded over the faulty dryers in the local Laundromat. She's waiting for you outside her place, smoking a cigarette.

"Just observing the local wildlife." She motions toward the couple arguing very vehemently across the street. "Come on in while I finish getting ready."

You walk into her building and down the stairs to her apartment. "Welcome to my closet," she says, beckoning you inside.

"As always, I love what you've done with the place," you deadpan, stepping gingerly between piles of magazines and newspapers. "The stereo is around here somewhere, isn't it?"

"Over in the corner. Careful with that pizza box, it's an antique."

You choose a CD while she applies her makeup in her minuscule bedroom.

"So," she shouts out over the music, "we want to get to Lindy's party so you can hook up with Mark, right?"

"Yeah," you yell back, "the problem being that we're not invited."

"Actually," she says, coming back into the room and sinking into an armchair, "we have a bigger problem than that. I don't know the address of Lindy's house. My cousin Nick knows, and he's invited, so we can tag along with him, but I'm not sure where he's going to be—and he must be out already because he's not answering the phone."

"So, how do we find Nick?" you ask, steeling yourself to the challenge.

"He usually starts his night in one of two bars. And if he's not there, we're bound to bump into one of his friends who'll know where he is."

"You're sure? I had hoped you might have concocted a more cunning plan than just wandering around hoping we'll bump into him."

"Trust me." She smiles. "Which lipstick should I go with—sluttish red or discreetly natural?"

"Go with your mood."

"Sluttish it is. Okay, I'm all set. Remind me to eat something tonight; I have a craving for Stoli and tonic, and you know what happens when I drink that on an empty stomach."

"If memory serves, there's usually an impressive dry-cleaning bill to deal with the next day."

You leave Suzy's and walk in the direction of the two bars Nick is most likely to be in—the Berlin, a new place that's attempting to be sophisticated, and Sullivan's, which is a little more down-market. Suzy checks her watch. "It's just after eight. Nick'll probably show up at the party around midnight, so we have loads of time to find him."

"Okay, which bar do you think we should check first?"

To go to Sullivan's, turn to page 9.

To go to the Berlin, turn to page 45.

The second you part ways, you realize you forgot to ask Dave for the fifty bucks he owes you. You're counting on having that money tonight, so you make a mental note to remind yourself to ask him for it as soon as he arrives at the Lunar Lounge later. Should have gotten that overdraft feature on your bank account, you big dope.

At the Lunar Lounge, you order a martini and take a seat at the bar. Mike and co. probably won't show for at least twenty minutes. Then you'll either convince them to stay for Dave's friend's band (if Dave even makes it back from the keg party in time) and go to the party with them afterward, or, if Mike's crowd doesn't want to stick around, you'll hightail it out of there with them. You hope Dave shows up with your cash before you have to go. Dave himself—tonight at least—you can take or leave.

Feeling self-conscious about being out alone on a Friday night as the bar starts to fill up, you decide you have to *do* something. The woman sitting next to you is alone, too, so you could strike up a conversation with her to pass the time. She looks a good deal older than you, but the years have been pretty kind to her, and you've always had a fantasy about being with an older woman. Maybe indulging in some harmless flirtation with her will satisfy your curiosity. You spy the pay phone near the door . . .

If you want to check your messages, go to page 19.

If you want to try to strike up a conversation with the woman next to you, turn to page 21.

It's crowded in Sullivan's, but you find a table for two near the back and Suzy orders the drinks, returning from the bar with your usual and a vodka tonic for herself. "I love that bartender." She sighs. "But I can't see Nick anywhere."

"What does he look like?"

"Tall with dark brown, floppy hair; not bad as far as cousins go."

"There's a guy over there with floppy hair." You point.

"Don't you think I'd recognize my own cousin?"

"That depends—aren't you the same Suzy who got in a taxi last weekend and drunkenly gave the driver the address of your mother's house, the one you haven't lived in since the age of twelve?"

She laughs and takes a gulp of her vodka. "Trust me; he's not here. We can just have these and then go check out the other place."

You scan the room, catching the eye of a guy who is drinking alone. He looks away and returns to reading his book.

Suzy turns to see whom you're looking at and then lets out a disgusted snort. "Why do people read in bars on a Friday night? Hey, I dare you to go ask what he's reading."

She sees your hesitation and nudges you in the arm. "Go on! He's kind of cute!"

You look over at him again. She's right; he is kind of cute, at least from this distance, but you're not sure you want to be dragged into one of Suzy's mad schemes right now. At least not while sober.

If you decide to talk to him, turn to page 11.

If you don't, turn to page 50.

"I've got an idea," you say to Dave. "Let's make a bet. I win, we go right to the Lunar Lounge. You win, I'll go to the keg party with you."

"What's the bet?" Dave is still more interested in Kate than he is in any wager, so you use this to your advantage.

"Whoever guesses Kate's bra size correctly wins."

"Oh yeah right!" Dave practically screams. "Like Kate's going to go for *that*! Why don't you just go offer her boyfriend a million dollars for one night with her and see what happens."

You just raise your eyebrows and shrug.

"What? You think she might actually let us guess?" There's no mistaking the hopeful look in Dave's eyes.

"Hey, Kate," you say, and she comes over to you. "Dave and I have a little wager going."

"Let me guess." She straightens a pile of beer mats and feigns a contemplative look. "Whichever one of you stays away from here the longest gets the 'No, Really. I'm Not An Alcoholic' award."

"Very funny," Dave says. The two of you have, in fact, sworn off the Pub before—only to go back the next night. And the next night . . .

"Our bet has something to do with you, actually," you explain. And then you give the specifics. You're prepared at all times to duck a punch.

"Okay," Kate says, rolling her eyes. "Hit me with your best shot."

"Thirty-six C." Dave wastes no time making his call.

You assess the bosom behind the bar. . . .

If you say, "thirty-four B," turn to page 14.

If you say, "thirty-four C," turn to page 13.

What the hell; here goes. I'll get us another while I'm at it." You finish your drink quickly and take the empty glass up to the bar, sidling close to your prey. Here goes.

"Excuse me, I wondered if you could tell me what you're reading?"

He gives you an accusatory glare. "Why?"

Yikes.

"Because my idiot friend over there dared me."

He grins, looks over at Suzy, and waves. He is, you quickly deduce, pretty bombed. Suzy pretends to be fascinated with her empty glass.

"It's a Nick Hornby novel, but you can make up something more impressive for your friend if you want."

"No, that's fine," you say. "I loved *High Fidelity.*"

"Me too. And this one's also pretty good. A friend lent it to me and I'm almost finished. I was going to give it back to him tonight. But if you want, I could lend it to you." He gives you a smile that is 65 percent Heineken. "No strings, really. My name's Bill. I come here a lot; you could meet me next week and give it back then."

Even though the acrid scent of Eau de Desperation is hanging heavily in the air, you take the book, thank him, and agree to be here at the same time next week to return it. Back at your table, you fill Suzy in on what happened, and she applauds your bravery.

"So, he was a little weird, but at least you got a pseudodate out of it. No, wait." She closes her eyes and puts her hands to her temples in mock-psychic pose. "Don't tell me. You don't want a pseudodate, you want Mark. Swami Suzy knows all, tells all." She starts flicking through the book, then jumps up in surprise. "Holy shit!"

"What's up?"

"This is my cousin Nick's book! Look, his name is on the inside page!"

"That guy said he was going to meet up with the person who owns the book later tonight," you remember, turning around to call out to Bill.

Too late; he's already gone.

"He can't have got far; come on." The two of you hurry to the door and spot Bill weaving his way down the street.

You shout his name and he glances back, then waits till you catch up.

"Hey, you're going to meet Nick Zorcik?"

"Yeah. You know him?"

"I'm his cousin, Suzy. Are you going to Lindy's party?"

"Nah, I don't know anything about a party. I was just gonna return the book and have a beer with the Nickster. He said he's gonna be drinking in the Upstairs Lounge for a while tonight."

"Upstairs Lounge?" You glare at Suzy.

"So I got the location wrong. At least we know where he is now, right?" She smiles sweetly at Bill. "Would you mind if we tag along with you? I need to see my cousin tonight."

"Sure thing, babe." Bill makes as if to put his arms around you both, but stops when he sees the look on your faces.

"Hey, no need to get defensive, ladies. Just being friendly."

"Maybe we should take a cab instead," Suzy whispers to you. "Do we really want Lassie here slobbering all over us the whole way there?" Then, "Hey, Bill, do you want to split a taxi?"

"Let's walk. It's only fifteen minutes away, and I'd prefer not to waste good beer money on a taxi," mumbles Bill.

"You do surprise me. Well"—she looks at you—"taxi or Bill?"

If you want to get a taxi, turn to page 15.
If you walk with Bill, turn to page 53.

"As much as I hate to admit it, Dave's right," Kate says.

"Hey," Dave says triumphantly, raising his glass. "You watch enough B movies, you pick these kinds of skills up. Anyway, I believe we have a keg party to go to."

Go to page 16.

"Thirty-four B it is," Kate says.

"No way!" Dave shouts. He hits you in the arm. "But *look* at her!"

Kate walks away, and you think she's out of earshot. "Wonderbra," you say solemnly, raising your drink. "Can spot 'em a mile away."

"Watch your mouth, pinky dick, or you'll never drink in this town again."

You turn, but she's not really mad; she's smiling. You wink at her and turn back to Dave. "The Lunar Lounge awaits." The two of you swiftly finish your drinks, then press on . . . the Lunar Lounge is a short taxi ride away.

The second you enter the place—a dimly lit, long, and narrow bar with a back room venue—Mike pulls you into a circle of people, most of whom you know. He introduces you and Dave to Tracy, Will, and Lisa, and a couple of new people . . .

"Okay," Mike says, with a firm hand on your shoulder. "You ready? Don't think too much, just say the first thing that comes to your mind."

"Anal sex," you say, without blinking.

"No, you idiot." Mike slaps you on the arm. "You have to wait for the question." He turns to his friends. "You believe this guy?"

"Sorry." You shrug.

"So anyway, the question is, what's the stupidest Oasis lyric you can think of? Think fast, come on, what is it?"

If you say, "Slowly walking down the hall, faster than a cannonball," turn to page 32.

If you think it's possible there's another Oasis lyric stupider than that and you want to say it, turn to page 29.

You hail a cab. Bill climbs, unasked, into the front seat and gives the driver the address.

"Nick said he'll be here until nine," he says. Then suddenly, "Hey driver, pull over on this corner for a second! Anton! *Anton!*"

The car pulls over, and a short, greasy-looking guy approaches the passenger's window. Bill leans out and starts gabbing excitedly.

"Anton! What's up? You wanna come to the Upstairs Lounge for a beer?"

"You know I don't drink beer." Anton opens a door to climb in beside Suzy and nods briefly at you both. "But I'll join you for a martini."

Introductions are made. Anton is an art director for a home-decorating magazine, and within thirty seconds he's mentioned that he went to Yale, adores Charles Bukowski, and rarely goes to see a film unless it's European and subtitled.

"You're hearing-impaired?" you ask dryly.

Anton is unbearable. You silently calculate the bodily damage that would be sustained by one pretentious art director falling out of a taxi moving at approximately fifteen miles an hour. Sadly, it doesn't seem worth it.

"We're nearly there," you say, to shut Anton up for a second.

"Let's go to that new place, the Temple, instead," interjects Anton. "I was there last week with my Chinese girlfriend, Lynn. I love Asian women."

"Sorry, we need to find someone at the Upstairs," you say. "He has directions to a party we're going to, that someone called Lindy is throwing."

"Lindy Graham? I heard she was having a party tonight, but her friends are too suburban for my tastes. No offense, of course. Why not have a drink at the Temple first?"

If you and Suzy get out of the taxi to go to the Upstairs Lounge, turn to page 18.

If you stay with Bill and Anton, turn to page 57.

After finishing your drink at the Pub, you go by Dave's place and get his car. Joe lives about twenty minutes outside the city. Loath as you are to leave the thriving metropolis you call home, the idea of seeing some trees and grass is kind of appealing. Maybe it's Sadie bringing on such urges; this is as close as you've ever come to nesting tendencies. Because trees and grass mean houses and houses generally mean families. And up until now the thought of having either one of those things hasn't appealed to you in the slightest. So why is it you're suddenly imagining Sadie's splendid laugh—the sound of promise—echoing through all the rooms of your suburban mansion, her hair blowing in the wind as you drive her home from a night out in the big city? In a car a lot nicer than this piece of shit, it must be said.

After a short drive, Dave parks on a tree-lined suburban street. He walks up to the door of a house not unlike the Bradys' and goes right in. You follow.

"Dave-o!" someone screams immediately. "Go no further!"

Dave stops dead in his tracks and you slam into him, then step back awkwardly. Everyone's looking at the two of you.

"Thou shalt not pass unless thoust doeseth a Jell-O shot."

This is going to be worse than you expected. Not that you've got anything against Jell-O shots right now, not if it'll help you through this. But what's with the medieval English crap? You and Dave do your shots and are welcomed into the party. On the way to the keg, Dave stops short again.

"Holy shit!" he says. "That's Steve Buscemi manning the keg!"

"Yeah." You're dripping with sarcasm. "And over there, look. It's Cameron Diaz. And she's talking to Gwyneth and Winona."

"I'm not shitting you, man." Dave nods toward the keg. "It's him. I swear."

"What would Steve Buscemi be doing at your friend's keg party?"

"I don't know. But that guy's everywhere these days. As a matter of fact, I've got a bone to pick with him. You coming?"

"You've got a *bone to pick* with Steve Buscemi?" You obviously don't know Dave as well as you thought you did.

"Yeah," he says. "You coming?"

If you say, "No way," go to page 24.

If you accompany Dave over to the keg to pick a bone with Steve Buscemi, turn to page 26.

Climbing out of the taxi, you spy the Upstairs Lounge across the street. Woohoo!

"I have a good feeling about this," says Suzy. "He's definitely here. I know it."

You walk in and Suzy gives a little whoop when she sees a floppy-haired guy playing pool. She was right; he's not bad for a cousin. Not bad at all.

You leave them chatting for a moment while you get drinks. It's time you got a little buzz going, so you drink yours pretty quickly and order another before Suzy and Nick are finished. Better remember to take some money out before you go to the party or you're going to be stuck. And maybe you should check your voice mail later.

Then, in the corner, you spy Clara Merton.

Clara, your high-school nemesis. Clara, the girl who stole your first serious boyfriend from under your nose. Clara, who was nicknamed Angel of Doom on account of her knack of always seeing the cloud behind the silver lining. ("You're going to San Francisco on vacation? Aren't you worried about the earthquakes?" "Your grandmother just gave you five hundred dollars? I've heard that old people often start giving away their possessions when they sense they're going to die.") Clara, who spread rumors about everyone, including that completely unfounded one about you and Joey Shipenberg getting caught behind the bicycle shed. You never went anywhere near the bicycle shed with Joey Shipenberg. It was Brian Christiansen behind the chemistry lab.

If you want to talk to her, turn to page 60.
If not, turn to page 20.

You ask the woman next to you if she'll watch your seat for a minute, then you go to the phone. You dial your voice-mail number, punch in your password, and listen to the animated voice. "You have two new messages. To hear—"

You hit 1.

"Hi sweetie. I figured you'd be out—"

You hit 2 to save your roommate's message, and wait for the next one.

"Mike here. Listen, we're not going to make it to the Lunar Lounge, but we should definitely try to catch up at some point. Tracy wanted to go out for dinner since it's her birthday, so we're here at Woody's and we still haven't gotten a table. We'll be here, and then we're stopping at Spinners to meet some other people—Alyssa and Sadie and those guys—then we're going to this party maybe eleven, eleven-thirty. Try to catch up with us somewhere, okay? Later."

You return to your seat and think.

If you want to go straight to Woody's for fear you'll miss them all later, go to page 36.

If you want to wait for Dave at the Lunar Lounge, go to page 41.

You decide to take a break and go to an ATM. The cool air makes you realize just how many drinks you've had, and you're glad to be outside for a while. After taking out fifty dollars, you wander back into the bar, stop at the pay phone, and check your voice mail.

One saved message. You hit 1. It's your old, dear, and crazy friend Peter.

"Hi sweetie. I figured you'd be out, but maybe you'll get this message in time. One of the bands playing Busters tonight fired its rhythm guitarist because of musical differences—basically he was always playing a different rhythm than the rest of the band—and they called and asked me to fill in . . . we go on at ten-fifteen. I know it's short notice, but it'd mean a lot if you could get your ass down there and lend little Pierre some moral support. I'll even let you buy me a drink afterward. Hope to see you later."

You erase the message and go to the bathroom, pondering the situation as you reapply your lipstick. Peter has been your friend for years. In fact, until you developed an interest in Mark, there was always a lingering hope that someday Peter would rethink his whole "women make such great friends!" policy and try going out with one of them, namely you. Though it's a good bet that he doesn't even know you'd be interested.

You join Nick at the bar and check your watch. It's a little after ten now.

"I guess we're going to hang out here for a while," he says. "Or if you want to go somewhere else, we can just meet you at McCormick's around midnight."

If you'd prefer to go see Peter and arrange to meet the others later, turn to page 22.

If you decide to hang out in the Upstairs Lounge, turn to page 63.

You smile at the woman next to you just as she orders her next drink. That's all it takes.

"And another for my friend here," she says to the bartender while looking right at you.

"Thanks," you mutter, unsure of how to proceed. She's crossed her legs to give you a better view of a pair of thin, shapely calves. She's got to be at least forty, but she's still got a great body. Even from this distance you can tell she smells good, too. When she takes an olive from her martini and puts it in her mouth seductively, you feel yourself getting turned on.

"What's a nice-looking boy like you doing out alone on a Friday night?"

You laugh nervously, then say, "I'm meeting some friends." Because you are. And you can't really ditch them to go off with some forty-year-old. Can you?

"Oh, that's too bad." She sighs exaggeratedly and takes a sip of her drink. "I was hoping to find a nice young strong man like you to *mow my lawn* while my husband's away."

You practically spit out your beer. Stuff like this doesn't really happen. Not to you anyway.

She brushes her leg against yours as she shifts in her seat, and it's clear it was intentional. You know it's crazy, but you're really turned on now. She knows this. She's just looking at you seductively, licking her lips. She kicks off one of her pumps, and you can feel her foot running up and down your calf.

After a few minutes she leans in close, her lips practically touching your ear. "What do you say, you up for the job?"

If you say, "After you," and make a sweeping gesture toward the door to lead your lady away, turn to page 44.

If you feel like you need another drink before you make a decision like this, then go to page 47.

You take a cab to Busters—this is proving to be a more expensive night than you bargained for, but you'd feel guilty if you missed the show. The band has already started when you arrive, and for once Peter seems to have found a group with a shelf life longer than warm milk. You recognize Peter's roommate, Doug, in the crowd and go stand next to him, chatting between songs. Peter looks nervous, but toward the end of the set he sees you and smiles, making a thumbs-up sign.

"I believe that's international guitarist's sign language for 'Order me a beer; I'm almost done,' " says Doug. "Can I get you one?"

A couple of minutes later Peter, sweaty and very happy, is downing his beer and yapping excitedly. "That was the best! I screwed up a couple of times, but considering we only rehearsed once I think I was awesome! They're gonna ask me to join, I can feel it. Thanks for showing up." He kisses you on the cheek. "You look great. What are you doing later? I feel like Mexican and margaritas to celebrate."

"I have to be at McCormick's at twelve. I'm meeting some friends and we're going to a party. But that gives me an hour, so . . . sure, why not?"

"Excellent. You coming, Doug?"

"Nah, I'm gonna hang out here for a while and see if I can convince that girl drummer to come home with me."

"Doug, you know she hails from the island of Lesbos, right?" Peter's shaking his head and laughing.

"I got a definite vibe earlier tonight."

"That would be her 'Stop staring at me, pathetic horny straight guy. I'm gay' vibe. This isn't *The Real World;* lesbians do not change their sexual preference overnight to make for better TV."

"Fuck it, it's not like I can do any worse with gay women than I usually do with straight ones. Have a good night, you two. Don't do anything I wouldn't do." And he gives Peter a look that almost—no, that *definitely*—means something.

"You mean don't drink twelve pints, complain to the bartender about not getting laid in six months, hit on her, and then crawl home alone, waking up covered in cigarette ash in the clothes I went out in. Okay, I can promise you that." A nice rebound, Pierre.

You go to Julio's, a Mexican restaurant that Peter loves because the margaritas are particularly strong, and he nabs his favorite table by the window for both of you. And now you have to make a judgment call. Based on prior experience, two of these babies, especially on top of the variety of drinks you've consumed so far, can knock you out.

Peter suggests getting a pitcher, and the idea is very tempting. But maybe you should just get a glass and play it safe.

If you have a glass, turn to page 25.
If you go for the pitcher, turn to page 66.

Hi there, stranger."

"Kristy! Oh my god. How *are* you? What are you *doing* here?"

Kristy is your ex-girlfriend. *The* ex-girlfriend. The only woman who's ever tamed your wandering eyes for more than a year. In fact, she did it for two and a half years. And you would have been happy if she had kept on doing it. Kristy, you see, is *it*. She's got it going on. She's fly. She's phat. She's all that. And then some.

"I just moved back. I finished school—finally—and now I'm looking for a job."

You can't believe your ears. Kristy, who has been hundreds of miles away from you in law school for the last three years, is going to be in the same city as you.

"I was going to call you." She leans in and gives you a light peck on the lips. "Things just haven't been the same since we've been apart."

They sure as hell haven't, you think to yourself. For starters, you haven't been getting steady, sweaty, loud, nail-digging sex since then. But of course you can't say that. So you pick something else: "I've missed you."

"You don't know how happy you've just made me." Kristy runs her fingers through her long blond hair, and you think you see her chin tremble. "I mean I know there are things we'll have to work out, but us getting back together, well, it just makes sense somehow because . . ."

And she's lost you. Who said anything about getting back together? What about Sadie? What about the fact that Kristy dumped you for another guy? But before you can protest she leans in and you can smell her—the only woman you've ever known who smells of aniseed. It brings back vivid memories, flashes of body parts, positions, things you haven't done with anyone since. She whispers, "Let's go somewhere," then takes your hand.

If you follow her, go to page 51.

If not, go to page 55.

"Damn, and I was hoping to get you drunk and make my move tonight, too," says Peter, and though he's laughing you sense that he's serious. You feel like you've just blown your first real chance with him, and wonder if you're going to be kicking yourself tomorrow.

The next time you check your watch it's almost midnight. Peter's got no plans, and it's pretty clear that he wouldn't mind going with you to the party. This is apparent from the way he clutches your sleeve desperately after you've split the check and says, "I wouldn't mind going with you to the party."

"Well, I dunno . . ."

"Come on, if I go home I'll be bored. I'll have to wander the streets, looking forlorn and dejected, like a male version of Ally McBeal."

"I have a tiny skirt and a briefcase you can borrow, to complete the look."

Arriving at the party with your best male friend may jeopardize your flirting potential later. Although there's also the possibility that seeing you walk in with another guy may heighten Mark's primitive, competitive instincts—men are so dumb that way.

You decide to come clean to Peter and tell him that you're hoping to get lucky later.

"That's fine; I can help! I'll get talking to this guy Mark and tell him how cool you are. I'll be your very own PR company—you'll be so glad you brought me."

"As glad as I was when I took you to Melissa's beach house last summer?"

"You're referring to her grandmother's antique china plate again, aren't you? Come on, you have to admit that it looked exactly like a Frisbee."

If you decline to bring Peter, turn to page 28.
If you bring him, turn to page 68.

When you get to the keg, "Steve Buscemi" is being turned upside down to do a keg stand. A handful of guys gathered around him are chanting, "Bu-shemmmmm-i, Bu-shemmmm-i," over and over as he guzzles directly from the tap lead. Since he's upside-down, you still can't decide whether you really believe it's him.

"Woohoo!" the scrawny little guy says, once he's put back on his feet. "Who's next?" He scans the faces around him and stops at you. "What are you looking at? Never seen a movie star before?"

You say, "Not doing keg stands, no."

"Hey," Steve says, elbowing the guy next to him with a chuckle. "First time for everything, right?"

"I've got a bone to pick with you," Dave cuts in. He's apparently knocked back a beer already and is working on his second.

"And pray tell, what would that be?" Steve says lightheartedly, rolling his bulging eyes.

"I'm sick of you showing up when I don't expect it. I think there should be some kind of warning on ads for movies you're in. Warning: this movie contains a completely gratuitous appearance by Steve Buscemi."

"What can I say," Steve says in that nasally voice of his. "Everybody wants a piece of me."

"I know what piece *I* want." A girl with long, curly, brunette hair—obviously drunk—has interrupted the conversation. She steps up to Steve and he refills her cup from the keg.

Dave steps up to the girl, who's making eyes at Steve. "I'm sorry, but I have to save you from yourself." He takes the beer out of her hand and sets it down on a nearby table. "Do you have a friend that can take you home before you make an even bigger fool of yourself for coming onto such a funny-looking specimen of man? And a married one, no less."

"Married, huh?" She mulls the situation over, teetering slightly. "Oh well. But for the record, I'd take him over some generic-looking frat boy any day."

There are boo's and ooh's and hisses.

"Obviously, my presence here is causing some trouble," Steve says, "so I think I'll be on my way. But as for you"—he points at Dave—"I'm going to take as many movie parts as I want, okay? So you just keep going to movies and keep watching close, because when you least expect it, baby, expect it. I'll be right there in your face."

After Steve leaves, Dave does a keg stand and spends some time catching up with friends. When you think you've paid your keg-party dues, you catch Dave's eye and point at your watch. He raises his plastic cup and says, "Down in one." You raise your cup and oblige. You can't wait to get back to the city, back on the track that will lead you to Sadie. You grab another Jell-O shot on the way out, to make up for lost time. Only then do you wonder if Dave's fit to drive. Hmmn . . .

If you turn to Dave and say, "Give me the keys . . . ," turn to page 59.

If you let Dave drive, turn to page 62.

Well, I tried. I guess I can't blame you for ditching a dear, trusted friend, who's stood steadfast by your side for years, and running off in search of a tawdry one-night stand instead."

"Glad you understand."

"You know I'd do the same for you, honey."

You say your good-byes and walk up to McCormick's. On the way you pass a deli, and, remembering Peter's reference to a tawdry one-night stand, you wonder if you should go in and buy condoms. You're feeling lucky, after all. Or would that be tempting fate?

If you decide to skip the condoms, turn to page 30.
If you go in, turn to page 72.

You say the line that popped into your head.

"Well that blows that!" Mike throws his hands up in the air, and the rest of the group moans.

"Why? What?" you ask.

"Everybody else I've asked said, 'Slowly walking down the hall, faster than a cannonball.' You blew it, big guy. It was going to be ten for ten." He shakes his head.

"Sorry," you say, and shrug.

Turn to page 65.

That Petrol Emotion is blaring from the jukebox in McCormick's, and a visiting Irish rugby team is taking up most of the space at the bar. You order a drink from the bartender and find standing room between two burly rugby players who are anxious to seem polite.

"Squeeze in there now," one says, smiling at you. "Move up, lads. Don't want her to think we're a shower of drunken yobs."

Just as you're taking a sip, Suzy approaches you with a guy in tow, and it's clear that she is completely bombed.

"Baaaay-beeee!" she squeals, running over and hugging you.

"Suzy! You're . . . damp."

"Phil and I were trying to see who could pick up a shot glass with their teeth." She nods at her companion.

"I'm betting that Phil won."

"You're sho funny, haha, yeah he did. Look, here's Nick. *Nick!* My perfect cousin!" She grabs Nick, who's been quietly minding his own business and trying to order a drink. "I love this guy! Y'know, mebbe I should have eaten something earlier," she says, swaying gently from side to side as if caught in a summer breeze. "I'm just going'a bathroom."

Suzy makes her way unsteadily down the stairs, and Nick rolls his eyes at you. "I don't know if I can take her to Lindy's place like this. In the taxi on the way here she was trying to rest her head in the driver's lap. I love Suzy, but letting her puke all over my friend's living room doesn't seem like standard party etiquette."

"So what do we do with her?"

Before Nick can answer, one of the Irish rugby players approaches you.

"Sorry, but aren't you with that girl who just came in? She's passed out downstairs. Completely bolloxed by the looks of her. I'll help bring her up if you like."

Downstairs, Suzy is slumped, in semifetal position, against the door to the women's bathroom. You try to wake her, but all you get is a mumbled "I shlipped" before she's out again. The Irish guy, who introduces himself as Liam, helps you bring her upstairs, and the two of you support her while Nick and Phil shuffle uncomfortably.

"What are you going to do?" Phil asks you in a grating English accent.

"*Me?* You're the one who's been plying her with shots; maybe you have another bright idea now?"

"It's not my fault your friend can't hold her drink," he grumbles.

Liam nudges him. "If stupid gobshites like you didn't have to get women plastered in order to get a shag this kind of thing wouldn't happen."

"Who are you calling a gobshite?" demands Phil, nudging him back.

"What *is* a gobshite?" puzzles Nick.

"Can we get back to Suzy now?" you ask. "Someone's obviously going to have to take her home. She's too out of it to get in a taxi by herself."

No one is enthused. Nick is whining about having to get to the party soon. Phil is glaring at Liam. Liam grunts impatiently.

"God, you're a useless bunch. Where does she live?"

"Not far; about a ten-minute drive away."

"I tell you what, I've got the van outside. I can drive her home, if you come with me and show me the way. The lads are going to be here until closing anyway; we can make it back in half an hour."

"That's very generous of you, but you don't even know us," you respond.

"I know, but it's no big deal. I could use a break from this crowd."

If you and Liam take Suzy home in the van, turn to page 34.

If you take her home yourself, turn to page 76.

"Yes!" Mike and company erupt, giving each other high fives and generally whooping it up. "That's ten for ten," Mike explains after the initial outburst. "I've asked everybody here and some other random people, and everyone's said the same line. Hey, while we're at it, Will here is stuck on this eighties song lyric." He turns to Will. "See if my buddy here knows it." Mike gestures to you.

Will opens up a book and reads a lyric: "Several years ago I said good-bye to my own sanity."

"Waoh, hold on a minute. It's in a *book*?" Mike takes the book, keeping Will's place, and reads the title aloud. "*Who Can It Be Now? The Lyrics Game That Takes You Back to the Eighties—One Line at a Time.*"

He looks at the place the book is open to, then turns the page. "The answer's right here, you bonehead," he says to Will.

"I know, I know. *Don't tell me!*" Will covers his ears and starts humming. When he stops he says, "It's no fun if you use the answer key."

Mike hands the book back. "What's the difference? You're asking everyone you know if they know it, so if somebody does it's like you're looking at the answer key anyway."

"It's not the same."

"How's it not the same?"

"The more people I ask that don't know it, the more vindicated I am in my belief that it's a ridiculously obscure lyric that no one in their right mind remembers."

"That's pretty sad, Will."

"I don't understand what the fascination is with all this nostalgia stuff anyway," Tracy cuts in. "Like, did you get that one rambling E-mail about how great our generation is. I mean, it's just this long—painfully long—list of TV shows and songs and celebrities that were popular when we were kids. And whoever wrote this stupid thing just strings them all together as if, there's enough of them, there's going to be some meaning that comes out of it. After a while you just want whoever wrote it to stuff it. I mean, come on, just because we all had a Sit'n'Spin and a Big Wheel and watched *Planet of the Apes* and read Choose Your

Own Adventure books doesn't make us one big happy family. Those really aren't the things that define a generation or a time. Other generations have toys and TV shows, too."

"I got that E-mail; I thought it was kind of cool," Will says.

"Sure, if you want to be reminded of some things from your childhood that maybe you forgot about. But there's no *meaning* inherent in it. I'm just sick of being part of a generation that has to relate every experience to some supposedly commonly shared pop-culture experience for lack of any real grasp of the futility of efforts to ascribe meaning to anything."

"Hey," Mike cuts in excitedly. "You sound like Daria. Didn't she just sound like Daria?"

"Oh my god, she totally did," says Will.

"I rest my case."

If you want to know what song the lyric is from, turn to page 67.

Otherwise, turn to page 65.

Unlikely as it might be, right now Liam seems to be the most reliable person in the bar, and at least it'll save on cab fare. After arranging to see Nick back here in half an hour so he can take you to the party, you and Liam take Suzy out to his van.

"Sorry there's no seats in the back, but we can put her lying down on that rug. She's probably too far gone to feel any bumps along the way. I just hope she doesn't throw up back there; I'm supposed to be driving down to Florida in this thing, and I could do without the smell of vomit traveling with me."

Within fifteen minutes you're parked outside Suzy's place. You lift her out of the van and half-drag, half-carry her to the door. Rummaging around in her pocket, you locate her keys and bring her downstairs.

Urging Liam to make himself at home, you take off Suzy's boots, pants, and shirt and put her to bed. As you're hanging her clothes up in the closet, silently congratulating yourself for being such a considerate friend, you spy the new suede jacket she bought last week, and finger it lovingly. You try it on—what the hell—and are admiring the effect in the mirror when Liam comes in and nods appreciatively.

"Suits you. You should borrow it, after what she's put you through tonight."

"Y'think? It cost her a fortune; she might freak out."

"Return it tomorrow; she'll be too hungover to argue. It really does look good. It, eh, accentuates your best points, if you get my drift."

"You're saying it makes my chest look bigger."

"Basically, yeah." He laughs. "Come on, borrow it—trust a man's opinion."

You hang your own jacket up in place of the suede one. Back at McCormick's, you buy Liam a drink and thank him for his trouble, and then rejoin Nick, who's talking to two of the rugby players. Phil is testing the seductive effects of his accent on some other poor sucker, and you're glad to be rid of him.

"Let's have a shot and go, okay? Lindy made me promise to be there early, and I've already screwed that up."

You drink a shot with Nick and head out.

Turn to page 38.

You walk across town toward Woody's, a hip little restaurant you've noticed before but have never gone into. When you pass a park on your left, two in-line skaters crash right into you—each of them clinging to you to try to keep from falling.

"Sorry, man," they both say, making sure you haven't lost your footing.

"No problem," you say, anxious to move on.

A few minutes later you arrive at Woody's, where Mike's gang is still hanging out at the bar. "You've got to hear this," he says, pulling you toward him with a strong arm. "Lisa here watched so much TV when she was little that when she got her period she freaked out because it wasn't bright blue."

"Oh, give her a break." That's Tracy, the birthday girl. "I mean those commercials brainwash women into hating their own bodies—not to mention brainwashing you into wanting a big white couch no matter how impractical it is."

"Watch out." Will drapes an arm around Tracy's shoulder. "Tracy's really got a thing about those commercials—especially the ones where they talk about wings and channels. The only ads she hates more are the ones about makeup that doesn't rub off on anything."

"Well, come on!" Tracy squirms her way out from under Will's arm. "They've got wings, channels, and four walls of protection. Are these people fucking civil engineers? And those makeup commercials. They show you that your foundation won't wear off on a litter of white puppies! And that's supposed to be proof! Lisa, when was the last time you nuzzled a litter of white puppies?"

"Hey, I'm on your side." Lisa leans over to get her Heineken off the bar. "I'm *still* upset about the whole blue blood thing."

In a lull, Mike reintroduces you to his friends. Will and Tracy both roll their eyes and say, "Mike, we've met a thousand times before." Lisa just smiles. She looks cuter tonight than you remember—something about the hair. Or maybe, like you, she's tweezed her eyebrows. Something about *some* kind of hair, anyway. Nonetheless, it's Tracy you're happiest to see tonight. She's your party connection—your *luv* connection.

Mike goes to change the head count for dinner to five so as to include you. You look up at the specials board over the bar nervously. When you see that entrees can cost as little as eight bucks—in spite of the ultratrendy crowd gathered in this cool, smoky restaurant—you order yourself a drink from the bar. Since you weren't able to collect your cash from Dave, the twenty in your wallet has to last until you can get to an ATM machine. And even then you'll be strapped since you can only withdraw about forty dollars. To your extreme pleasure, when Mike returns he insists on paying for your drink along with his own. And now that you think about it—now that you've had a few drinks—you're not even all that hungry. The group gets a table and the waiter starts taking orders. . . .

If you decide to eat dinner at Woody's, turn to page 70.

If you tell the group you've had dinner and just drink while they eat, turn to page 74.

Outside Lindy's house, Nick gives you an appraising glance while he rings the buzzer.

"Is it my imagination or did your chest get bigger within the past hour?"

"Typical guy—you don't notice the different jacket but you notice the breast size."

"We *always* notice the breast size, babe, it's in chapter one of *The Big Book of Things Guys Do.* Aha, I hear our lovely hostess approaching."

A tall, very blond woman opens the door.

"Nick! You bastard! I *knew* you'd be late. But it's okay; everyone else just arrived within the last half hour. Come on in."

Lindy's house is beautiful, not that you can see that much of it given the number of people crammed in here. To your disappointment, Mark is nowhere to be seen.

"Shit, I forgot to pick up some beer," Nick mutters to you. Lindy, who's wrapping herself around an incredibly good-looking guy at least ten years younger than she is, overhears and points in the direction of the kitchen, shouting happily, "Don't worry about it; the place is overflowing with booze. Martin's making martinis in there; help yourselves. Haha, Martin's making martinis! Martin, Martinis! That's funny!"

"Riotous, Lindy. Wow, what *is* that music they're playing?" Nick asks as you both make for the kitchen.

"You're not a fan of modern jazz?" says a voice to your right, and there, lurking behind the kitchen door, polishing off a drink, is Mark. Even the way he sucks back a martini is attractive.

"No, can't stand the stuff," says Nick, weaving toward Mark and a table where a dark-haired, middle-aged guy—Martin, obviously—is mixing drinks. "You know Mark?" Nick asks you.

"Yeah, we've met a few times," you say, hoping the jacket is doing its trick.

"How are you doing?" Mark asks, giving you a quick head-to-toe glance. "I haven't seen you in a few weeks."

"Not since Gillian's party." You immediately want to bite your tongue, since it was at Gillian's party that Mark and his now ex-girlfriend Meg had a very public fight.

"How could I forget." He laughs, semiembarrassed. "I guess you heard that Meg and I broke up not long after that."

"I hadn't heard." May God strike you down! "Sorry."

"It's not that bad. You know the saying If you can still be friends after you've broken up with someone, then you were never really in love with them? Well, we're still friends, so you can work it out for yourself."

Nick hands you your drink. "Better go mingle. It's time someone took control of the music and put on something more appropriate. There must and shall be dancing!"

If you stay in the kitchen, turn to page 40.

If you play it cool and go with Nick, hoping Mark will join you, turn to page 79.

Half an hour later you and Mark have downed another drink each and are getting on famously. You are also getting tremendously drunk . . . Martin makes a mean martini. People have been trickling in and out of the kitchen, and Lindy has popped in once or twice and given the two of you some curious looks, but mostly you have the place to yourselves, just you, Mark, and Martin. You're wondering if the time has come to make your move, while your courage is at its peak. Just then, Lindy rushes into the kitchen and grabs your arm.

"Darling, you must tend to Nick; he's in the bathroom and throwing up all *over* the place. And Mark, are you going to hide in here all night? Come out and dance with me. I insist."

She stands there smiling, but it seems pretty clear, even to someone as drunk as you, that she wants the competition out of the way so she can make a move on Mark. You're very reluctant to leave her alone with him. Maybe you should get her to come with you while you go see how Nick is doing.

If you go to Nick alone, turn to page 42.

If you ask her to come with you, turn to page 83.

Dave shows up right after you order your next drink. He went all the way out to the keg party only to realize it's next weekend. You tell him that Mike and his gang are going to Spinners and that you're planning on catching up with them there in a little while.

"Cool." Dave looks at his watch. "You want to check out my buddy's band? That should be them going on now."

You hear a couple of random bass notes and a few drum thumps.

The two of you pay eight dollars each—Dave, thankfully, has your fifty dollars—and go into the venue. When the band takes the stage you think they show promise. They've got a definite "look"—one that inspires Dave to immediately wonder whether they'll sound, as they look, like a cross between the Wonders from *That Thing You Do* and Spinal Tap. Then they start to play, and *you* immediately wonder whether they sell earplugs behind the bar. The band's as loud—and just about as tuneless—as a garbage truck at 6 A.M. Dave, however, seems pretty content to watch, his head bopping along to the beat in as much as there is one.

If you turn to Dave and say, "This sucks. Let's get out of here," turn to page 78.

If you decide to hold your tongue until they're done, turn to page 81.

Nick is crouched over the toilet in the bathroom, looking pitiful.

"Oh god, I'm sorry about this," he groans, in between retches. "Must have been something I didn't eat," he adds, glancing up at you and attempting a smile.

"You realize you may just have ruined my chances of winding up with Mark, don't you?" You sigh, handing him a towel.

"Mark? Wow, so you *do* like him."

"What do you mean?" Suddenly you're feeling remarkably sober.

"Well . . ." Nick retches again and then attempts to sit up. "We were talking last week and he mentioned that he wanted to ask some friend of Suzy's out on a date—and I'm guessing that'd be you—but wasn't sure if she, meaning you, would be interested, especially because he felt like such an asshole after fighting with his girlfriend at some party."

"Shit, couldn't you have told me this earlier? I just left him dancing with Lindy, and before the night is over they'll probably be playing Hump the Hostess."

"Lindy? Don't worry about her. She and Martin have been married for years. She flirts all the time, but she'd never actually cheat on him; she's far too attached to his money. Excuse me a moment."

With that he's retching again, and you decide to go find him something to eat. Maybe it'll settle his stomach. In the living room, Mark and Lindy are dancing, but from the way Mark grins as you walk past you know you've nothing to worry about.

"You're not going anywhere, are you?" he asks.

"Just be a second."

The only suitable thing the kitchen has to offer is a loaf of bread, so you take two slices back to Nick and hand him one. He reaches out blindly and . . . wipes his face with it.

"Oops," he mumbles, handing it back to you. "Didn't they have anything softer than multigrain? I have to get out of here so I can go throw up in the comfort of my own apartment."

"Go home; you're pathetic." You laugh, throwing the bread and the towel in the corner and helping Nick to his feet. "I'll give your regards to Lindy."

"I guess I don't have to tell you to enjoy the rest of your evening," he shoots back as he stumbles toward the door.

Five minutes later you're dancing with Mark to the Spice Girls' "2 Become 1," and he's singing in your ear.

"I asked them to play this," he whispers.

"You like this song?" you ask, incredulous.

"No, but I was hoping that if you hated it as much as I do, you might be persuaded to leave the party and come home with me."

"I guess I could do that. Of course, I didn't exactly plan for this to happen."

"Me neither, naturally. Let's go."

The End

Your lady friend's car is parked right in front of the bar, and you both get in. She seems to have sobered up the second she got behind the wheel.

"So," she says. "Tell me about your girlfriend."

You figure she gets off on this kind of stuff—the idea that she's doing it with some young girl's boyfriend—so you decide to invent a girlfriend. You proceed to tell her about this girl you've been seeing for a few months, and what a great, fit body she has and how you have sex more times a day than you can keep track of.

Before you know it you're pulling up to the gates of a mansion in a wealthy suburb. She pulls up the circular driveway and stops right in front of the door. A butler comes out and takes the keys from her, and you follow her inside. There's a chambermaid waiting in the lobby.

"Janice here will show you to the guest suite," she calls over her shoulder as she ascends a massive marble staircase. "And in the morning someone will show you where to find the lawn mower."

She disappears into a room upstairs, and Janice looks at you sympathetically.

"Told her about the girlfriend?"

"Yup."

The End

There's a band playing in the Berlin tonight. The Daytrippers are a local group who specialize in alternative versions of Beatles songs, and if enthusiasm was the sole criterion for success, they'd be playing Madison Square Garden instead of a poky bar with a toilet the size of a matchbox. Perhaps thankfully, enthusiasm is *not* the only criterion for success—the world will survive quite well without the Daytrippers' rap fiasco, "Yo Jude."

The Berlin has dubious charms—there are plush red booths along the walls, most crammed with martini-drinking ad exec types and the kind of girls who spend far too much time and energy maintaining washboard stomachs. But there are at least two good reasons to come here, not including the possible presence of Nick. There's the drinks—lethal and delicious. And there's Dan, Bartender to the Gods.

"Do you think Dan has any idea how good-looking he is?" Suzy asks, scouring the bar for a couple of seats.

"Hmm. Well, judging by the way he gazes longingly at his reflection in every pint glass he polishes, I'd say yes. Hey look, two stools over there, next to those guys."

Over you go, and Suzy, giggling like a schoolgirl the whole time, orders drinks—a Stoli tonic for herself, as always, and your usual. Nick is nowhere to be seen, but Suzy suggests that you may as well stay here for a while anyway; her decision is possibly influenced by the fact that Dan is hovering nearby and occasionally smiling in her direction. They engage in a little mindless chatter, and you, more than willing to let her flirt—you'll get your chance later—look around for other distractions. The guy sitting next to you is waving a CD in the air as he argues with his friend, and accidentally knocks you on the head with it.

"Wow, I'm sorry. I didn't see you there," he apologizes.

"No problem." You nod. How remarkably polite you are tonight. Amazing what the prospect of seeing Mark can do. Barely a minute has gone by and you're settling back, taking another sip of your drink, when the missile thwacks you again, in the arm this time. Another brief apology, and you nod, more brusquely this time. One more chance before you get angry. . . .

Thirty seconds later your CD-wielding friend has clipped you in the arm with his new purchase, and not even an apology this time. Suzy's still engrossed with Dan. Either you can confront this asshole beside you or find somewhere else to sit.

If you confront him, turn to page 85.
If you find another seat, turn to page 87.

You and your new lady friend are getting on swimmingly now that you've got a buzz going. You've moved over to a table in a far corner of the bar, and she's feeling your package through your jeans. Your hand can be found up her skirt, caressing her inner thigh through her nylons. You're so caught up in the pleasure of your arousal and the thrill of being touched so intimately in a public place that you lean in to kiss this adventuresome woman you've had the good fortune to encounter. Busy sucking face, you don't see Dave come in.

"What the fuck!"

You pull away from the kiss and see your friend looking at you in shock. "What's wrong?" you ask.

"What's *wrong*?" Dave's practically screaming, and a few people have turned around to see what the problem is.

"Dave, it's not what it looks like."

And now you're the one that's in shock. Because those words didn't come out of your mouth. They came from your lady friend, who has gotten up, straightened her skirt, and gone to Dave's side.

"You two *know* each other?" You're stunned.

"I guess you haven't been properly introduced," Dave says bitterly. "This is my aunt Mary. That would be my uncle Bob's *wife*."

Aunt Mary, who has suddenly sobered up, starts to put her jacket on. "I think I should go. Dave, I'm terribly sorry you had to see this. I can't really justify my behavior, but I'd obviously prefer if we kept this between you and me. I assure you it won't happen again."

Dave says, "Just leave. I don't want to look at you another second. I'm going to get a drink."

Aunt Mary turns to you. "I'm sorry. I didn't mean any harm." And she's gone.

Dave returns with his drink, and another for you—which you take as a good sign. You apologize profusely, but he doesn't say much. You sit in silence for a while, then finally he speaks: "My family is so fucked up, man. My parents just told me last week they're getting divorced. Apparently they've been miserable for years. They said they stayed together at first for my sake and were going to get a divorce when I went away to college, but by then they'd gotten so accustomed to an 'arrangement'—they were openly having affairs—that they didn't see what the hurry was. And now my aunt Mary! It's like no one in my family is capable of having an honest relationship. Lord knows my track record isn't too hot. I don't know why they even told me all this. Now I just feel like it's my fault they stayed together and were miserable."

"It's not your fault, Dave."

Dave just sits there, staring into his pint.

"No, look at me," you insist, and Dave turns. "It's not your fault."

"I know," he says, nodding somberly.

"It's not your fault," you say again.

"I know, man."

"No, really, it's not—"

"Shut the fuck up, man. I'm sitting here spilling my guts to you, and the best you can do is start acting out *Good Will Hunting*? Next you'll be telling me I'm so money and I don't even know it—or, worse yet, making me promise I'll never let go." He clutches your arm and impersonates a melodramatic female. "I promise I'll never let go, Jack. I'll never let go."

You stare down at his hands on your arm. "If you don't let go now, *Rose*, I'm going to kick your pretty little ass. Anyway, I thought you said you didn't see *Titanic*. That you were never going to see *Titanic*. That you were going to make a point of never seeing the most popular movie of all time."

"And I'm sticking to that"—Dave nods his head sharply once—"meaning that I will live the rest of my life and never watch *Titanic* in a theater or on video. I was, however, unemployed when it came out, so I was watching a lot of TV, so I figure I've practically seen the whole thing anyway, just not in the right order—like an interactive CD-ROM."

"Surprised James Cameron hasn't thought of that."

"Oh, it exists. I was actually going to pick it up if one of the options was to rearrange events so that that egotistical maniac doesn't win an Oscar, but it can't be done." Dave takes a deep breath and looks around the room dejectedly. "I need a picker-upper. You want to do a shot?"

You shrug.

"Oh come on. You jump, I jump, right?"

Dave comes back from the bar with two shots and a flyer. "So we missed my buddy's band. But this beautiful baby just gave me this and says we can get a free drink if we go to some club around the corner."

You know that Dave really needs you tonight. But what about Mike and the others? What about Sadie?

If you want to go to the club and forget about everybody else since Mike hasn't shown up anyway, turn to page 84.

If, instead, you check your messages—and therefore find out that Mike and co. are at Spinners, and you want to go there, turn to page 302.

If you want to take a break from your adventure to indulge a fantasy that James Cameron didn't win any Oscars, turn to page 86.

"No, I'm not going up to him," you say decisively. "He might be weird."

"How many people do we know who fit into any other category?"

"Point taken. But I'm not in the mood for a meaningless fling."

"The night is young." Suzy slurps her drink.

You feign annoyance. "I'm insulted you think I'm that kind of woman."

"You are that kind of woman, sweetie."

"True. I'm just insulted that it's so obvious." Another slurp. "So what now? Ask the barman if Nick has been in, maybe?"

"Ooh, that's an idea. Wait here."

A minute later she's back, and grinning. "That was inspired. Nick *was* here before—he told the bartender to tell anyone who came looking for him that he'd be in the Upstairs Lounge for a while. Finish that drink, we're moving on up!"

You gulp it back, follow Suzy outside, and get in a taxi.

"You know where this place is, right Suzy?"

"Of course I do! Have I ever led you astray?"

Before you can answer, she taps the driver on the shoulder. "Pull in here!"

Turn to page 18.

Kristy leads you to a remote bedroom in Joe's house. She pushes you back so you're forced to sit on the edge of the bed, then drops to her knees and goes to work. If there's anything to be said for Kristy—and in truth there are a lot of things, but none of the other ones matter right now—she knows the way to a man's heart.

You take hold of her blond hair as she runs a hand up your shirt. You can't believe how good what she's doing to you feels.

"I knew it!" Dave busts through the door, and you and Kristy scramble to make yourselves presentable. "It's the Licorice Lady. I could smell her a mile away. It's like Steve Martin in *Roxanne*—how his huge-ass nose leads him to a fire no one else knows is going on."

"Hello, Newman," Kristy says bitterly, wiping her mouth with the back of her hand.

"Come on," Dave says, grabbing you by the arm. "We're outta here."

"What the hell!" You're pushed through the crowd, out to the curb, before you can get a word in.

" 'What the *hell?*' " Dave is practically shouting. "You're asking me, 'What the hell?' *I'm* the one that should be asking *you* 'What the hell?' That's the fucking Licorice Lady, man. She's right up there with that *Chasing Amy* chick in terms of fucking with your head. You *know* that. You don't want to go there again, man."

"Maybe I do." The Jell-O shots have gone to your head—yes, that head, too—and you're feeling an awful mix of loneliness and horniness.

"Are you out of your mind, man? This is the woman who used to make you sing 'I Want Candy' before you could get sex."

"Hey, whatever happened to Bow Wow Wow?"

"Not the point." Dave gets into the car, and you follow suit. "The point, my friend, is that you're in a much better place now. A place where you know you deserve better than a two-timing girl like Kristy. A place where the women you go out with wear *real* perfume. Stuff that smells like flowers and shit."

Dave starts to drive, and you don't stop him. A few miles down the road you say, "Thanks, Dave. You're right." Because he is. "But couldn't you have waited a few more minutes before busting in? I'm all jived up now."

"Sorry, man." Dave laughs, shaking his head. "If I'd a known I would have. . . ."

You ride in silence for a while. "You know what the funny thing is," you finally say. "I've got this intense craving for candy now. Any kind of candy."

"There's a Seven-Eleven a few miles up this way," Dave explains. "But if you want me to stop, you're going to have to sing a little 'I Want Candy' for me."

If you start singing Bow Wow Wow's "I Want Candy" at the top of your lungs, go to page 88.

If you think that's the stupidest thing Dave's ever asked you to do and want to go straight to the Lunar Lounge, turn to page 92.

It may be only a fifteen-minute walk to the Upstairs, but it's going to be a very long fifteen minutes, full of bad jokes, pathetic attempts at flirtation, and Bill trying to disguise his farts by coughing loudly. Any distraction would be welcome, so when Suzy hears whimpering, peers under a parked car, and announces, "It's a tiny doggie!" you gladly stop.

"He looks frightened. Think we can coax him out?"

"If Bill stands far enough away, sure."

Bill just grins. Good old oblivious Bill.

Reaching under the car, you manage to grab the dog's collar and pull it out. It really is tiny—some kind of chihuahua, well cared for but petrified. You hold the dog's head gently and Suzy checks the tag around its neck. "Oh it's a girl doggie!" yelps Suzy. "Her name's Margarita. Aw, that's cute! And there's an address . . . I think it's one block over. Should we bring Margarita home?" She tickles the dog under the chin. "You want us to take you to your houseywousey, diddums? Does ickle Margarita want to go home to mumsie and dadsie then?"

Suzy always gets like this around small animals. She blames it on her parents' never giving her enough Barbies when she was young.

It's agreed that you have time to bring Margarita home to her mumsie, who turns out to be an elderly woman who squeals excitedly when she opens the door. "You found her! Oh you angels! She's been gone for three whole hours, haven't you, missy?" She takes the dog and ushers you all inside. It's a small, cramped apartment; clearly Margarita's mumsie is not exactly rolling in money, so you and Suzy instinctively refuse when she starts rummaging in her bag for "a little reward."

"No really, it was no trouble." Suzy smiles.

"Well, I wouldn't say *no* trouble," Bill mutters.

"Oh what a shame," Margarita's mumsie continues, "I don't seem to have much spare cash anyway . . . but look, I have these!" She holds up two scratch tickets for the state lottery. "I always buy two on Friday . . . my little weekend treat!" she explains. You smile weakly. This is heartbreaking stuff. "But I want you to have them. The two girls can have one, and the nice gentleman can take the other! Now go on! I insist! You girls pick first! Left or right hand?"

There's no refusing her. Suzy motions for you to do the picking.

If you pick the left, turn to page 89.
If you pick the right, turn to page 91.

Whoa," you say. "Slow down, Kristy. We can't just get back together and jump into bed like nothing happened."

"Why not?"

Good question, really. But for some reason you're not letting her off that easily. She left you for another man. And we all know the male ego bruises as easily as an anemic on a protein diet. "You dumped me, Kristy. And it really hurt."

"I know. I'm sorry. I was a total bitch to you. Breaking up with you was the biggest mistake I ever made."

"You can't just say that and expect it to be all better right away, though. I mean maybe you've been thinking about this for a while, but this is like a total shock to me. I have a whole new life now—one without you in it—and I like it. And being with you, well, I don't know. It'd have to be a lot different this time around. I've grown a lot. I'm a different person now."

"Well, I hope you're not too different. I liked you the way you were. But can't we spend some time together and see if there's a chance?"

"Well, I guess so."

"I've got an idea. I'm going to a wedding tomorrow and I RSVPed for two, but then the friend I was going to take got sick. Will you go with me? I don't know many people who are going to be there—it's a friend from my old neighborhood who I haven't really seen much—and I don't want to go alone. Please, it'll be the perfect chance for us to catch up."

"You haven't called me in years and now you want me to go to a *wedding* with you and see if maybe we have a *future* together?"

"Yeah, basically. Is it really so hard to believe we still might?"

You look at her and know that your answer is no. Not hard to believe at all.

"No, that's not what I mean." You don't really know what you mean.

"So you'll come with me?" The hope in her voice melts your insides.

"Okay." You really are a sap when it comes down to it.

"Great," she says. "I'll drive you home; we've got an early morning ahead of us. The ceremony's at ten."

"What?"

"What, you don't want to go now?"

What about Sadie and your plans for your Big Night Out? Is it really worth it to give it all up—give up the prospect of something new and meaningful or maybe even something new and meaningless—for the chance at a reconciliation with Kristy?

Well, apparently you think it is. You tell Dave you ran into Kristy and that it's a long story but you're leaving, sorry. He understands immediately. You're tucked in your bed, sound asleep, by 11:30. You dream that tomorrow's your wedding day and wake up in a cold sweat.

The End

The Temple is a cocktail bar with a pretentiousness quotient that's rocketing through the roof. Naturally, Anton is in his element.

"So classy!" he sighs, moving toward the back. "There's a little table here that I like to call my own. Ah, Roland!" He waves to the bartender.

"The bartender is called Roland?" says Suzy incredulously. "Hey Anton, they have any good beers on tap?"

"No beers," he sniffs. "An impressive martini menu though."

"That's okay; I'll just have a Stoli and tonic. Hell, put a slice of lemon in it; I'm feeling adventurous."

You order a martini. Sitting at the table next to you are three guys who look to be having a far better time than Anton could ever provide. Suzy obviously thinks so, too—she leans back in her chair to catch their conversation, then glances at you, raising an eyebrow as if to ask if she should try to butt in. Shielding your mouth, you give a tiny yawn and point to Anton, then point to the guys beside you and give a thumbs-up. Suzy looks quizzically at you, points at Anton, and mouths, "What?" You nod vehemently, trying not to let Anton see you.

She mouths, "What?" again.

"Yes! Yes! Go talk to them!" you practically shout.

"Jeez, okay." She grins, gets up, and moves to their table, leaving you to listen to Anton's diatribe about the inferiority of Kieslowski's later films.

"I wonder how many people would watch those movies if the director cast ugly chicks," is Bill's contribution. "Y'know? All those subtitled movies have good-looking women. That Juliette Binoche, she's pretty hot. And the Julie girl, the one who was in that movie with Ethan Hawke?"

"Julie Delpy."

"That's her! Amazing body!"

"You're such a philistine," sneers Anton.

"Yeah, well, you're such a . . ." Bill struggles a moment for a suitable comeback. "a . . . nipple, man."

"I'm such a *nipple?*" fumes Anton. "You freaking boor."

"Freaking? *Freaking*?" Bill stands up and starts ranting. "Why can't you just talk normal, man! Say the word *fucking*! Go on! What's your problem? You scared?"

Maybe it's time you joined Suzy. Checking your watch, you realize that Nick may have already left the Upstairs Lounge, which would make Anton your only hope of getting the address of Lindy's party.

If you join Suzy, turn to page 93.
If you stay with Anton and Bill, turn to page 96.

Dave stops and looks at you funny. "Are you fucking joking? You're bombed!"

"I am *not* bombed. You're the one who was doing keg stands."

"Yeah, but you were sucking down those Jell-O shots like they were pussy-flavored."

"What? I had, like, three!"

"There's no way you're driving my car, man."

"Well there's no way I'm getting into the car with you."

"Well then you're shit out of luck. Because I'm your ticket back to town. Unless you want to settle down out here, maybe get a paper route."

"Dave, if you get stopped again for anything, your license is going to be suspended."

"Too late." Dave gets into the driver's seat, and you talk to him through the open door.

"You're going to drive drunk with a suspended license?"

Dave suddenly turns pensive. "Alright, man, you're driving. But you're not going above forty, hear me?"

"Deal." Within minutes you find yourself on a generic two-lanes-in-each-direction highway of sorts, with fast-food restaurants and car dealerships on either side.

"You think we should eat something?" Dave asks.

If you want to eat, turn to page 90.

If you want to press on to the Lunar Lounge, turn to page 92.

This is just too good an opportunity to pass up. You have to talk to her, especially as you know you look better than usual tonight.

"Clara! It's been years!" You're about to add "And not enough of them!" but it's a little early for deliberate bitchiness.

"Oh hi!" She untangles herself from the guy she's with and stands up to blow an air kiss in your direction. "Wow, you look terrific! You've really improved since high school. It's amazing what a good haircut can do." Not too early for Clara, apparently.

"Gee thanks. You haven't changed." You grimace.

"Well, I guess most people have put on a few pounds since then"—she looks you pointedly up and down—"but I've always been able to eat whatever I want."

"That's right, I remember you always had a fondness for stuffing things in your mouth."

"Anyway, this is Serge." She drapes an arm possessively around the guy sitting next to her. "We got engaged last week."

"That's such great news. I'm so glad you two found each other." It'll save two other people, you think. "Let me buy you a drink."

"Very kind of you," says Serge. It speaks!

Back at the bar, you deliberate what to buy. Clara could never hold her liquor. Tequila, in particular, made her sick.

"Three shots of Cuervo, please," you call. "Make one of them extra-large."

Clara looks at you with thinly disguised horror when you arrive back with the shots. Serge even registers shock. "Baby, I didn't know you drank tequila."

"Clara? Oh sure, she's always had a strong stomach," you cut in. "Real party girl. Remember, Clara, the time we all went to a party given by my boyfriend? And you had a couple of shots and next thing we knew you were dancing topless with him on the lawn and using the plastic flamingo as a prop? Hilarious. Clara was just so much fun to be around. One of the things I admired about her in high school. That, and her basic generosity of spirit."

"Well actually, I don't . . . ," she sputters.

"Come now, don't pretend you can't handle it! Drink up!" You hand her the biggest shot, and all three of you knock them back.

"I'd better be getting back to my friends." You wipe your mouth and wait for the aftertaste to disappear. "Congratulations again. Have a great night."

Nick and Suzy are playing pool, and they've put your name up on the board. As you stand in front of the jukebox rummaging in your pocket for change, there's a tap on your shoulder. It's Serge.

"Hey, Clara wanted me to say good-bye to you. She wasn't feeling well so she went, y'know, home."

"That's too bad. I was looking forward to chatting about old times later."

"Can I buy you a drink?"

Now this is unexpected. "Sure, I guess so."

Twenty minutes later it's clear that Serge's interest in you is not platonic. He's complimenting you on your shirt . . . which for some reason he has to touch in order to appreciate.

"Y'know, Clara and I aren't really, y'know, engaged." He's leaning very close and you can sense that the Lunge is going to happen any second now. "I mean, we've, y'know, talked about it, but I don't feel ready yet. I'm not really, y'know . . ."

Pause. Not really, y'know, articulate? Not really, y'know, ready to commit to a full sentence?

". . . at that place in my life right now. So it's a sort of . . . y'know . . . open engagement." He leers suggestively.

"Open engagement, right." Serge is not the type you—or any other sentient being—would normally be attracted to, but there's a tiny, vindictive part of you that wants to finally get back at Clara for breaking your teenage heart when she stole Tony Mill . . . Millhouse? Milton? Miller? Whatever. And it's not like it's your fault that Clara has chosen to settle for someone with the morals of a weasel. Then there's the fact that you're feeling pretty drunk right now . . . why didn't you and Suzy have dinner?

Shit.

If you try to escape from Serge's clutches, turn to page 98.

If you go along with it, turn to page 100.

After driving for a few minutes, Dave realizes he's too drunk. He pulls into a McDonald's, and the two of you stuff yourselves. Dave drinks loads of coffee to sober himself up, but you refrain; you're working on a buzz. On full stomachs, you proceed.

Go to page 92.

Why move? The Upstairs Lounge has everything you need—a seat, a jukebox, alcohol, a toilet to relieve yourself of same. The next time you look at your watch it's pretty late. Nick gulps back the rest of his beer and suggests you get going.

He reaches behind him, expecting to find his jacket on the back of the chair. It's not there. It's not on your chair either, or on the floor, or on any of the chairs around you. Panicking now, he asks the bartender if anyone's handed in a leather jacket. No luck.

"Fuck. I know it was on this chair. You're sure no one put it behind the bar?"

"I'm sure, and I've had a lot less to drink than you," replies the bartender. "Look, what can I tell ya, someone must have taken it. Happens, especially with leather jackets. Leave your name and address if you want, and if it turns up I'll let ya know."

Nick is understandably annoyed. Suzy finally drags herself away from the guy she's been flirting with to find out what's happening. "At least my wallet wasn't in it," Nick fumes. "Nothing was in the pockets except, oh fuck, my address book. Shit, shit, *shit.*"

"What a drag," you cluck sympathetically. And then something occurs to you. "But you must know a lot of the addresses in it by heart, right? Like, say, Lindy's?"

He glares at you. "No, I don't know her address by heart; that's what the address book is for. For addresses. Thanks for being so fucking sympathetic."

Yikes. "Sorry."

"Forget it. No point turning the night into a total disaster. I know I've got her address written down at home. You wanna come back with me and get it?"

Suzy is so wrapped up in her new man, whom she introduces as Phil, that you'd feel awkward staying in the bar without Nick, so there's no option but to leave with him. You get a cab to his place and wait while he sorts through a pile of papers on his desk to find Lindy's address. "Got it! Knew it was here somewhere." He beams.

"What are all these trophies for?"

"Those? Oh, bowling mostly. I used to be pretty good. Still am, in fact. . . . *Hey!* Why don't we play a quick game? There's a bowling alley right up the block! We'll just stay for half an hour, okay? Come on, I insist. I need something to cheer me up."

There's no talking him out of it; Nick is adamant. He promises to get you back to the Upstairs in time for the party, but he won't budge till he's played a game. Grudgingly you accompany him to Bowlorama, keeping an anxious eye on the clock.

Nick might be a champion bowler, but his game is definitely off tonight, doubtless a result of all the Maker's Mark he's been throwing down his throat. You're beating him, and he's growing increasingly sullen and irritable. If he loses, he might sulk all night—maybe he'll even refuse to go to the party. The male ego being what it is, you toy with the idea of deliberately losing just to make sure that doesn't happen. But you *want* to win. You *deserve* to win. Nick's a big boy; surely he can cope with being beaten by a woman?

If you throw the game, turn to page 102.
If you play to win, turn to page 106.

Among those you've just been introduced to for the first time is Chris, and you find yourself making eye contact often as you both observe what's going on. Something deep within you stirs. This is no ordinary eye contact, and it's obvious the two of you need to talk.

When you do, you can't help but feel this is the first time you've ever been understood in your whole life. Chris seems to know exactly what to say to you, even seems to be able to anticipate what you'll say in return. Is it possible that soul mates really do exist? And that you've found yours in this most unlikely place, on the very night you set out to end up with someone else entirely if it was the last thing you did? You've never before felt so strong an attraction, not like this anyhow . . .

If Chris is short for Christopher, and the person arousing such strong emotions in you is, perhaps to your own surprise, a man, turn to page 95.

If Chris is short for Christine, and the person arousing these strong emotions is a woman, turn to page 99.

A pitcher it is then, sweetie. Let's get trashed, shall we?"

Within half an hour you're ordering another pitcher and feeling giddily bombed. Suddenly the world, and everything Peter says, is hysterically funny, and only the fact that a burrito the size of a torpedo is already congealing in your stomach is keeping you from slumping over the table.

"You know," says Peter, waving a tortilla chip in your face and adopting the trademark French accent he always resorts to after a few drinks, "Eet truly ees a gurrrrreat playzure to be een your company."

"Really, Monsieur, you are exqueeseetly kind."

"You theeenk? Non, petit Pierre ees just eeen 'onest mood. So eef there ees anything you want to ask Pierre, ask away."

"Any theeeng?"

"Mais oui. To you, Mademoiselle, Pierre ees an open book."

You think about it for a moment, not very lucidly. By now you're tempted to blow off the party altogether and just see what happens with Peter. He's never seemed this interested in you before—that is, if it is interest, and not just tequila. How can you tell the difference? Hey wait a second, that's not a bad question.

If you ask him, "Are you interested in me or is it just the tequila?" turn to page 109.

If you wait and try to think of something else, turn to page 111.

I Don't Mind at All" by Bourgeois Tagg

To resume your adventure, go to page 65.

"Fine, you can come."

"I can? Hurrah! Pierre's going to a party!"

By the time you get to McCormick's, the place is heaving with sweaty bodies, two of them belonging to Suzy and a guy she introduces as Phil. They're pawing each other unashamedly. Somehow, though, you manage to persuade her to take her leg out from between the guy's thighs long enough to get to Lindy's.

Lindy's house is gorgeous, and she's assembled a pretty good crowd, including—*yes!*—Mark. All alone! In the kitchen! Sans annoying girlfriend! Now that you've finally got here, you're not going to lose any valuable time . . . You march right up to him and start a conversation. You're starting to inch perceptibly closer when the sound of raised voices in the next room leads him to investigate.

He returns a few seconds later. "There's some asshole in there who's taken control of the stereo and is playing 'Sheena Is a Punk Rocker' over and over again," he fumes. "I don't think Lindy even knows who he is. Why do idiots like that think they can just take over?"

"Sheena Is a Punk Rocker"? That's Peter's favorite song. You don't even need to peer out the door to know that it has to be him. The song starts up for what must be the sixth time in a row, and Mark bangs his glass down on the counter.

"Okay, that's it. I'm going to put an end to this."

It's hard to know which is more annoying—Peter's holding the stereo hostage or Mark's acting like a rutting stag. You take your drink and wander into the living room just in time to see Mark punch Peter squarely in the face. Peter punches right back. It continues in this vein for a few seconds, both men aimlessly beating the crap out of each other, until Lindy hears the scuffle from the next room and tries to intercede.

"Break it up, you morons. The little testosterone display will have to take place somewhere else."

Peter stands there looking sulky, and Mark makes an elaborate display of putting his arm around Lindy. "Sorry about that. Didn't mean to cause a scene. But this little dork with his pathetic Ramones fixation . . ."

He gets no further than that; Peter yells, "Alright, that's it!" and swings again, but this time Mark ducks and Peter's fist collides with

Lindy's jaw. She sinks to the floor and Peter gazes at her, horrified. You hear someone talking about calling the police. Grabbing Peter, you drag him out of the room and toward the door.

"Wow, you're leaving the party to save me?" he asks as you hurry with him up the street, hoping to find a taxi before someone chases after you. "Are you my best friend or what?"

"You have no idea." You grimace.

The End

You're feeling confident now. You look good and you're pleasantly drunk; within a few minutes you'll be seeing Mark at the party and it makes sense to be prepared. You give yourself a little pep talk as you stand at the counter, trying to decide what brand to buy. This is your night! Nothing can go wrong now. Mark wouldn't want flavored, would he? Nah, that's tacky.

"Actually, I find the ribbed ones are best. 'For her pleasure,' you know?"

That voice behind you . . . under any other circumstances you'd be overjoyed to hear him, especially to hear him addressing you, but right now—with a packet of featherlight Trojans in your left hand and the lime ones that you were toying with in your right—you can think of nothing worse.

"Mark!" You put the condoms back and try to turn your grimace into a smile. "What are you doing here?"

"Just buying beer." Holding up a six-pack of Sam Adams as evidence, he lets out a laugh eerily reminiscent of Beavis. "Not as interesting as what you were buying, I admit."

"Haha, very funny."

"Wow, you've turned bright red. Hey, were they meant for me? They were, weren't they? I'm flattered! But I usually bring my own—buy 'em in the big boys' store."

Oh no, Mark, please don't do this. Don't turn into an asshole now, just when it was all going so well. But he's ogling your chest, and you can feel all traces of lust fading from your loins. This is terrible. Mark continues making inane comments, and you finally put the condoms back on the counter.

"Not buying them?" He winks. Actually winks.

"No . . . I don't think I'll be needing them. Think I'll have an early night instead."

"That's a shame. Guess I have to find someone else to use these on." He pats his jacket pocket and laughs again.

"My loss, no doubt. See you around, Mark."

As soon as you get to McCormick's, you push your way to the bar and order a shot. After knocking it back, you look around for Suzy. She's already making her way toward you, looking drunk and happy.

"Ready for the party?" she beams.

"Can we skip it? I'd rather just stay here and get bombed."

"Sure, if that's what you want. I didn't have any reason to go anyway. Did something happen? Do you want to talk about it?"

Shaking your head, you hold up your empty glass. "Here's to beautiful illusions."

The End

You have a couple of beers while the rest of the crowd chows down at Woody's. The food looks awesome, and if you had more money you would probably eat. As it is, you're too anxious to keep your buzz and get on with the evening's main event: your seduction of Sadie, the laughing lovely.

You're thrilled when Mike decides that the group's animated conversation about the greatest sequels never made—his personal favorite is *There's Something Else About Mary*, but you still think *I Know What You Did Two Summer Ago* is kind of funny—will have to be stopped and resumed again at Spinners.

You divide up into cabs and head for the next stop. There, in a barn of a bar filled with fraternity types, you resume your drinking. No one else seems to be keeping pace, but you don't mind. At least not until they start complaining that they're not feeling well. When Tracy moans about feeling sick, you panic. She's your ticket to the party Sadie's going to be at. Your ticket to *ride*, as it were.

When she disappears to the bathroom for an inordinate amount of time, you get edgy. What if Tracy bails?

Sure enough, Tracy comes back and says she's got to go home. Mike, who has also been complaining of not feeling well, says he just puked in the bathroom and needs to leave before it happens again. Will is going to go home with Tracy, obviously. And Lisa decides she might as well just share a cab with Mike since he's on the way; she's not feeling so great either. They deduce they got some kind of food poisoning at Woody's. Much as you're glad you didn't eat, this is a disastrous turn of events.

With no one to go to the party with, you admit defeat. There will be other chances to see Sadie, surely. Under better circumstances. You head toward the Pub to see if anyone's around and, because there's no one you especially want to hang out with there, you put your name up to play pool and drink heavily. Last call—and the last game of pool—are called just before your name comes up. You go home alone, pissed off and positively shit-faced, having consumed almost one alcoholic beverage for every hour you haven't eaten (sixteen). You wake up with the sensation that someone's grabbing the front of your brain and squeezing it really, really hard. There's not a painkiller in sight.

The End

"It's very nice of you, but I think I should take her home myself."

"No hassle; whatever you want." He shrugs, looking slightly offended.

Nick says he'll be leaving McCormick's in half an hour, enough time for you to drag the semiconscious Suzy home and get back to the bar. A taxi is just pulling up, thankfully, and you bundle Suzy in before the driver gets a chance to see how drunk she is. The fare uses up the last of your cash, but not to worry, there's a bank near Suzy's place. As soon as you've helped her to her door, found her keys, escorted her to her room, and bid her good-bye as she cries "Thanksh for the great nishe!" you head for the ATM.

You've just taken out fifty dollars and are shoving it in your purse when, in the glass of the ATM machine, you see the reflection of three girls standing directly behind you. Their gaze is practically burning a hole through your bag; it's like they're all looking out of the same pair of eyes. Shit.

One of these girls you could tackle, maybe even two. But three? Not a chance. And it's a good bet that they're carrying something a little more dangerous than lipstick in their pockets.

"You got any change?" One of them, the self-appointed leader, addresses your back.

Deciding to brazen it out, you spin around to face them, say "No" in as authoritative a voice as you can muster, and start to walk away.

"Hey, where ya going?" she persists. They're following you now.

"Home."

"I don't think so. I think we should hang out for a while now that we're all friends."

You stay silent and keep walking. They're about three feet behind you.

"Hey, you hear me?" she continues. "I'm talking to you! Don't be so fucking rude!"

The street is deserted apart from the four of you, and there's no way you'll be able to outrun them for very long—your new boots may look swanky, but they weren't bought for sprinting.

"Just give us the money," says one of the others. Her mouth is almost level with your ear—you can smell her chewing gum. She makes a grab for your bag, and impulse takes over. You run. You didn't even know you could run this fast. If only there was a store nearby, something . . . Then you spy it—about a hundred feet in front of you, across the street, there's the twinkling sign of the local taxi company. They're still open. *Thank God.* You race over and hurtle through the doors, colliding with one of the drivers who's hanging out having a smoke.

"Hey, you need a taxi or an ambulance?" He chuckles, grabbing your shoulders. "Slow down!"

Panting and sweating, you lean against the wall, loving every shabby poster and morsel of flaky paint in the place. Through the glass door you can see the trio hanging back on the corner. "I need a car to get me home," you gasp at last.

"Sure, two minutes. Sit down and relax, okay? We'll get you home."

The End

next thing you'll want to move in. I just couldn't handle the commitment. Meg, you even put out a clean towel for me."

"You've *got* to be kidding." This was supposed to be said quietly to yourself, but in your exasperation you blurt it out loud.

"Who was that?" sniffs Meg. "Is someone else on the line?"

For a second you hesitate and then decide you have to speak. "Um, I just happened to pick up the phone and . . . that part's not important. The point is, the reason the two of you broke up is because you asked him to feed the fish and he freaked out, right?"

She snuffles affirmatively.

"You're such a jerk, Mark," you say.

"Wait a sec, who is this? What does it have to do with you?" he responds angrily.

"Absolutely nothing, you're totally right. But you know what? Women have to deal with this kind of male paranoia all the time, and it's ludicrous. I mean, how selfish of her. Better to let the fish starve than that you should have to deal with the colossal pressure of owning a set of keys."

There's a click on the line.

"Did he hang up?" asks Meg.

"I guess so," you mutter, suddenly ashamed at your outburst. "Shit. I'm sorry."

"Oh, hell, maybe it's for the best." She blows her nose. "I can't believe he made such a big deal about keys. I've got to go, okay?"

You hang up and hand the phone back to Nick. "What happened?" he begs.

"Meg and I both realized that we could do better." You sigh.

You pass Mark on your way downstairs, and he gives you a hostile look.

"It was you, wasn't it? Bitch." He shakes his head as you walk out the door.

The End

You start tapping a foot, thinking maybe you're being too harsh. There must be something redeeming about this band. You try listening to the lyrics:

"Baby, baby, baby, maybe, maybe, maybe, that baby ain't mine

Baby, baby, baby, save me, save me, save me. Tell me that baby ain't mine."

You decide that some sentiments—while entirely valid—just weren't meant to be put to music. The solution: drink more. You remember once actually enjoying an episode of *Home Improvement* after drinking a six-pack in an hour; surely with a few more beers you'll think this band is the greatest thing since Viagra (not that you need it, virile man that you are, but it's nice to know it exists).

You turn to Dave. "You want another?"

"No, man. These guys suck. Let's get out of here while we can."

He turns to leave and you follow, not speaking until you're outside.

"*Man*, those guys sucked." He's shaking his head in disbelief. "I don't know what the hell I'm going to say to Jack when I see him. Maybe if I'd caught a different bus and gotten here five minutes earlier or something they would have been awesome and I would have met the girl of my dreams in the crowd."

You and Dave start walking, and he tells you that he had the dream again last night. It's a recurring nightmare he's been having ever since he saw *The Truman Show* many months ago. In it, his life is a TV show and he doesn't know it; only it's not a wildly popular show like in the movie, but one that gets canceled after three weeks. You're not really paying attention, though, what with the possibility of seeing Sadie tonight. You're fantasizing about tickling her, of her laughter showering you like rain.

Suddenly, it gets darker. You look up. A dark, purplish gray cloud is rolling toward you and the wind picks up, blowing a sheet of a newspaper so that it gets caught on your leg. You turn around to kick it free just as you feel the first drop, and when you turn back, you can actually see the sheets of rain coming at you.

"Holy shit." Dave stops walking. "I feel like I'm on the set of *Twister*."

In under a minute you're both soaked to the bone.

"What are we going to do, man, look at me. Look at this." Dave holds out his hands, and rain collects in his palms in tiny puddles. "I look like Clint Eastwood in that totally hokey scene in *The Bridges of Madison County*. I mean what are you supposed to take from that, that standing out in the rain with what little hair you have pasted to your forehead is a sign of true devotion? Give me a break."

You look around. The only establishment on this block is a strip bar.

If you point at it and shrug, turn to page 107.
If you decide to head for Spinners, turn to page 110.

Maybe you could show me where he is." You smile sweetly. "And where the clean towels are?"

She mutters something under her breath but leads the way out, waving a glass of red wine precariously as she goes.

"Here he is!" she shrieks.

Nick looks pitiful. He groans when he sees you and promptly throws up again.

"You should take him home, darling."

"I'm sure he can make it home himself, can't you, Nick?" You thump him softly with your boot.

"Ugh. I need to call a cab," he moans, reaching out to wipe his face with the nearest available soft object, which happens to be a bath mat.

"I really think you should take him," Lindy repeats, more icily this time. "Just to be sure."

"Is there some reason you don't want me around?" you inquire.

"I can't imagine what you mean," she sneers, waving her hand around for emphasis . . . the hand that is holding her glass of red wine. It lands all over the jacket you're wearing. *Suzy's expensive suede jacket.* Swearing loudly, you grab a towel and start to wipe it off frantically.

"You did that deliberately, didn't you?" you yell.

"Are you out of your tiny mind? Why would I do that?"

"Mark, maybe?"

"Mark?" she spits. "You're crazy, you know that? I've heard enough. Get out of my house. And you, too, Nick . . . go vomit somewhere else and take your trampy little friend with you."

"Lindy, she didn't mean anything," he starts.

"Yes, I fucking did!" you roar.

"Get out now!" Lindy yells, shoving you and the frazzled Nick out of the bathroom and toward the front door. "I'll make sure Mark doesn't get lonely without you," she leers as the door closes in your face.

The End

Sounds good," you say to Dave as you finish the rest of your drink. "This place is dead anyway."

He smiles at the movie reference, and the two of you head to a new club called Plush. You exchange your flyer for free drinks at the bar, then find yourselves on the dance floor. It's so dark you can barely see the faces of the people around you and so loud you couldn't have a conversation if you tried. So you don't. Instead you find yourself bumping and grinding with a scantily clad woman. She's practically humping your leg, and you're getting really turned on. When she pulls you to her and slides her hand down your pants you're stunned. But almost instinctively you do the same to her. Before you know it, the two of you are fondling one another awkwardly while dancing close enough so that no one can see. Not that they'd be able to if they were looking directly at your crotches, it's so dark. She slips a condom on you minutes before you lose it; presumably this is to avoid the mess. But after you climax, the condom and the girl both disappear.

At closing time, you and Dave find each other on the street.

"What the hell *was* that place?" Dave says.

You can tell by the color in his cheeks he had an experience similar to your own.

"Did something weird happen to you in there?" he asks. "A girl maybe?"

You nod.

"And a disappearing condom?"

You nod.

"You think they *do* something with it?"

The End

You nudge him in the elbow, and he glances around.

"Please stop hitting me," you say. Slight smile, firm tone of voice, nicely handled.

"Did I do it again?" He shifts around in his chair to get a better view. "Sorry, really. I'm playing a round of our favorite bar game with my friend Bryan here, and he's getting me all riled up."

You just give your most withering look.

"Don't be mad," Bryan chimes in. "Let us make it up to you. Tell you what . . . you play our game and if you win, we'll buy you and your friend, let's see, two drinks each. And even if you don't win we'll buy you one anyway. Nothing weird, I swear."

Suzy's still smiling inanely at Dan, and it's clear there's going to be no chance of moving her on to another bar for a while, so why not have a go.

"Okay. Buy me a drink first and tell me how to play."

CD-thumping guy, who's tall and burly and introduces himself as Graham, dutifully buys your drink, while Bryan, who looks unnervingly like Jon Cryer circa *Pretty in Pink,* explains the rules. "Okay, this game is called Snowball's Chance in Hell, and it's very simple. First you have to pick a category. Tonight we're offering Spice Girls, heavy metal, or, my personal favorite, Tony Bennett."

Silently praying that this won't involve removing items of clothing or doing something lewd with an olive, you pick heavy metal.

"Good choice. Okay, here's the deal. We all have to think of the most unlikely words to appear in a heavy metal song. Like, for example, *hyacinth.* The best word wins. If we can't choose a winner between us then your friend can judge, okay? Graham, you start," he prods his friend. "The category is heavy metal."

Graham opens with *endocrine.* Bryan counters with *deciduous.* The words that are springing to your mind are, for some reason, *scone,* and *Nutella,* which must be your mind's way of suggesting that you really should have eaten something before going out.

If you go for *scone*, turn to page 114.

If you go for *Nutella*, turn to page 116.

HOLLYWOOD NEWS
That Ole Sinking Feeling
James Cameron Resurfaces After Academy-Induced Breakdown

For the first time since his labor of love—*Titanic*—lost all the Oscars that writer/director/producer James Cameron himself was nominated for last year, the director agreed to talk with *Hollywood News*. Devastated by what seemed to him—and indeed to much of the filmmaking world—a deliberate snub by the Academy, Cameron has only just begun to rebuild the life that fell to pieces starting after the March 1998 Academy Awards.

Alright, that's enough of that. Go back to page 49 and make another choice.

You're not in the mood to start an argument, so you take your drink and look for another seat while Suzy continues chatting to Dan. A couple sitting near the stage are preparing to leave, so you snag their table. Suzy gestures that she'll be over in a minute. Meanwhile you settle in to listen to the show.

The band is playing its last song, a slow, pretty version of "Across the Universe." Whatever the talents of the other members, the singer's got a certain charm. You can't help noticing that he's also got incredibly blue eyes, and they're focused on you right this minute. He flashes you a quick grin, and, caught off guard, you smile back. The band finishes up, and two minutes later the singer is back onstage, packing up gear. Again you exchange brief smiles—there's something about this guy that makes it impossible not to smile at him, even at the risk of looking like a dork. He finally climbs down from the stage, hovers around your table looking endearingly awkward for a few seconds, then takes the plunge and asks if he can buy you a drink. You say, "Sure, why not," and soon he's sitting opposite you.

"My name's Ed. I hope you don't mind me barging in on you like this. What did you think of the show?"

"Great," you lie. "Well, John Lennon isn't rolling over in his grave yet, anyway."

"It's okay, you don't have to be polite. We stink. Believe me when I say this isn't exactly the type of music I want to be playing, but it pays the rent. I'm in another band, a lot different than this crew—maybe you'll come see us play sometime."

The conversation drifts on pleasantly, and it takes a while before you register that Suzy is waving at you from the bar and beckoning you over.

"Can I get you another drink?" Ed asks.

If you say yes and ignore Suzy, turn to page 119.

If you go over to Suzy, turn to page 123.

You start singing at the top of your lungs. . . .

"I know a guy who's tough but sweet . . ."

You pound out a drumbeat on the dashboard.

"He's so fine he can't be beat."

Dave cuts you off as soon as you get to the "I want candy" bit. "Alright, that's enough of that. Go get your stupid candy." He's pulled into the 7-Eleven parking lot. When you get out of the car you realize you're drunker than you thought. You stumble a little as you slam the car door behind you.

Inside you buy a selection of candy and a Coke to sober you up, if only temporarily. You pick up one for Dave, too. You pass the stuff through the driver's-side window to Dave and tell him you're going to check your voice mail.

You call your answering service, punch in your mailbox number, and find a message from Mike. He tells you they're having dinner at a place called Woody's. But the next message is newer. "Alright buddy, I'm leaving you all these messages. I hope you're not blowing us off tonight. We're leaving Woody's now and going to this bar called Spinners. You know Spinners. You took me there once. Anyway, we'll be there until about eleven, then we'll hit the party. Hope to see you there." You check your watch and see that you'll just make it to Spinners in time.

You hop in the car and tell Dave to step on it. A mile down the road he gets pulled over for speeding, and they ask him to step out of the car. He can't walk a straight line, and they give him a Breathalyzer test, then arrest him for drunk driving. You accompany him to the police station and spend the night trying to track down his lawyer father—or anyone who can bail him out. Lo-hoo-hooser.

The End

You take the card from her left hand.

"Isn't this exciting?" The old lady, who insists you call her Millie, gives the other card to Bill and leans over your shoulder to watch you scratch.

"Do it slowly!" she urges. "You girls go first . . . one panel at a time! Wait; use my lucky scratcher!"

Her 'lucky scratcher' turns out to be the lid of a bottle of Tanqueray, flattened into a disc. This is getting more pitiful all the time. Millie's gaze is glued to the card. "You need three matching numbers to win, don't forget! Look, a fifty dollar! A ten dollar! Ooh, a five hundred dollar! Another ten! Another five hundred! And, oh dear heavens, another . . ."

"Another five hundred! We won five hundred dollars!" yells Suzy. "Millie? *Millie?*"

Millie is on her knees, clutching her throat. Her face is purple, and she seems to be having some kind of seizure.

"Oh fuck, she got so excited she's having a stroke. Or is it a heart attack? What does it mean when your face turns the color of eggplant?"

"It means it's time to call an ambulance, Suzy."

"I didn't win anything," sighs Bill, holding up his card.

"*Bill!* Call a fucking ambulance!"

Five minutes later Millie is being placed on a stretcher. "I'll go with her to the hospital," offers Suzy. "Maybe someone should stay with the dog; it's going berserk." Margarita is whining frantically, running around in tiny circles.

Bill shakes his head. "I can't deal with dogs, man."

"Oh, go home, Bill. I'll stay," you snap.

"Once I see that Millie's okay, I'll get a cab back here, okay?" suggests Suzy. "I'm sorry we're gonna miss the party, but maybe we'll have time to get a late drink."

You nod dumbly, close the door, then settle down on Millie's couch for a night of television. "Look, Margarita, *Oklahoma!* is on. Exciting, huh?" you whisper.

The End

You and Dave stop at Denny's and have an all-you-can-eat buffet dinner. By the time you leave you're so stuffed that you don't know how you'll even put away another beer. The temptation to just go home and sit on the couch all night watching TV is enormous. Still, your Big Night Out awaits.

You and Dave hop back into the car and go to the Lunar Lounge, hoping Mike and co. will still be there.

Turn to page 92.

Thanks very much, very kind of you." You take the card that was in her right hand.

"Scratch it here! Scratch it here!" she insists. Clearly this woman craves excitement.

You dutifully scratch off the silver panels to reveal . . . absolutely nothing. Not a sausage. Bill, on the other hand, has grabbed the other ticket without a second thought and is scratching off the last panel, his face turning pink with excitement. "Yes . . . yes . . . *Yeeess! Haha-haha!*"

"No luck, Bill?" Suzy pipes up.

"One hundred dollars! I won a hundred bucks!"

"Well, isn't that lovely!" beams the old lady.

"I'm gonna go cash this thing. Where did you buy it? The store on the corner? I'm gonna go get drunk! Thanks, ma'am," he calls, already on his way out the door. "I'll see you girls around . . . tell Nick I said hi."

"What an incredible asshole," Suzy mutters, once the two of you have finally persuaded the old lady that no, you don't want a Fig Newton, thanked her again, and left. "Can you believe he didn't even offer her any of the money? Jerk."

"Forget about him. Let's just find a taxi and get to the Upstairs quickly, before Nick leaves, okay? You know where the place is, right?"

"Sure," she insists, flagging down a cab. A couple of minutes later, she taps the driver on the shoulder and orders him to pull over.

Turn to page 18.

You and Dave swing by his place to drop off his car, then hop into a cab to get to the Lunar Lounge. You look at your watch, and so does Dave.

"Think they'll still be there?" he asks.

"I hope so." You wonder if Mike'll be pissed off you're so late. "What about your friend's band? Are we gonna make it in time?"

"Nah." Dave waves his hand dismissively. "That's okay, though."

You get to the Lunar Lounge, and to your dismay there's a line stretching around the corner. Hopeful, you step right up to the bouncer. "We're just looking for someone in the bar."

"Yeah, pal." The large man in black doesn't even look at you. "You and everybody else on this line."

"What's this line for anyway?"

"Elizabeth Albern's playing tonight."

Why does that name sound familiar? You and Dave look at each other with puzzled expressions on your faces. Clearly, it's familiar to him, too.

You strike a deal: you give the bouncer your wallet, then go in to search for Mike while Dave waits outside. It's dark and hot and crowded and smoky, and there's no sign of Mike and co. anywhere. You meet Dave back out on the street and find a pay phone. "Maybe they called."

"Hey." Dave is talking to you while you dial your answering service. "I figured it out. We went to camp with an Elizabeth Albern. You should remember. You're the one who kissed her, then blew her off. You think that's her?"

"Nah," you say as your messages start to play. "Couldn't be."

If you and Dave have already eaten dinner tonight, turn to page 308.

If you haven't eaten dinner, turn to page 113.

You have to escape from this conversation at any cost. There's an empty chair beside Suzy, so you slide over.

"Meet my new friends!" Suzy exclaims. "This is Andrew, Andy, and Andrew!"

"Three Andrews?"

"No, I'm Andy, the others are Andrew," explains the middle guy. "Scots Andrew and I are old friends—we call him that because he's from Scotland."

"Very cunning. And the other Andrew?"

"I'm just Andrew," says the other Andrew. "Don't worry, it's only confusing in the beginning. Usually it's just me and Andy, but Scots Andrew is in town for a couple of weeks, isn't that right?"

"Aye." Scots Andrew grins.

"What are you here for?" you ask.

"Wait till you hear!" squeals Suzy. "This is the best bit! You're gonna love it."

"Well," begins Scots Andrew, "I'm actually here to see my cousin. We're good mates, likesay."

You turn to Suzy, puzzled. "What's so great about that?"

"Ask him who his cousin is!" You've never seen Suzy this excited. Except for that time when her favorite bar was hosting a Stoli promotion, with free flavored shots.

"Okay, who's your cousin, Scots Andrew?"

"Ewan McGregor," he answers.

Suzy was right, this *is* good.

"You're kidding! Really? Wow."

"Tell her the rest!" Suzy pleads.

"We're meeting Ewan later," Scots Andrew continues. "He's staying here in town for a few days. We just told your wee mate that she could come with us if she wants. That goes for you, too."

You turn to look at Suzy. Her eyes are sparkling and she's nodding her head ecstatically.

"Ewan McGregor! We have to go! Come on, you've seen *The Pillow Book*, haven't you?" She nudges you, and you remember exactly what she's talking about. Those nude scenes. My god . . .

"Aye, all the lassies love that film," says Scots Andrew. He leans over the table and whispers to you, "Y'know, me and Ewan used to compare equipment when we were young, you know what I mean? And if I do say so myself, he can't hold a candle to me. So to speak."

"Really?" Now that *is* interesting. Unthinkingly, you start caressing an empty beer bottle in front of you.

"Aye." He grins. "Just something to bear in mind, ken?"

"So are we going then?" Suzy asks you, hope shining in her eyes.

"Lead the way."

The End

You find yourself talking to Chris to the exclusion of all others and occasionally look over to make sure Dave's okay; he doesn't always like hanging out with Mike's crowd. Tonight, however, he's talking excitedly to Lisa and seems pretty happy about it. For that matter, so does Lisa. They'd actually make a good couple; not that you'd ever thought of it before.

"Are you in a relationship?" Chris's question seems to you a non sequitur.

"Excuse me?" you say.

"You and Dave over there. I was wondering if you were together."

"No, no, no. I'm not, I mean, well he's not gay, um, neither am I."

"You're not?"

"No."

"Oh, I'm sorry. It's silly, it's just that I thought we—oh, it's not important."

"No," you say, surprising yourself. "Don't be embarrassed. There is something going on here; I'm just not sure what. You're great. It's just I've never felt this kind of connection with a man before."

"Does the idea of it totally turn you off?"

"I don't know, really. Right now I feel like I could do anything with you. But I'd hate to act on impulse and do something I'd regret."

"I totally understand. I'd like to get to know you either way, though."

"I'd like that."

"Hey, you want to play pool?"

Just then Dave comes over. "What do you say? You going to come back and watch the band?"

If you want to play pool, turn to page 121.

If you want to watch the band, turn to page 144.

Truly, there can be no greater love than that which compels you to stay and listen to Anton and Bill argue the merits of the word *freaking*, rather than miss a chance to see Mark at the party. The tension between the two of them subsides, only to explode a few minutes later when Bill accuses Anton of being a dumbass drama queen, and Anton retaliates by insisting that Bill is a brain-dead moron who needs a diagram to figure out which shoe goes on which foot. The situation is getting ugly—not that it was very aesthetically pleasing to begin with.

"You wanna take it outside?" yells Bill at last.

"Don't be stupid. We don't have to fight like freaking barbarians."

"Yeah? *Yeah?* Well, I think we do, asshole! Get outside or I'll drag your fairy ass out!"

One of the bartenders shouts over, asking them to keep the noise down. Next thing you know, Bill is dragging Anton out the door. Maybe you should call the police, or at least get the bartender to keep Bill from pounding Anton into the ground?

Nah.

Anton staggers back in, holding his nose, which is bleeding profusely. He charges into the men's toilets. Bill never returns. Suzy comes over to ask what's going on.

"Looks like Bill beat the shit out of Anton; that's all I know. He's been in the bathroom for a while now; maybe I should check up on him?"

"We'll both go; come on."

As soon as you enter the bathroom, you see Anton's legs sticking out from under the door of the last stall. Suzy rushes over. "My god, it looks like he collapsed. There's a cut on his head, and I think his nose is broken."

You don't want to get involved—it'd be easier to just slip out of the bathroom, and the bar, before anyone sees Anton. On the other hand, Anton did say he knew where Lindy's place was. An idea strikes you . . . totally selfish, admittedly, but still . . .

"Hey, Suzy, does he have an address book or diary in his pocket? He said he knew Lindy; maybe her address is written somewhere?"

"Y'think? I don't really want to touch him; he's all bloody."

"Here, I'll do it." You crouch over him and check his jeans pockets. Nothing there. Maybe the chest pocket in his jacket. You're just pulling out his wallet and rummaging around for anything that looks like an address book when the bathroom door opens and someone yells, *"Hey!"* very loudly. It's the bartender.

"What are you two doing? Mugging the guy? Did you beat him up, too?"

"No, we just found him here, he's sort of a friend and we were . . ." Suzy's voice trails off. There's no good way to explain this.

"You were checking if he had anything worth stealing? And you're friends of his? Jesus. I'm gonna call an ambulance. And the police—maybe you two should stick around till they get here."

"But we hardly know him!" wails Suzy. "Really! We just have to get to a party, okay?"

"Sorry, but you're not going anywhere for a while."

"You watch too many bad cop shows, you know that?" complains Suzy as he hauls you back into the bar to wait for the police.

The End

Serge puts his hand on your shoulder and you gingerly lift it off.

He protests inarticulately for a few seconds, with copious "y'know"s thrown in, and then, as if on cue, Nick arrives.

"You're up. We're partners, playing Suzy and some English guy named Phil."

"See ya, Serge."

Though you and Nick play a good game, your opponents are too skillful. Afterward, Suzy and her new friend huddle together in a corner, flirting with all the subtlety of a bad sitcom, and Nick asks if you want to join him at the bar.

If you decide to check your messages and go to the ATM machine now, turn to page 20.

If you join him, turn to page 126.

You've only been talking to Christine for a few more minutes before you're scared for your life. She is what you like to call a member of the SWAT TEAM: Single Woman Approaching Thirty, Tries Entrapping All Men. She already has you married and living in a big house with three kids, working sixty-hour weeks so she can be a stay-at-home mother. She's clinging to you, and she's already started calling you by a pet name—Moo Moo. When you find out that she's going to the party with everyone else, you fake a stomachache and leave. Sadie will just have to wait. But can those raging hormones of yours do the same?

You decide to swing by the Pub.

Go to page 299.

This is petty. Mean. Degrading. Beneath you. But not far enough beneath you. Could it be that you're so drunk and horny that the prospect of a surefire revenge fuck is better than trying, and possibly failing, to get together with someone you really like?

Apparently so.

"Can I, y'know, tell you something?" asks Serge. "You're very pretty."

"Thanks. Do you often cheat on Clara?"

"Well, not often, y'know. But I like you. You've got a full bounty."

"A full bounty? Does that mean what I think it means?"

The answering grope leaves little doubt. Suzy is staring incredulously at you while Nick takes a shot. You find it hard to concentrate on being cheap, duplicitous, and trashy while you're being watched. "Why don't we go somewhere else?" you suggest.

His place is, conveniently, just a couple of blocks from your apartment. You mumble good-byes to Suzy and Nick and apologize for missing the party. Suzy tells you to have fun and be careful. She's busy flirting with some English guy but promises to leave a message on your machine telling you where the party is, just in case you can make it.

Serge's place is impeccably neat. Even the *Playboy* magazines on the bookshelves are arranged chronologically in special binders. When he sees you examining them, he gives a boyish, rueful grin.

"Guy stuff. Would you like something? Y'know, beer?"

"Got anything stronger? Y'know, vodka? Gin?" "Chloroform? Sedatives?" you mouth to yourself as you perch on the sofa. Can you really go ahead with this? Maybe you should just try to get it over with as quickly as possible.

If you retire to the bedroom right now, turn to page 129.

If you delay the action a little longer, turn to page 131.

Come on," Lisa says, hooking her arm around yours. "You probably left it on the bar or something." She tells Mike you'll meet them at Spinners.

A short cab ride later—Lisa's wearing new shoes, so she insisted—the bouncer asks you for ID. You reach for your wallet, forgetting for a second that that's why you're here in the first place. Duh!

"I don't have it," you say.

"Sorry, pal, can't let you in."

"But—"

"No buts about it. No ID, no par-tee."

Lisa holds out her ID. "I'll go in and ask. Wait here; I'll be right back."

The bouncer checks Lisa's ID, then lets her in with a sweep of his arm. "Right this way, young lady."

In a minute or less Lisa returns to your side. "I was right." She hands you your wallet. "Let's go."

"Hold on a minute."

"What?"

If you decide to go in and check to see if Dave showed up, turn to page 124.

If you say, "Nothing, forget it," and decide you're better off heading straight uptown without Dave and his backward baseball cap, turn to page 191.

"Woohoo, the Nickster triumphs again!"

It's been like this for the past ten minutes. Nick promised to leave as soon as the game was over, but since he won—since you let him win—he's been parading around, congratulating himself and boring the pants off anyone who'll listen.

"Still got it, I guess!" he bellows. "Still the best, the king, the natural!"

"Hey, Mr. Wonderful, you gonna pay for that beer?" yells the bartender. "Or maybe one of your hordes of adoring fans is buying it for you?"

Nick reluctantly hands over the money, and the bartender rolls her eyes at you sympathetically. You smile weakly. "You want another?" she asks. "It's on me—my shift's just finishing. And you look like you could use it."

You gladly take the drink, trying to ignore Nick while he rambles on and on about his bowling prowess. Now that you've refused to play anymore, he's scouting for another partner. "What about the party?" you howl.

"I don't think I'll go. Having too much fun here."

"Then give me the address."

"What? Oh . . . no, I don't think I can do that. I mean, it's not fair to Lindy to send complete strangers to her party."

Surely, *surely* he is joking. But no; Nick absolutely refuses to give you Lindy's address, and nothing you say makes any difference. You sit there weighing your glass in your hand. If only he wasn't a blood relative of Suzy's. If only you could beat him up without feeling guilty about it.

Still, better to do something mature, like storm outside in a huff and bum a cigarette from somebody. The bartender, now finished for the night, is leaning against the wall outside, and she offers you a smoke. "Good night?" you ask.

"Lousy. Though I'm glad I was on my side of the bar serving the freaks and not on your side, bowling with one of them. Who was that asshole? Not your boyfriend?"

"Hell no . . . just some dimwit I was hoping would bring me to a party. But once he won the game he became unbearable. And the worst thing is, I let him beat me so he wouldn't feel bad."

She inhales deeply. "If they win, they never let you forget it; if you win, they hate you for it. My old boyfriend, he thought I was the greatest woman in the world until we both took an IQ test and I got a higher score than he did. He couldn't handle it. He figured that because he went to an Ivy League school and I was bartending, there was no way I could ever be smarter than he was. As if I want to stay here forever. It's just an easy part-time job. What I really want to do is finish my screenplay . . . but I won't bore you with that. Hey, you wanna get a beer somewhere? If you're not going to that party? My name's Jane, by the way."

Might be fun to hang out with Jane for a while. The alternative is going back to the Upstairs, presumably to watch Suzy slobber all over her new friend.

If you go with Jane, turn to page 133.

If you decide to go back to the Upstairs, turn to page 137.

When you and Mike get to the Lunar Lounge and there's no sign of your wallet, your mind suddenly flashes back to your run-in with the in-line skaters. With perfect recall, you feel your wallet being lifted out of your back pocket when the collision occurred. How could you have been so stupid and not known it at the time? Then again, you were hardly going to go after a pack of teenagers on skates and demand that they return your wallet.

"I don't fucking believe this." You're shaking your head.

"What?" Mike asks.

"I got mugged and I didn't even know it."

"What are you talking about? You probably just left it somewhere by accident. Maybe some good samaritan will find it and you'll get it back in the mail or something in a few days."

"Hellllooo," you say. "What color is the sky on your planet? These in-line skater guys rammed into me on my way to Woody's and they took my wallet."

"You sure?"

"As sure as I am that I'm not going to get laid tonight the way things are going."

"C'mon." Mike goes for the door.

"Where are we going?"

"This is my brother's precinct. We're going to report a crime."

"But . . . what about the rest of those guys? And the party and all that?"

"Listen, if you're going to have to mooch off of me all night, you're going to at least be a good citizen first and report the crime perpetrated against you. The law's useless if we don't all participate as best we can in helping law-enforcement officials to do their job. That's what my brother always says. Actually that's what they all say. All three of my big brothers are cops."

"Jeez," you mutter. "I can see it now. The Hamilton family sitting around watching *America's Most Wanted* together on Thanksgiving."

"I told you about that?"

Mike leads you a few blocks to the precinct house. Just as you're about to go inside, someone calls Mike's name and you both turn around.

"Hey, Bobby." Mike goes back down the stairs and gives the policeman getting out of the patrol car a handshake and a backslapping half-hug. He introduces you to his brother and explains you've been mugged.

You spend the next forty-five minutes filling out a report and sitting in a room with a phone, canceling your credit cards with numbers from a master list Bobby provides for you. When you're finished, he offers you and Mike a ride up to Spinners. On the way there, however, when stopped at a light, the three of you witness a robbery in progress. Bobby springs into action, radioing for backup, drawing his weapon, and telling you two to stay put and keep your eyes peeled. As witnesses, you and Mike get held up for questioning and never make it to Spinners or the party.

Civic duty can be a real bitch sometimes.

The End

"Beaten by a woman!" Fifteen minutes after you wipe the floor with him, Nick is pacing the bar area, downing his fourth cup of beer, pointing at you and ranting to anyone who'll listen. "See her? She beat me! Beat *me*! It's a fluke, I tell ya!"

"What the hell is your problem?" you yell. "So I won! Big deal, it's just a game! You've had a lot to drink." Why are you even indulging this moron? Because you want to see Mark, that's why. And now it's after midnight and Suzy's going to be wondering where you are. "Look, can we go now?"

"No! I can't leave yet. One more game! Come on, I'll buy your beer!"

"Nick, I'm not playing again. It's over, I won, deal with it. If you want to stay here, fine. Just give me Lindy's address."

"Won't," he sulks. "S'not fair."

"You won't give me Lindy's address?"

"That's right." Nick has folded his arms and is glaring at you.

"You're an idiot, you know that?"

"Maybe, but I'm an idiot with Lindy's address." He smirks.

"Screw you, and screw Lindy's party." You crumple up your empty cup and toss it at him. "I'm going back to the Upstairs."

Furious, you occupy yourself during the short ride back by imagining scenarios in which Nick is horribly maimed by a bowling trophy. Probably Suzy won't even still be at the Upstairs. Probably you'll end the night raiding the refrigerator.

Turn to page 137.

Hello, boys." A scantily clad girl meets you at the door. "Ooooh." She steps up to Dave. "You're really cute."

"I'm all wet." He backs away.

"Not as wet as I am," she whispers, but loud enough for you to hear.

"You boys want a table?" She leads you toward the stage area, where several girls in G-strings are wrapping themselves around poles. You instantly get an erection.

"How about that table there?" You point at a prime table.

"That's reserved."

You look around the room and see that only one other table is occupied, by a scummy-looking man in his sixties. You decide to try your luck. "Well, the joint isn't exactly jumping and we're here now. Can't you give the other party another table?"

"I'm afraid not. That table's for Howard Stern. We always accommodate him when he wants to come here."

"Alright," Dave pipes up. "We'll take the table next to him, then."

You sit down and order some drinks, then settle in for the show, which you have to say is pretty lame. Not that you won't maintain your erection for its duration, but you don't find any of the girl's faces all that attractive. You try to put Sadie's head on top of one of their bodies but then you feel kind of sleazy. Sadie deserves better. Dave elbows you when Howard Stern and his entourage show up, as if you could miss them. You give Dave an irritated look; you don't want to seem like a stargazer. But Dave doesn't seem to catch on; "Hey." He elbows you again. "That's one of the Baldwins."

"Which one?" You're actually curious.

"I never did get them straight. I don't think anyone knows for sure."

The show picks up once Howard's there—not because the girls are doing anything differently, but because it's funny to listen to the shock jock's running commentary, easily audible over the cheesy music.

"Oh yeah, that's gooooood."

"You are so *hot*!"

"Mmmmn. Look at that ass."

"I'd like to take a bite out of that."

The man seems to have an endless supply of this kind of stuff. You don't know if you should be laughing at how pathetic he is or taking notes.

The waitress comes over and asks if you want a third round.

On Howard . . .

You look over at him and though you can't make eye contact since he's got his sunglasses on—what's the deal with that anyway?—he nods his head in recognition.

If you say, "Yes, thanks. We'll have two more margaritas," turn to page 128.

If you say, "No thanks; got to go," turn to page 130.

Even as you're asking the question, you realize that you've overstepped the bounds of your friendship and are now making your way toward a little patch of Very Shaky Ground. Peter's grin has turned to stony discomfort, and he starts dipping his finger awkwardly into the salsa.

"Ah, I thought you might start with sometheeeng a leeetle less personal," he demurs, "like, whether I prefer dogs or cats or something. But since you ask, I guess I've always assumed that we both knew what the deal was."

You look questioningly at him.

"Well you know," he continues, "that we like each other and maybe there's a certain spark but we don't act on it, because then it'd ru . . ."

He's actually going to utter the words. Those words. The phrase that ranks right up there with "It's not you, it's me" as a relationship death sentence. He's going to say "It'd Ruin the Friendship." You experience a temporary self-induced deafness until he's finished his little speech and is gazing at you apologetically.

"Sorry if that's not what you wanted to hear," he adds, wiping his finger on a napkin.

"Not quite. Still, at least you didn't start your reply with 'Are you out of your fucking mind?' " you offer.

You split the check between you and make your way outside. He gives you a good-bye kiss on the cheek and promises to call.

One rejection down and it's not even midnight. Feeling glum, you make your way to McCormick's.

Turn to page 30.

When you and Dave get to Spinners, soaked, it's clear you're not the only ones who got caught in the storm. Women all around the room keep pulling at their shirts to stop them from clinging to their breasts. Thank the lord for those skinny strappy things that prevent women from wearing bras. Everywhere you look there's an erection waiting to happen. Uph, too late. Look at the pair of silver dollars on that—

"Sadie!" You hope she didn't see you gawking. She should have checked the forecast before wearing white.

"Hey," she says, pulling at her shirt. You can tell she's self-conscious, so you make an extra effort to maintain eye contact and not let your eyes wander. "Who's this?" she asks you, eyeing Dave.

You introduce them, and both of their faces seem to light up.

"I know it's kind of wet," Dave says, stripping off his button-down shirt. "But do you want this? I'll be okay in my T-shirt."

"I would be eternally grateful." Sadie shyly takes the shirt, though nobody's admitting to knowing exactly why he's offered it and why she's taking it. "Can I buy you a drink in return?"

"Sure." Dave shrugs at you as she leads him away to the bar.

"Mike's over there," Sadie calls over her shoulder.

You find Mike just as he, Will, Tracy, and Lisa are leaving for the party.

"What about Sadie—and Dave?"

"Sadie knows where it is." Mike basically pulls you out of the bar with him. "They'll just follow in a while."

The party is totally lame and Sadie and Dave never show. You decide to go home via the Pub.

Go to page 299.

Even though you're itching to know, something—be it instinct, innate sense of timing, or just cowardice—tells you to back off for now. Just as well, because at that second there's a tap on the window and you look up to see none other than Mark grinning in at both of you. He's with some guy you've never seen before, and you beckon them inside, warning Peter not to say anything embarrassing.

Soon Mark is standing by your table, smiling beatifically down at you both like . . . well, like a very tall guy in a suede jacket smiling down at two drunken people. "Just thought we'd say hi," he begins. "This is my friend Jay, an old high-school buddy who's in town for a couple of days. Are you two going to Lindy's party?"

"Oh, it's *Lindy's* party?" says Peter, nudging you. "Isn't that the one you were telling me about last week, where you were hoping you'd see some guy who's just split up with a girl you said looked like a . . . owwww fuck!"

You kick him under the table with your new boots and then shoot him a withering look. Luckily, before Peter can say anything else, Jay has asked if he can help himself to your pitcher of margarita.

"So," Jay says, "you guys both coming to Lindy's? Mark was telling me she throws a killer party."

A killer party, in the company of Mark, is exactly what you're in the mood for. You suddenly like Lindy.

"You know her well?" says Peter pleasantly.

"Oh, Mark knows her pretty well alright," chuckles Jay, with a meaningful leer. He gulps down his drink with frightening speed.

You suddenly don't like Lindy.

"We went out a couple of times years ago, before she got married," explains Mark, glancing at you. "Nothing serious."

So maybe Lindy's not so bad after all.

"I was planning to go to the party, yeah," you say.

"You?" Mark nods in Peter's direction.

"I haven't been invited, technically."

"Hey, come along!" presses Jay. "Are you going to finish that drink, by the way?"

"Help yourself," says Peter.

Jay needs no second invitation.

You explain that you need to meet friends in McCormick's, and, after leaving Julio's, all four of you walk in that direction. On the way, you pass Mecca, a bar that's been open for just a few weeks. Jay stops. "Hey Mark, isn't this the place you were telling me about? Let's go in."

Mark seems keen to just get to McCormick's, but then Peter pipes up.

"I've heard about this place from someone—can't remember who—but it looks *très* glamorous. Come on!" and with that he's disappeared through the steel-and-glass doors.

If you follow him inside, turn to page 140.

If you shout for him to come back out, turn to page 143.

Dave says something right as you're listening to a message from Mike. You try to signal for him to keep quiet, but he's not looking at you. So you get the gist of the message, that they've all gone on to the party, but you can't quite hear the address when Mike leaves it. Four sixty-seven Tenth?

"Shhussh, I can't hear anything."

You go to play the message again, but since you haven't eaten dinner the alcohol has gone straight to your head and you're drunk, so instead of hitting 1 to hear this message again, you hit 3 and erase it.

"Fuck!" You slam down the receiver.

"What?" Dave is oblivious.

You explain that you erased the message before you could get the address of the party.

"Why'd you do *that*?"

"I didn't do it on *purpose*. If you hadn't been babbling about Elizabeth Albern, I would have heard it the first time."

"Well, excuse me, hot shot. You know, just because you want to get laid tonight doesn't mean the earth revolves around you." You and Dave stand there in silence for a minute. "Well, I'm beat and I'm bombed. I'm going to go pick up some Chinese, rent a couple of movies, and head home. What are you gonna do?"

If the mere mention of Chinese food has your stomach doing cartwheels out of sheer excitement, turn to page 322.

If you're determined to find the party, turn to page 118.

Scone! Scone! I love it! It's the best! It rules! You're a genius," raves Bryan passionately. "Scone!" he exclaims again, prodding Graham in the chest for emphasis.

"Alright, enough. Were you going to let me win no matter what I said?"

"Well maybe, but who cares? At least you get another drink out of it, and two for your friend, and now you won't go away thinking we're complete assholes."

"That's a pretty big leap of logic, but I'll take the drink anyway. Suzy, you want two free Stoli tonics?"

Other questions in this category would be "May I give you enormous wads of money?" and "How about I go down on you and you don't have to do anything?" The only thing that can drag Suzy's attention away from a man is the adjective *free* in conjunction with her very favorite word: *Stoli*. She asks for no explanation, merely beams at you, thanks the guys, and goes back to gazing at Dan, who's flirting gently while he slices limes. Bryan and Graham are pleasant company, but you're starting to get a little impatient—it's nine o'clock, Suzy shows no sign of wanting to leave, and you have to find Nick if there's any chance of making it to the party. As soon as Dan wanders down to the end of the bar to serve a customer, you suggest to Suzy that it's time to go somewhere else.

"Oh, come on, he's going to ask for my number any minute now!" moans Suzy. "I can't leave. And besides, he's giving me free Stoli shots!"

"Exactly how many free Stoli shots can you have crammed into the forty-five minutes we've been sitting here?"

"Four! Not bad, huh!" Her cheeks are flushed, and the needle on your internal disasterometer begins to rise.

"What happened to the plan to eat something?"

"Oh, yeah, I said that, didn't I? But I'm not very hungry anymore. Anyway, they have peanuts! Look! Honey-roasted!" and she thrusts the dish in your face, smirking like an inebriated Cheshire cat.

"Suzy, I really—" At that second a girl wearing a long Indian skirt and standard hippie regalia interrupts you with: "You two want tarot readings? Very accurate, only five bucks!"

Suzy looks semi-interested. Maybe if you can get her to think about something other than Dan for two minutes you'll have more luck getting her out of here.

If you persuade Suzy to have her cards read, turn to page 146.
If not, turn to page 149.

Nutella?" Graham frowns. "I like it, but you can't use proper nouns."

"You never said that," you protest.

"I'm sure I did . . . I must've."

"No, you didn't."

"Well, I meant to."

"That's not the same thing, is it?"

This is going nowhere. Clearly they're just trying to squirm their way out of buying your second drink. A familiar voice behind you tuts disapprovingly.

"Bickering already! Can't take you anywhere, can I?"

You swing around to see Hayley, your high-school drinking buddy, and one of your very best friends. She was the kind of childhood friend that parents automatically, and with reason, label a "bad influence." You and Hayley don't see each other much since she got into a serious relationship with Cole, a possessive character who objects to her spending time with her former buddies. Still, she seems happy with him, so maybe he has hidden depths. Very well hidden depths.

Hayley hugs you and says hi to Suzy—they know each other slightly. You're so pleased to see her you abandon the Nutella debate and go and sit at Hayley's table, leaving Suzy engaged in happy flirtation. Hayley's by herself; Cole was supposed to show up, but he just beeped her to say he won't be able to make it—something came up at work—though he asked her to make sure she's home by midnight. "So I'm free to party with you for a few hours instead!" She beams. "Like old times!"

Old times with Hayley! Ah, happy memories. Actually, your memories of nights out with Hayley tend to be not just misty and watercolored, but utterly blurred . . . Hangovers were so inevitable following an evening with her that you started to refer to them as "Hayleys," as in "Man, my head is killing me. I've got an atrocious Hayley," or "The only thing that cures a really bad tequila Hayley is three Advil and a can of crushed pineapple."

In any case, you explain to her your need to find Nick, in order to see Mark later, and she suggests going to Sullivan's right now, if you can drag Suzy away.

You try, but no dice—Suzy is drunk enough, thanks to free Stoli shots from bartender Dan, to be extremely obstinate. She wants to stay here talking to him for at least another half hour and suggests you go to Sullivan's to try to find Nick.

"But I have no idea what he looks like," you protest.

"Ask the barman there—he knows Nick pretty well. I tell you what, if you want to go on to Sullivan's, I'll follow you there in half an hour and if Nick still hasn't shown up, we'll try and come up with Plan B."

If Plan B is as stunningly ineffective as Plan A, it's going to be a fairly dismal night, but it seems like those are your only choices.

If you want to go to Sullivan's with Hayley and hope that Suzy follows you, turn to page 153.

If you decide to stay with her in the Berlin, turn to page 158.

"Four sixty-seven Tenth." You say this to yourself repeatedly as you watch Dave walk away toward home. "Four sixty-seven Tenth. Four sixty-seven Tenth."

You're going to go to that address and see if there are signs of a party. In the meantime, you've called Mike and left a message that said to leave you another message, if he gets your message, telling you where the party is because you erased his message. You're not at your most articulate at the moment.

In your drunken haze, you decide you might as well walk up to Tenth. On the way there, you have a vague sense that people are staring at you, though you're not sure why. What you do know is that if you don't concentrate all your energy on walking, you'll find yourself all over the sidewalk. When you decide to squat down in a doorway to try to clear your head and regain your balance, someone actually tosses some spare change at you. You can't be looking too good.

Still, you press on. You have to see Sadie. This, after all, is your big chance. A girl like Sadie won't be on the market for long. So when you discover that there is no 467 Tenth—at least not one where people live; it's a Kinko's—you're crushed. Still, you're sure the address is just slightly off.

If you suddenly remember with perfect clarity that it's 467 Ninth, turn to page 132.

If you suddenly remember with perfect clarity that it's 457 Tenth, turn to page 135.

If what Suzy wants is important, she can come over, you reason. And refusing a drink from Ed now that you're getting along so well would be rude, wouldn't it? Of course it would.

A little while later, you reason that refusing a third drink would be exceptionally impolite indeed.

Later still, it seems logical that refusing a fourth drink would be unforgivable. So you don't. Suzy is still glancing over and making gestures behind Ed's back that are no doubt supposed to be significant. Something is Definitely Going On, and if you were more sober, and if Ed wasn't quite so cute (and getting cuter in direct proportion to the amount you drink), you might feel inclined to go over and see what it is. But, ah, fuck it.

"Look," says Ed, as you sink the last of your fourth drink, "me and the rest of the band are thinking of going somewhere else soon—the drummer's friend Lindy is throwing a party and . . ."

"Lindy? Not Lindy Graham?"

"Yeah, that's it!" He beams. This town is really too small. "Why don't you come along? You're here alone, aren't you?"

"Well actually no, I'm here with somebody; she's over at the bar, breaking her personal record for alcohol consumption. But we were thinking of going to that party anyway."

"Which one's your friend?" he swivels around to look.

"Right th . . . wait a second. She's gone. Maybe she's in the bathroom. I'll go find her."

The bathroom in the Berlin has recently been painted, but it already hosts an impressive display of graffiti. Here are the usual inept drawings of various body parts, a couple of alcohol-related quotations, including "I'm no longer living, just looking for excuses to drink," plus the obligatory lines of tearjerkingly bad poetry, and the equally obligatory review "Get a fucking life!"

The only person in the bathroom is an aging Patti Smith look-alike searching for somewhere to do a line of speed. Long live the eighties. No Suzy anywhere to be seen. Maybe bartender Dan knows what's happened to her.

"Suzy? She left a few minutes ago," he says, running a hand through his hair thoughtfully, then checking his reflection in the mirror. "But she left this for you."

He hands you a napkin covered with Suzy's unmistakable scrawl. It reads:

"Sorry for rushing off like this. I realized I know that guy you're with, Ed. He's someone I'm trying to avoid—long story, I'll explain later. I didn't want him to see me here tonight. If you ditch Ed and want to find me, I'll be in Sullivan's for a while. Or I'll leave a message on your machine. Love, Suzy."

Well, that's just great. She could at least have said why she was avoiding him—what can his problem be? Psychotic tendencies? Deranged ex-girlfriend? Penis that bears a startling resemblance to Iggy Pop? Maybe you just have to take your chance.

If you stay with Ed, turn to page 161.
If you go to find Suzy, turn to page 165.

Playing pool at the Lunar Lounge is somewhat akin to having sex in the backseat of a car. The pool table is located in a small alcove toward the end of the bar, an alcove too small to comfortably hold a pool table. Still—and here, too, the backseat-sex analogy holds—if there's a short stick on hand (or should that be a hand on a short stick), people generally find a way.

At the moment, two women are playing what you quickly deduce must be the longest game of eight ball in history. After watching a few shots, you start to wonder whether they're actually trying to get balls in the pockets at all; maybe there's some kind of boccie equivalent people play on a pool table? Regardless, beating these two is going to be a cinch. The chalkboard hanging on the wall is clear of names, so you approach and put yours up there, claiming the next game.

"Oh." One of the women, a short stocky blonde, looks up when she sees you. "We're just messing around. You guys can have the table."

"Thanks." You turn to Chris. "Guess we're playing each other."

Just then two guys appear in the alcove. "Well, look who it is," one of them says to Chris. He's tall and lean with a tight black ribbed T-shirt and deep blue jeans; he turns his gaze to you, taking you in from head to toe. "And this must be your new friend."

"It's not like that, Thomas," Chris says.

"None of my business." Thomas covers his ears with his hands and shakes his head from side to side. "Just looking for a friendly game of pool. I see you already have a *partner*. Vince here will play with me."

"Okay, I guess." Chris looks at you and shrugs.

Thomas's partner, Vince, starts to rack up the balls, and you take a minute to assess the situation. You're sure this is the first time you've played pool with three gay men; you admit to yourself that you didn't even think gay men played pool. As stereotypical as it is, if you associate gay men with a recreational sport it'd more likely be Rollerblading—even bowling. You wonder whether Thomas and Vince are going to be any better than the two women who spared you the hassle of wiping the floor with their butts a few minutes ago.

Chris breaks and gets two balls in—one solid, one stripe. He follows up by sinking another two stripes. Thomas pulls a cue stick out of

Vince's hands, obviously determined to go first for his team. He proceeds to sink three solids.

You take a shot on a stripe and miss.

Vince misses a solid.

Chris makes his next three shots, including a tricky combination shot.

"You always were a show-off," Thomas mutters. Then he proceeds to sink all of his team's remaining balls. He misses his shot on the eight ball, however.

You're up. You sink the nine ball, the last remaining stripe, then assess the position of the eight ball. It's almost directly in line with the cue ball, but on the opposite side of the table. About three inches off the far bumper.

If you think you can cut the eight ball into the right corner pocket, turn to page 139.

If you want to bank the eight ball and bring it back to the pocket nearest you, turn to page 142.

"Thanks, but I should be getting back to my friend now," you say. "Nice meeting you."

Suzy greets you warmly. "I had an idea!" She beams. "I'm gonna check my voice mail and see if Nick called!"

You're genuinely impressed. Considering the amount of vodka Suzy has been knocking back, this is a master plan. On your way to the phone, you and Suzy stop to listen to the guitarist from the band onstage announce that they're going to hold a little competition—he'll give a mystery prize to the first person up on stage to tell him which actress, formerly linked with Woody Allen, also has a Beatles connection.

"I know this!" squeals Suzy. "It's Diane Keaton! I'm absolutely positive! No doubt whatsoever. Though, wait a second . . . it might be Mia Farrow. Shit . . . you pick one."

If you choose Diane, turn to page 167.

If you choose Mia, turn to page 170.

You explain to Lisa that your friend Dave's supposed to be here and that he owes you money. If you don't find him, you won't be able to pay her back for dinner tonight. Or do much of anything. You didn't get to the bank in time to cash your check.

"Some date you are." She smiles coyly as she goes back inside, you trailing behind her.

Inside, the bar is packed and it's a good ten degrees warmer than it is outside. You don't see Dave and wonder if he's in the back watching the band. You look at your watch and figure that it's his friend's band that's onstage now. You could really use that fifty bucks—if Dave even has it on him. But you have to pay a cover to get in.

"Well, what are we doing?" Lisa's standing really close to you, making it seem like she has to because of the crowd.

"I don't know, he could be in the back, but I don't feel like paying if he's not."

"Oh come on! Live a little. The band sounds pretty good; let's do it. But first I think you should get me a drink, for recovering your wallet."

"Okay, what do you want?"

"A Long Island Iced Tea. I need to get a buzz going."

"Are you sure? Those things are pretty strong." You know this because your personal experience with Long Island Iced Teas is rather intimately linked to your experience with puking into washing machines. On top of that, Lisa's already so buzzed it's a wonder she has anything more than a quarter inch of hair on her head.

"Sure I'm sure."

Long Island Iced Teas in hand—Lisa forced you to get one for yourself—you use the rest of your cash to pay the eight-dollar cover to get in to see the band. Lisa pays her own way in with a joking huff. There's a sizable crowd gathered, but with the exception of a few people dancing near the stage, they're just standing there, staring at the stage. "Come on," Lisa says. "Let's go up front."

If you can't resist Lisa and head for the front of the crowd, go to page 160.
If you say, "No, I'd rather hang back here and look for Dave," go to page 163.

No doubt the alcohol is helping to lubricate the conversation, but still, you feel comfortable with Nick. There's a girl sitting near you, evidently waiting for someone. "She's about to meet a blind date," declares Nick.

"How can you tell?"

"She's too nervous to be meeting someone she already knows. Look at the way she's fiddling with that straw in her drink. And I bet she's had her hair cut today . . . see the way she keeps reaching up to pat it, like she's not quite used to it yet? This is definitely the first time she's meeting someone. You ever been on a blind date?"

"Lots of blind drunk dates, if they count. You want to ask her and see if you're right?"

"If I'm wrong I'll buy you a drink."

A couple of minutes later he's back. "I was half right; she's meeting a guy she talks to on-line. They've exchanged photos but never talked on the phone."

"I guess that's a deaf date then. Very perceptive of you all the same."

"Yeah well." He grins. "When I was little I wanted to be a private detective. I can tell, for instance, that Suzy and that guy over there are going to go home together tonight, but that she'll probably never hear from him again. He's got nipplehead written all over him. Every time Suzy's not looking, he stares at that blond chick who's playing pool. His eyes are *glued* to her ass."

"Assuming you're right, why don't you say something to Suzy?"

"Why ruin her night?" He shrugs. "And I don't think she cares that much—she's just having fun. And as for *you,* young lady . . ."

"What have you concluded about me?"

"Well, Suzy already told me you want to see that guy Mark tonight, so I won't take credit for noting that your thoughts are elsewhere. But can I tell you something? And it's only because I like you, so don't take offense."

"Go on." There's a sinking feeling in your stomach.

"I know Mark pretty well. And he's not over his girlfriend yet. They were together for two years, you know? I'm not saying you don't have a chance with him; in fact, I don't doubt you could get him tonight if you wanted. But if you want more than a one-night stand, you should wait till he's got his act together. I'm not trying to interfere, honestly."

"What happens if, in waiting till he has his act together, I wait too long and he starts going out with somebody else?"

"Why would he want to go out with someone else if he could go out with you? Alright, that sounded corny, but . . . I'm not saying wait for months. But don't ruin it by rushing in." He pauses. Then: "Come outside with me for a minute."

"What for?"

"Just trust me."

He's smiling innocently, but there's been a definite shift in the direction of this conversation. Is his concern just a thinly disguised pass? Should you be flattered or annoyed?

If you go with him, turn to page 174.

If not, turn to page 177.

After your first drink on Howard, you and Dave have loosened up a good deal. So has Howard's party, all of whom seem to be knocking back drinks faster than the waitress can bring them. You end up joining their group but, unfortunately, hardly have any contact with Howard. Instead, you find yourself being monopolized by this guy whose voice you're sure you recognize from the show; he's that guy who's always talking, always making you want to tell him to just shut up and let somebody *funny* talk. Like much of the party, he strikes you as someone whose sole source of self-esteem is the fact that he works for Howard Stern.

When the guy on your other side starts to tell you what he thinks is a fascinating story about how he came to be an intern at the Howard Stern show—he's a fucking *intern!*—you decide you need to start drinking faster. The next time the waitress comes by, you order two drinks for yourself and another two for Dave, who's talking to the Baldwin.

Before long, you're completely sloshed and big chunks of the night start to disappear. Eventually, you look at your watch, and when you see that it's 12:30 you're stunned. You get up to retrieve Dave from the other side of the table—you've got to find Mike, the party, Sadie!—but you trip on your way over and fall into Howard's lap.

"Hey, get the fuck off me, man. Not my idea of a lap dance."

You get up and make your apologies, then try to talk Dave into leaving, but you're having a hard time making sense. Dave isn't in any better shape, and Howard apparently notices. He signals over to the door, where his driver is sitting at a table alone.

Before you know it, you and Dave are in a limousine and the driver's asking you where you live. Dave gives his address and you fall asleep. When you wake up, it's because Dave's getting out of the limo and poking you. "I'll call you tomorrow, man. Do you believe how great this night was? Howard Stern, man. Howard Fucking Stern. And his limo!"

The driver asks where you live and you tell him. You pass out on your bed, fully clothed, and wake up the following morning having wet yourself.

The End

Unsurprisingly, Serge reacts keenly to the idea of moving the action to his room. In fact, you're barely in the door before he's grappled you from behind and is playfully tugging at your shirt while ripping his own clothes off. This is becoming more unappealing by the second. Then, he grabs you, spins you around, you look down, and . . .

Oh my god.

You take a second look just to make sure.

Oh dear, dear god.

It's tiny. You'd no idea they even came in sizes this small. This is something you'd have trouble finding in the dark. Even with the lights on . . .

Inadvertently, you giggle. The fatal mistake. Now it's not just tiny; it's tiny and sad.

"I'm sorry," you gasp, now lost in paroxysms of laughter, "I just . . . it's not . . ."

Serge is pulling his pants back on, and you have at least enough sense to take this as your cue to leave. Mumbling another apology, you inch out the door. Poor Clara.

Outside Serge's place, you realize you're just one block from your local, the Pub. You could stop in and see if any of the regulars are around. Or you could just go home and check your machine . . . maybe Suzy called.

If you go to the Pub, turn to page 179.

If you go home, turn to page 182.

"Hey, listen," you say to Dave. "Let's not tell anybody we were at a strip bar tonight, okay?"

"Not tell them we saw *Howard Stern*?"

"Yeah, that, too. Women aren't always impressed by these things."

"I guess you're right."

"Deal?"

"Deal."

Turn to page 302.

He mixes you a drink and puts on a CD. Barry White.

"Subtle. Does the couch revolve, too?"

"Hey, enough talk," he growls, and pins you down.

Then, just as his tongue is foraging around in the general area of your tonsils, you realize that you don't have to sleep with Serge to make Clara suspect something. You just have to make it look as if you, or someone, was here. And really, it's not such a mean thing to do. Actually you're doing her a favor by letting her know what he's like. Sort of.

"Could you excuse me a minute?" you say, clambering to your feet and making your way to the bathroom.

On the bathroom shelf you spy a small flowery washbag. Clara's. Inside is a compact, a toothbrush, tampons, deodorant, and various standard girlie bits and pieces. You take out the toothbrush and smear a little lipstick on it, so it looks as if it's just been used, then leave your own lipstick in the bag.

Back in the living room, Serge has sprawled out on the sofa and is examining you with all the finesse of a small child eyeing a cookie jar.

"Freshened up?" he inquires.

"You know, Serge, this really isn't a good idea. I'm going to go," you say sweetly, pulling on your jacket.

"What? You can't!" he wails.

"I just don't feel like it anymore. Not feeling too well actually."

"What's wrong, are you marinating your steaks?"

Seeing the blank expression on your face, he continues. "Expecting a visit from Aunt Flo? Jamming, y'know?"

"Serge, y'know, see ya," you snort, and make for the door.

Back outside, you realize you're just one block from your local, the Pub. Maybe you could pop in and see who's there, and check your machine from their phone—Suzy might have left a message. Or you could just go home and check from there.

If you go to the Pub, turn to page 179.

If you go home, turn to page 182.

To your extreme glee, people are coming out of the front door of 467 Ninth, others going in. You run to catch up with an arriving group so you don't have to guess what buzzer to press. They're all carrying brown paper bags, and you realize you're going to have to mooch your booze. No hassle. You're just thrilled to be here. You're on a natural high. You think you can imagine how all those Outward Bound types feel when they spend twenty-four hours alone in a forest. You're at the party! You made it. Against all odds. You're as good as gold.

You find Mike and his whole crowd hanging out in an oversized kitchen and join them. Mike is first to spot you. "Hey, ace! What the hell happened to you?"

"Long story." You go to the fridge and grab the cheapest beer in there.

Returning to the group, you crack open the can, the crisp sound of the splitting metal like music to your ears. And as you lift the can to your lips, imagining how good this beer is going to taste, even though it's Carling Black Label, you hear Mike, practically in slow motion, saying, "You just missed Sadie. She had another party to go to."

The can connects with your mouth, and you don't stop drinking until it's empty. You make an attempt to be social with Mike for about a half hour before deciding you're in too much of a foul mood to rally. The room's crowded, and you're sick of being brushed against. In spite of two quick beers, your hangover's already setting in. You go home and get into bed. Your upstairs neighbors are having a party that keeps you awake until 4 A.M.

The End

Jane suggests going to a place called the Three of Hearts. You've never been there before, but it's a cool little basement dive, dark and cozy and not too full. Jane knows the guy behind the bar, and the first couple of rounds are on the house.

"So," she says, once your irritation at Nick has been replaced by a warm, fuzzy glow, "you must have a good reason for wanting to go to that party if you were willing to put up with such an annoying little shit. What was it, some guy?"

You nod.

"You're better off without the hassle. Men—can't live with them, can't attack their genitalia with a food blender." She laughs, flicking her ash to the floor. "They want to fuck every woman they meet, but they can't deal with women who actually like sex for its own sake. Then there are the ones who think they want an equal, and are scared shitless when they find one. You know what the answer is, don't you?"

"Lesbianism?" you respond instinctively.

"Exactly." The way she says it is a little too firm to be a joke.

"Have you ever thought about it seriously?"

"I've done more than think about it. My friend says I'm just going through an adolescent lesbian phase ten years too late. Maybe she's right. Or maybe it just took me a long time to realize the obvious, that I prefer women. Am I making you uncomfortable? I'm not hitting on you, don't worry."

"Oh, sure, I know," you answer, feeling the slightest twinge of disappointment. Might have been nice if *someone* had hit on you tonight. Someone you actually like.

"Would you like me to?"

"Pardon?" You jump. It's like she was reading your mind.

"Hit on you. Not that I usually go for straight women; it's confusing as things stand . . . I mean, I only split up with my boyfriend eighteen months ago and I have enough trouble convincing people I'm serious about this. But if you want, I'd be willing to bend my rules." She smiles. "Or we can just stay here and get drunk. Your call. No pressure."

If you go for it, turn to page 184.
If you don't, turn to page 186.

You've barely gotten a chance to look at the names on the buzzers at 457 Tenth—not that you have any idea whose party it is that you're going to anyway—when a cop car pulls up right in front of the building.

"What's your business here, young man?"

You're too startled to respond.

"I said, state your business."

"I'm going to a party," you mutter, but apparently not loud enough that they can hear you.

One of the cops is leaning out the passenger's-side window. "Listen, son, we got a call about a suspicious man wandering around this block, and we're guessing that's you. So state your business once and for all."

Just then a woman with an overstuffed garbage bag comes out of the building you're standing in front of. You can't believe your eyes. It's Sadie. She sees you—obviously recognizes you—then sees the cops. "*There* you are!"

You look at her in shock.

"I'm sorry, officers," she says. "Is there a problem?"

"Do you know this gentleman?"

"Yes, officers, I do. This here's my brother. He's not, well, not quite right. We were just starting to get worried. We usually let him go out for ice cream alone, but I guess we won't be doing that anymore, will we?" She pats you on the head.

"You sure everything's alright, miss?" The police obviously aren't too worried as they haven't even gotten out of the car.

"Yes, fine. Sorry to trouble you." Sadie escorts you inside after she drops her trash into one of the cans out front. "You look like hell," she says flatly.

"Oh my god, Sadie." You grab her by the arm. "I'm so glad to see you. I can't believe this, though. What a coincidence."

"Not exactly." She starts up the stairs, pulling her silk robe tight around her waist. "I'm not Sadie."

You just look at her, dumbfounded.

"I'm Amanda. Her twin sister, and her roommate."

"You're shitting me."

"I shit you not."

"How do you know who I am?"

"Sadie showed me a picture of you. Come on in." She waves you along. "You look like you could use some coffee."

"I was looking for the party Sadie's at, actually." You start up the stairs. "Do you know where it is?"

"Yeah, but I'm not letting you go there until you've had some coffee. It's for your own good, trust me."

You perch yourself on a high stool in the kitchen as Amanda starts to make some coffee. As you watch her move around—the spitting image of Sadie—you realize there's no reason you shouldn't be just as attracted to Amanda as you are to Sadie. That movement in your crotch indicates you are. You wonder if the two of them have ever been with a guy together.

If you see fit to ask Amanda this out loud, turn to page 341.

If you ask her, instead, "Sadie ever say anything about me?" turn to page 353.

Despondently, you push open the bar door, fearing the worst, only to have Suzy welcome you with a grin.

"At last! What took you so long? And where's Nick? We found his jacket—it had fallen under a table. A little damp but all intact, including his address book!" She waves it in your face. "Hey, isn't Nick coming?"

"No, he decided to stay at home." Tomorrow will be time enough to explain what really happened. "Let's go to the party anyway, okay? We can explain that we're friends of Nick's—I'm sure Lindy won't mind."

Suzy, you, and Phil walk to the address listed under Lindy's name. The journey is long enough for you to regain your enthusiasm for the evening. At Lindy's place, a lean, fortysomething man answers the door and smiles pleasantly at you all. "Thanks for coming! Come in, come in, make yourselves comfortable."

"Which one do you think is Lindy?" whispers Suzy as you nod politely at the other guests, some of whom are eyeing you quizzically.

"No idea," you whisper back. "Maybe that guy was her husband? I can't see Mark anywhere. Not really the kind of crowd I was expecting. Kind of sedate. Kind of . . ."

". . . old." Suzy finishes, nodding. "Maybe I'll go mingle, see if I can get a drink."

She's gone for fifteen minutes or so and returns just as you're running out of things to say to the very drunken Phil. "We're leaving," she mumbles out of the corner of her mouth. "Now. Let's go."

"What's wrong?" you ask as soon as she's dragged you outside.

"This isn't Lindy's apartment. Lindy moved two weeks ago. This," she opens Nick's address book and points to another address, written on the page opposite Lindy's name, "is the right address, way across town. I was looking for a beer in the kitchen and the guy who answered the door asked me how long I'd known Winston. 'Winston who? By the way, where's the booze?' I said. 'Winston, the guy I'm holding the intervention for,' he said. 'I thought you were friends of his. He's supposed to show up any minute now. And there is no booze. You mean to say you're not here to help get Winston into AA?' " She hides her face with her hands. "I've never been so embarrassed in my life. Can we go home now please?"

You nod wearily—by now it's too late to show up at the other place anyway.

"You know," Suzy continues, as the three of you wait outside the apartment building for a taxi, "on the bright side, one day this is going to seem really funny. Hey, it'll make a great story to tell Mark."

"Yeah, great story." You sigh. "When and if I see him again."

The End

You overcut the shot and miss. The cue ball bounces off the bank and goes into the corner pocket nearest you.

"Figures you'd end up with a loser," Thomas says to Chris.

Irate, your new friend's entire countenance changes. "Well, at least my loser's great in bed. Which—and I hate to admit I know this first-hand—is more than can be said for *either* one of you."

Thomas turns and looks at Vince in horror, then storms off.

"That was really mean, Chris." Vince shakes his head and gives Chris a disdainful look. "Particularly because it's not even true."

"How do you know Chris and I haven't slept together?" you ask.

"He means that *he* and I have never been together," Chris explains.

For some reason, you find it kind of refreshing that men can be just as vindictive as women.

"So this isn't your new boyfriend?" Vince asks.

"I'm not even gay," you say. It's all you can do to stop yourself from adding "not that there's anything wrong with it."

Vince looks you over. "Yeah, whatever you say . . ."

"No wait!" You want to find out what he means, but Vince is gone before you get a chance.

"He's right, you know," Chris says.

"About what?"

"You may not know it yet, but you're definitely gay. You probably think you're looking to score with some woman tonight—maybe you even know what woman—but she's not going to satisfy you any more than any of the others."

You decide it's time to accept the possibility that you go both ways. So for tonight, at least, you give up on Sadie so you can sort through your feelings. You and Chris order some more drinks and talk the night away.

The End

Mecca has the crisp, clinical smell and spotless interior of a very new bar. The furniture is tastefully modern and at the back you can see a small elevated platform; it looks like they're getting ready for some kind of show. It's pretty crowded, and you notice that the ratio of men to women is decidedly in your favor. Peter is already putting songs on the jukebox—he's gone for his all-time favorite, "Sheena Is a Punk Rocker" by the Ramones—but through the glass door you can see Jay and Mark standing outside, having what looks like a heated discussion. Still, Peter has finished picking his songs and is ordering your usual, so you take a seat.

Mark wanders in, looking uncomfortable. "Hey, how about finishing those real quick and going to McCormick's before your friends give up on you?" he says.

"No hurry," you say soothingly. "It's barely midnight. I thought Jay said you liked this place?"

"Mark!" calls the bartender. "You're not on tonight, are you? I thought you swapped shifts with Mikey."

"No, I'm not on; just here for a very quick drink with some friends."

"You bartend here?" Peter asks Mark.

"Mark?" The bartender laughs. "Hell, no." He hands Peter a flyer. "Mark couldn't mix you a Screwdriver if you gave him an instruction manual. But he does the best Mariah Carey impersonation in the city, don't ya, Mark?"

All the margaritas in the world couldn't have prepared you for this. You can actually feel your jaw dropping, and Peter, giggling hysterically, gingerly takes the drink from your now shaky hand.

"Holy shit!" is all he can say. You can't even manage that much. The flyer features a photo of three drag queens, with a caption beneath saying "Shows nightly." And sure enough, one of them is quite obviously Mark.

"Nice calves," notes Peter. "You look a little like Cher."

"You'd probably have preferred if I looked more like Sonny," Mark says to you, looking flustered. "The thing is, hardly anyone knows about this. It gets exhausting explaining to people that I'm not gay, so I don't bother explaining what I do for a living."

"He's been dressing up as a woman ever since our class did *A Street-*

car Named Desire in high school," interrupts Jay. "All-boys Catholic school, so some of us played women. Mark made an awesome Blanche DuBois."

"I know it seems a little weird," continues Mark, in what you feel to be one of the record-breaking understatements of the century, "but really, it's just a job. I don't usually dress up as a woman except at work."

"You don't *usually*?" you sputter.

Peter tugs your arm and whispers, "This is getting a little weird for me. You want to forget the party and just go somewhere else?"

If you decide to stay with Mark and Jay, turn to page 189.

If you think that now would be a good time to leave with Peter, turn to page 192.

You line up the shot as best you can, then shoot. The eight ball rapidly hits the bank and sails effortlessly back toward you and into the corner pocket.

"*Nice* shot." Chris steps forward to shake your hand.

Vince comes up and shakes hands with you and Chris both, but Thomas says "What*ev*er" and walks away. Vince apologizes for Thomas's behavior, then follows him back to the bar.

Chris turns to you. "You want to play another?"

If you say yes, turn to page 148.

If you decide that you want to go watch the band instead, turn to page 144.

Hearing you holler, Peter returns.

"Hey, why don't we go in? It looks cool in there. The bartender said there's a drag show on later."

"I'd prefer to just get to the party," snaps Mark.

"Is there a problem?" Peter asks, in a tone that's a little too polite.

"No problem; I'd just prefer to go somewhere else."

"Whatever." Peter gives an exasperated shrug. "On we go." But he grabs your arm, and when the others have walked a little ways in front, he addresses you in hushed tones.

"Am I right in thinking that Mark is the guy you like?"

"Yeah, and thanks for almost ruining it before."

"I don't know if you stand much of a chance anyway. Has it occurred to you that Mark might be gay?"

"What?" You laugh. "Where the fuck did you get that from?"

"I dunno, it's just . . . Jay said he's mentioned that bar Mecca, and from what I could see, it's definitely a gay bar."

"Then how do you explain the fact that he just broke up with a long-term girlfriend?" you counter.

"Wake up, baby; it's not like he'd be the first guy who's afraid to come out. Or maybe he's bi. All I know is he reacted pretty strangely when we wanted to go in there, and yes, I'm drunk, but not so drunk that I can't see there's more going on than meets the eye."

Mark and Jay have stopped up ahead and are waiting for you.

"Look, I don't think I'm imagining this," continues Peter. "But it's up to you—I'll leave right now if you like. The last thing Pierre wants is to get in the way."

If you tell Peter to go home, turn to page 195.

If you want him to stay with you, turn to page 199.

Chris decides to leave; he's supposed to meet some friends across town anyway. On your way back to see the band, you decide that you haven't been drinking nearly enough, so you stop at the bar and do a Kamikaze shot. You also get a pint of Sierra Nevada.

You find your friends in the back and stand next to Mike, since Lisa's making every effort to dominate Dave's attention and is apparently succeeding. When the band comes on, you recognize Dave's friend Jack behind the drum kit. There are two more guys onstage, and then this absolutely beautiful waif of a woman steps onstage and approaches the mike. She's wearing this dress—god, how to describe it. You have absolutely no idea what material it is, but the way it clings to her body is amazing. And the way it changes color in the light. Is it green? Or blue? Or gold? Oh, who even cares! She's got a body to die for and gorgeous long jet-black hair. When she starts to sing, the slightest smile appearing on her face, you're convinced she's the most amazing woman you've ever set eyes on. In a flash, you see you and her leaning in intimately in conversation, kissing timidly, perhaps even touching each others' . . .

And then it hits you.

That woman up there, that woman who makes you just want to take her somewhere and do all sorts of unmentionable things to her, well, she's . . . *Elizabeth Albern!* You went to camp together when you were, like, twelve. And the two of you snuck off to the lake one night and you kissed her and groped her (though admittedly there wasn't much to grope at the time). But then when word spread around camp that you'd kissed Elizabeth Albern you wanted nothing more to do with her. You were too embarrassed, afraid everyone would find out what you and Elizabeth knew. That was the first time you'd gotten an erection in the presence of a girl, the first time you'd even shown the goods to a girl. To this day, you still get a hard-on whenever you're by a lake.

But lordy lord, look at her now. If you'd known back then how she was going to turn out, you would have proclaimed your love for her and bided your time, then moved to whatever state it is that allows fourteen-year-olds to get married. She's not just hot. She's otherworldly. And when she bends at the waist to pick up a tambourine, flashing her bra-free cleavage to your segment of the crowd—if only for a second—your dick gets hard.

You're going to have to talk to her. You need to get another drink to bolster your courage. But right now you can't take your eyes off of her, can't tear yourself away to go to the bar, fearing you might miss something—perhaps another glimpse of that cleavage. Finally, when she says they're about to play their last song, you make a mad dash to the bar. Just as you return, the heavenly music ends, and your friends turn and stare at your drink.

"What'd you get that for?" Mike points. "We should hit this party before it gets too late. And we're supposed to stop at Spinners on the way."

If you say, "Give me the address; I'll catch up with you either at Spinners or at the party," turn to page 155.

If you say, "I know, I know. I had a silly idea about reintroducing myself to the lead singer. We went to camp together as kids. But it's dumb. She won't even remember me. Help me drink this, and then let's go," turn to page 151.

Sure, we'll do it. Suzy, you go first."

The hippie girl, whose name, inevitably, is Summer, drags a stool over, perches between both of you, and asks Suzy to select ten cards. "Can I find out about the immediate future?" begs Suzy, glancing in Dan's direction.

Like, which street corner are you going to be throwing up on by eleven o'clock? you wonder. "Yeah, I'd like to know that, too."

Suzy pokes you in the ribs. "Ssssshhh! I'm *concentrating*."

Summer lays the ten cards out in the shape of a cross.

"Present position . . . three of cups . . . you're feeling celebratory. The knight of pentacles is crossing you . . . a dark-haired male figure might cause you some problems."

"Dan is dark," says Suzy glumly.

"Wow, yes, you're right," you sigh, "and shit, he's the only dark-haired man in town! I mean, look around you—the room is jam-packed with albinos!"

Summer just smiles sweetly and continues reading. "I sense that you're looking for a particular person—both of you, though he's someone closer to you perhaps?" she glances at Suzy. Your ears perk up at this.

"You couldn't tell us exactly where he is, could you?" you plead. "No chance of seeing any particular bar names in there? An address?"

"He's not where you expect to find him, that's all I can see. Though I sense he's trying to contact you, too. Hope you find him. Have a good night, ladies."

"Hell, yeah, tonight we're gonna party like it's nineteen sixty-nine, right?" says Suzy happily, as Summer scouts around for another customer.

"I don't think you should insult hippies, Suze. Bad for your karma. Anyway, she may have been helpful—what if Nick is trying to contact you? Did you think about checking your voice mail?"

"Y'think?"

"Yes, Suzy," you say patiently. "That way, maybe we'll find him and actually get to the party, instead of staying here, where I don't need tarot cards to predict that I'll spend the night wiping the drool off your chin and playing bar games with Ducky and his henchman."

Bryan, who's been engrossed in another round of Snowball's Chance in Hell, arguing that the word *welding* would never appear in a Spice Girls song, pipes up with a good-natured "Hey, I heard that!"

"No offense, it was really nice meeting you both. Come on, Suze," and you drag her off in the direction of the pay phone.

On your way, you pass the stage . . . the band is taking a break between songs and the guitarist announces that they're about to hold a little competition—he'll give a mystery prize to the first person up on stage to tell him which actress, formerly linked with Woody Allen, also has a Beatles connection.

"I know this!" squeals Suzy. "It's Diane Keaton! I'm absolutely positive! No doubt whatsoever. Though, wait a second . . . it might be Mia Farrow. Shit . . . you pick one."

If you choose Diane, turn to page 167.

If you choose Mia, turn to page 170.

Will you rack 'em?" Chris asks. "I've got to go to the bathroom."

The second Chris leaves, Thomas reappears.

"I bought you a drink. A peacemaking gesture." He hands you a fancy cocktail. "Sorry I was so pissy. And do me a favor; don't tell Chris. I'm embarrassed enough as it is."

"Thanks," you say, taking a sip of what proves to be a rather tasty drink.

Hours later, you wake up in your bed and feel woozy, like you've got seltzer pumping through your veins. Chris is at your side.

"What happened?" Your voice sounds strange to you.

"I don't know." He shakes his head. "You just passed out by the pool table. You must have had too much to drink."

You think back on the evening's events. You know you didn't have more than you could handle. Then, because it's true—but more because you've always wanted to say it—you sit up in bed and shout, "Somebody slipped me a mickey!"

The End

It's unlikely that some patchouli-scented Woodstock throwback is going to make any impression on Suzy, given her current state, so why waste the money. You decline, and the girl smiles beatifically. "I understand. You have a lovely aura, by the way."

"She bought it in Banana Republic. Big sale on auras," interrupts Suzy, laughing loudly at her own joke.

The hippie chick moves on to other prospective customers.

"Hey, Suzy, you're not going to get totally wasted, are you?" Even as you're asking you realize how pointless this question is. Suzy has already leaped over the divide between sobriety and drunkenness, and is galloping toward calamity even as you watch.

"I might be a little bit wasted already, but just a little. A *soupçon*. A smidgen. *Un petit peu*."

Oh shit.

"Listen honeybunch," she continues, "why don't you go on to Sullivan's and I'll meetcha in a while? Ask the bartender there if Nick is around—he knows him. I'll be there in a half hour, tops."

Do you really have a choice? It's not like you can force a grown woman out of the bar, and bludgeoning her with an ashtray, temporarily satisfying though it might be, isn't an option either. You might stain your shirt.

"Fine. See you there. And you'd better turn up." You snatch your wallet from the bar and march outside. A taxi pulls up just as you reach the curb; the first bit of good luck you've had tonight. It's only when you reach Sullivan's and go to pay the driver that you realize that, in your hurry, you took the wrong wallet off the bar. This is Suzy's. Still, it doesn't make much difference, you figure . . . she'll be turning up soon, and there's enough cash in here to cover your immediate expenses.

It's only after you've been sitting in Sullivan's for an hour, feeling like the most pathetic woman on the planet, with no Suzy in sight and the bartender claiming that Nick hasn't been in all night, that you grasp the extent of your error. What were you thinking, expecting an already drunken Suzy to leave a bar where not only was she talking to a guy she liked, but he was serving her free drinks? It's like trying to tempt a rottweiler away from a juicy steak by offering it a brussels sprout. And with Dan plying her with shots, Suzy probably hasn't even realized that she's got your wallet. You can take a taxi back to the Berlin to see if she's still there . . . or at least you could take a taxi if you hadn't spent the last of Suzy's cash on drink.

Annoyed and tipsy enough by now to try anything, you find the nearest ATM machine. There's one card in her wallet. You've been with her many times when she's taken out cash and though you're not exactly sure of the password, you *do* know that it's a four-letter word that has something to do with alcohol. *Beer?* You try it, no luck. Not surprising; Suzy's never been much of a beer drinker. Maybe it's *Stol,* short for Stoli. You key in the word, but again, nothing. There's one more chance before the card gets swallowed. What is that word? Not booze but . . . something like it? *Booz!* Maybe that's it. Sounds familiar. Or is it *buze?* Spelling was never her strong suit.

If you try *booz*, turn to page 202.
If you try *buze*, turn to page 355.

"Are you serious?" Mike gets that awful glimmer in his eye, and you're sorry you said as much as you did. A simple "Okay, let's go" would have done the job.

He steps forward and pinches your cheeks. "We can't leave until this little guy here gets to say hello to his little long-lost girlfriend. Come on." He grabs you by the arm. "If we wait for you to do it, we'll be here all night."

"Mike, what the hell!" You protest, but Mike is pulling you toward the side of the stage, where Elizabeth is selling CDs.

"Excuse me, excuse me," he says as he works his way through the crowd. "Man with a baby coming through!"

You're unbelievably mortified and extra-glad you chugged about half of that last pint before relinquishing it to Dave as Mike pulled you away.

"Excuse me, ma'am?" He called her *ma'am*!!! "This gentleman here is a friend of mine and he claims that he went to camp with you. But I bet him ten bucks he's full of shit."

She looks at you, smiles, then turns back to Mike. "Looks like you owe your friend here ten bucks."

"Shucks, lost again. Well, I'll leave you two to get reacquainted. We'll be just over there, ace, when you're ready."

"How are you doing, Elizabeth?" you manage, before letting out a huge, stinky beer burp. "Excuse me," you add, hastily covering your mouth.

She eyes you curiously. "I always wondered what happened to you. You look great. Better than you smell." She waves a hand in front of her face to move some air around. Then she smiles.

"No, you're the one that looks great," you say. "Really, you look incredible. I almost didn't recognize you. No, that's not what I mean. You were cute back then, it's just that now, well, now, look at you, you're, like, amaz—"

"Okay, okay." She laughs and touches your arm lightly. "I think you've made your point. Now I'm embarrassed."

"Emb*ar*rassed? I'm the one who should be embarrassed."

"Why? Everybody burps. Hey, wasn't that an R.E.M. song?"

You laugh. "I didn't mean the burp. I mean, that's embarrassing, too.

But I meant the way I treated you back then. When we were in camp. I was a real jerk."

"Yeah, well. We were kids."

"I know. It's just, well, I've always felt bad about it. I always hoped I'd get a chance to tell you you deserved better." So what if you haven't even had a passing thought about the woman in over a decade. It sounds good. And she's buying every word. Eating it up, as it were.

"It's really sweet of you to say so, thanks."

"Hey E. B.!" It's one of the guys in the band. "Quit your yapping and sell some CDs, will you?"

"Fuck you, Nat!" The reply comes effortlessly, as if that's what she says in response to everything this Nat person says. "You know"—she squats down and starts slamming discs around, putting them all back into a box—"I've about had it up to here with this fucking band." She looks up at you—again with the cleavage!—"Can we go somewhere?"

Your eyebrows practically shoot off the top of your face. "Yeah, I mean, sure."

Just then Mike appears at your side. "You ready to go, ace?"

If you say, "Yeah, sure," then turn to Elizabeth and say, "You want to come to a party with us?" turn to page 176.

If you say, "You guys go ahead. I think I'll skip it," turn to page 178.

You get to Sullivan's and sit at the bar, waving to attract the bartender's attention.

"Hi, you know Suzy Armstrong?" you ask.

"Small, dark girl, cries if we run out of Stoli?"

You nod. "I'm looking for her cousin Nick."

"You know his last name?"

D'oh. "No, but she said he might be in here tonight."

"If it's the guy I'm thinking of, he's not here. But he usually does come in on Fridays, a little later. You want to stick around and I'll let you know if he turns up?"

You nod and order drinks, feeling—and looking—royally pissed off.

"Why so glum?" asks Hayley as you fumble for your money.

"Because Suzy's being a jerk, and Nick's not going to show, and at this rate I'd have more luck finding Mark by using a divining rod." You slam ten dollars on the bar.

"You've been listening to your old Leonard Cohen albums again, haven't you? Woman, what happened to your enthusiasm? Your lust for life? The night's going to go fine—you're in the capable hands of Hayley now!"

"I guess . . ."

"Look at me." She grabs your chin. "Who's the girl who single-handedly put our prom on the front page of the local newspaper? Who managed to get us backstage passes to the R.E.M. show in the days when Stipey still had hair, before they lost the plot?"

"That was you," you quietly admit.

"Can't hear you." She holds a hand to her ear and leans forward. "Who was it?"

"You, Hayley," you say, laughing helplessly.

"Damn right it was me! So if I can do all that, not to mention the time I rubbed the principal's bald head like a Magic Eight Ball and said 'Answer unclear, try again later'—and got away with it—don't you think I can locate some stupid guy for you?"

"He's not stupid." You pout, but you're already feeling better.

"Whatever, whatever." She shrugs. "No doubt he's Mr. Fucking Wonderful and hung like Moby Dick, but the point is, you'll never find out if you keep moping around like some helpless girlie. No offense, but

Suzy's not going to get up off her ass to help you tonight—all she's worried about is screwing that narcissistic bartender."

"So, what do you suggest?"

"Well, something a little more constructive than traipsing into every bar in the city hoping that Suzy's cousin is going to appear and grant you access to the sacred sanctum of Lindy's party. Do you know Lindy's last name?"

"Yeah . . . Lindy Graham."

"And did you think of just looking up her address in the phone book?"

"Of course," you lie. Damn she's good. How come you didn't think of that? "But the point is, we need Nick because he's invited, and we're not. I don't think it's gonna be the kind of party you can just crash."

"Even better; the more sophisticated she's trying to be the less chance that she's going to make a scene. We find the address, go to the party, and act like we belong . . . maybe Nick and Suzy turn up, maybe they don't. Either way, you see Mark, get lucky, and then Hayley can go home happy in the knowledge that she's done an old friend a favor. Now I'm going to ask if they have a phone book behind the bar, so sit here and put some more lipstick on."

A minute later she's back, thumbing through the local phone book. "Voilà, only one L. Graham. Must be her. We can have a few drinks here and go straight to the party."

"Shouldn't we call and see if it's the right L. Graham?"

"We could," she considers, "but that might make her suspicious. . . . I vote for just showing up."

If you call, turn to page 204.

If you decide there's no need to call, turn to page 207.

You watch the rest of the band's set, becoming more mesmerized by Elizabeth Albern as each moment passes. When they're done playing and you see she's settled into a table in a far corner of the bar—alone—you make your move.

"Excuse me, Elizabeth?"

She looks up blankly.

"I don't know if you'll even remember me, but we went to camp together when we were kids. My name's—"

"I know your name." She smiles, but it looks as though she's trying not to. "Every girl remembers the first guy who treats her like shit."

"I'm sorry, I didn't mean to bother you. I'll go. But I am sorry about that." You start to walk away.

"You can buy me a drink next door at Peju," she calls after you. "To make up for it."

"I'd like that."

She goes to get her stuff, and then the two of you go to Peju. It's a dark and romantic little spot where they make killer cocktails. As in *strong*. So you're taken aback when the waitress comes over to your quiet table in the back and Elizabeth orders two drinks for herself. Not one to make a woman feel uncomfortable about her drinking habits, you do the same. You've already had a number of beers, so the idea of two martinis isn't exactly sending chills of anticipation through your spine. But on the other hand, the idea that Elizabeth might become affectionate after her two Cosmopolitans is sending strong sensations through another body part.

"Are you expecting someone, too?" She takes lipstick and a mirror out of her bag.

"Excuse me?"

"You ordered two martinis." She reapplies the color on both lips. "Who's joining you?"

"I, uh, I thought . . ."

"Oh my god, you thought these were both for me!" The drinks arrive at that very moment. "What kind of alcoholic do you think I am? I'll barely finish this one before I'm sloshed. I told my boyfriend to meet us here."

"I see." You're avoiding eye contact.

"You didn't think . . . ?" She points at you, then at herself. "You and me?"

"No, no," you say a bit too adamantly. "Of course not."

Suddenly a guy dressed from head to toe in black—mostly leather—sits down next to Elizabeth and slides an arm around her. "Hey, babe," he says, planting a wet kiss on her mouth. You detect an English accent and dislike him and his arrogant rock-star vibe immediately.

Elizabeth introduces you to Nat, who takes a hearty swig of the second Cosmopolitan. "You know I hate these poncey drinks," he says to her. Then he turns to you. "So, how is it that you know E. B.?"

E. B.?

The drinks you've had are taking effect. They're making you obnoxious. "Well I don't know about *E. B.*, but *Elizabeth* and I went to camp together when we were kids."

"Right, fascinating." He takes another swig of his drink and pulls out a pack of cigarettes. The three of you sit in silence as he lights up a smoke.

"And what is it that you do now?"

You tell them.

"Right." He looks at Elizabeth, as if to ask how the hell someone as cool as she is knows you. "And do you like that line of work, then?"

You suddenly feel like the biggest loser going. You must escape, and fast.

"You know . . ." You take a big swig of your martini, finishing off the first one. "I do actually like it, but the hours are a real bitch. I should really get going; I've got so much work to do." You're about halfway through the second drink by the time Elizabeth responds.

"Don't be silly." She grabs Nat's cigarette and takes a drag, in what strikes you as an annoyingly couply moment. You want to be couply, too. Or at least coupl*ing*. And Sadie's miles away. Where you're supposed to be.

You say, "Well, it was nice seeing you," and head for the door. You vaguely hear Elizabeth say something—maybe "But we hardly talked," or "What a fucking dork."

You're out on the street, with the address of the party in hand, before you realize you left them with the bill.

If you go back in and give the bartender a twenty-dollar bill, turn to page 181.

If you think stiffing them with two stiff drinks was a stroke of genius, albeit an accidental one, and treat yourself to a cab with the money you've saved, turn to page 183.

You plant yourself on a bar stool and order a drink, and one for Hayley.

"So, you're not leaving?" asks Suzy, in surprise.

"No. If I leave, I won't see you for the rest of the night—instead of following us to Sullivan's you'll stay here ogling Dan, and what if Nick doesn't show up there? Or what if the barman who knows him isn't working tonight?"

"I'm sure he'll be there. And I told you I'd turn up." Suzy sounds petulant now.

Hayley, who has followed you over, mumbles something under her breath, and Suzy spins around to face her.

"You say something?"

"Just that I'd forgotten how selfish you can be."

There is a decidedly pregnant pause.

"Oh yeah?" replies Suzy.

"Ooh, good comeback," sneers Hayley.

"Since when did you get to be such a complete bitch? Let me guess, since you realized that the guy you're going out with has been fucking other people for the last six months?"

Hayley turns pale. "You don't know what you're talking about."

"If you say so." Suzy shrugs.

"Do you know about this?" Hayley asks you.

"No, I've no idea what she's talking about," you say truthfully. "Suzy, you're drunk and you're talking through your ass. Let it drop."

But there's no stopping Suzy now. "You're so naive, Hayley. Everyone knows Cole's a jerk. Why do you think he gets so edgy when you go out without him? It's not because he's possessive of you—he just doesn't want you to meet someone who'll tell you what he's up to when you're not around. I'm telling you this for your own good. Half the women in this bar have slept with him, for chrissake."

"Including you, I'll bet."

To your amazement, Suzy turns bright red, even as she's replying, "Me? I'm not that desperate."

"I don't believe it." Hayley shakes her head. "You lying little bitch. You slept with him, didn't you? What's the problem . . . can't sustain a relationship so you have to fuck up everybody else's? I had no idea you were so pathetic. And now you're hitting on some brain-dead, narcissistic bartender who'd never touch you in a million years, not while there are dogs in the street, honey. But if you want to sit here shoving your puny tits in his face in hopes that he'll eventually feel sorry for you and let you suck his dick, go ahead. I'm leaving."

With that, Hayley picks up a half-full glass of beer that someone's left behind, and throws it in Suzy's face. While Suzy's still spluttering in shock and looking around for something to retaliate with, Hayley turns to you and says, "Sorry to be so *Melrose Place*. But you, babe, had better watch your back where this little slut is concerned. I'm serious. You coming with me?"

If you go with Hayley, turn to page 210.

If you stay with Suzy, turn to page 214.

Lisa takes your hand and leads you into the crowd, pushing past people without so much as an "Excuse me" the whole way. She stops at center stage, about two lines of people back from the stage. You suddenly notice that she's five-feet-two and you're not. Somebody else notices, too.

"Hey, asshole."

He can't be talking to you. *Please, let him not be talking to you.*

"Hey, *ass*hole."

If you ignore him, he'll go away. *Please, let him go away.*

"What is it about assholes like you who think you can show up half-way through the show and push up in front of people who got here early to get a good spot?"

"Sorry, man," you say.

"Sorry, my ass," he says. "Or better yet, move *your* sorry ass back to the back of the crowd."

You're about to do just that when Lisa pipes up. "Hey, dickhead," she says to your intimidator, "why don't *you* move *your* sorry ass to a Sting concert so you can hang out with the rest of the old farts."

"Funny, I don't remember talking to you," the guy says. Then he says, "Bitch," barely audibly. That sends Lisa over the edge. She pushes him with her drink-free arm, knocking him over. . . .

If you use this as an opportunity to grab Lisa and escape, turn to page 168.

If you extend a hand to help the guy up and make peace, turn to page 172.

Ed smiles broadly when you tell him you'll come with him to the party. "Great, I look forward to having you."

"Scuse me?"

"Having you around, y'know?"

"Right."

"We have to drop the equipment back at my house before going to the party, so why don't you come, too? It's not far. We'll unload the stuff, I can change, and then we'll take my car back to Lindy's."

Soon you're sitting in the Daytrippermobile, relatively comfortable in the passenger seat, while the drummer, Crispin, and the bassist, Jerry, jolt along and drink beer in the back, telling bad jokes that rank only one step above fart noises. Ed drops Crispin and Jerry at their apartment, arranging to pick them up in an hour or so and drive on to Lindy's.

Round about now is the time it occurs to you that Ed's intention may not be simply to change his clothes back at his place. There's not really any other way to interpret the way he shoves his right hand between your legs as he drives along. You remove the offending paw and drop it back in his lap.

"Something wrong?" he says, feigning surprise.

"Not yet. Are we almost there?"

"Yup, this is it," and he pulls into the curb.

You give a hand unloading the gear and then sit in Ed's living room watching TV while he changes clothes. It's a pretty big place he's got here, especially for one person. Maybe he's got a roommate. Now that you have time to think quietly, you start to wonder if going to the party with Ed is such a good idea. True, he's cute, but he also seems a little sleazy, and maybe it's not worth jeopardizing your chances with Mark by showing up with him.

Ed wanders out into the living room wearing only an undershirt . . . well, an undershirt and an alarming amount of body hair. Amazing how many human beings look better with clothes on. This really was a bad idea. Ed sits beside you on the couch and again makes an unsubtle pass, and the lurching sensation in your stomach tells you this is definitely not a love connection. You scramble to get up, but he tries pinning you down on the couch, and you're toying with the idea of delivering a swift kick to the balls when the sound of a key in the front door stops him from getting any further ideas. You have to get out of here.

"Shit, my roommate's home." He sits up hurriedly.

"Okay, this is my cue to go . . . I'm calling a taxi."

"I thought we were going to go to Lindy's party together?" he whines.

"Did I hear someone mention Lindy's party?" comes a voice from the doorway. "Could you give me a ride . . . I told her I'd try and be there early." Your stomach lurches, again, and you look up to face the unbelievable truth.

"I guess so," mutters Ed. "Oh hey"—he turns to you—"this is my roommate, Ma . . ."

"Mark," you finish. "Hello, Mark."

"Hey." Mark nods. "Didn't know you knew Ed."

"Didn't know you lived with him." You grimace. This is disaster. Could things get any worse?

"Erm, your shirt's open," says Mark quietly.

Well, that answers that question.

You close the buttons and grab your coat.

"Maybe we can see each other again sometime?" Ed calls as you head for the door.

You don't bother to answer.

The End

You quickly find Dave and introduce him to Lisa. He decides he doesn't care much about seeing his friend's band one way or another. You ask him if he wants to come with you to Spinners. He does. The three of you get a cab.

About halfway to Spinners, however, in a neighborhood you don't know well at all and don't care to, the cab begins to move in fits and starts and to spew steam or smoke from under the hood. Before long, it dies. Right smack in the middle of nowhere, on a street full of warehouses and shuttered doorways. The driver opens the hood, more fog steams out, and he throws his hands up, helpless.

"Great," says Lisa, as you all get out of the car. "Now what?"

Dave steps out into the street, foolishly optimistic. "We just get another cab." He assesses the complete lack of traffic. "Or we walk?"

"Walk? Are you kidding me? I'm wearing new shoes."

"Ohhhh, poor baby. You want me to carry you?"

Ten minutes pass and there's still no sign of another taxi.

Lisa turns to the two of you accusingly. "Does either of you know what general direction Spinners is in so at least if we're walking to get a cab we're walking the right way?"

Simultaneously, you and Dave say "Thataway." But you're pointing in different directions.

"Great," Lisa huffs. "This is just fucking great. Well, I'm going this way. You coming?"

You and Dave shrug and follow. After a few minutes of awkward silence, Dave starts singing: ". . . and when the car broke down they started walking. Where were they going without ever knowing the way? . . ."

Just as you turn to tell him to shut up, Lisa says, "Hey, you've got a really good voice."

Dave takes this as encouragement and continues more confidently, adding a little melodrama and vibrato to his voice, the happy melody gaining resonance. "Anyone can see the road that they walk on is paved in gold; it's always summer, they'll never get cold. They'll never get hungry, never get old and gray . . ." You think you hear Lisa harmonizing to the catchy tune and suddenly everything seems somehow cheerier.

Then, seemingly out of nowhere, a man jumps out at Lisa. "Spare a quarter?"

If you empty the change in your pocket, turn to page 185.

If you mutter, "No, sorry," along with Dave and Lisa and quicken your pace, turn to page 187.

Ed comes over to the bar as you're standing there pondering your options. "You coming back over?" He smiles brightly.

"No. Thanks, but I have to go find my friend."

"You don't want to go to the party?"

"I really do need to find Suzy. Sorry." If you show up with Ed, you ruin your chances of landing Mark, and if it comes down to a simple question of whom you want more, you have to admit that Mark wins, hands down. Pants down, too, with a little luck. Of course, it might be awkward if you manage to get to the party with Suzy and Ed is there.

"I'm not sure I really want to go either, now," Ed says. Thank god for that. This is getting too confusing to think about after so many drinks. "But can I give you my card? Maybe we could get together sometime."

"Sure, great."

Next thing to do, after seeing Ed safely out the door, is check to see if Suzy called you. You stop by the bar to order another drink on your way to the pay phone.

There are two messages, one saved, one new.

The new message is from Suzy. She just checked her own messages and—hallelujah—there was one from Nick. Suzy says that Nick's going to be in McCormick's, and so she's going to meet him there around midnight. Then you can all go on to the party together.

The saved message is from Peter, one of your best friends. There's a little more to it than just friendship, on your side at least. Sometimes you wish that Peter would consider turning his platonic-pal status into something a little juicier, but so far he's never shown an interest and you've kept your feelings to yourself.

"Hi sweetie. I figured you'd be out, but maybe you'll get this message in time. One of the bands playing at Busters tonight fired its rhythm guitarist because of musical differences—basically he was always playing a different rhythm than the rest of the band—and they called and asked me to fill in . . . we go on at ten-fifteen. I know it's short notice, but it'd mean a lot if you could get your ass down there and lend little Pierre some moral support. I'll even let you buy me a drink afterward. Hope to see you later."

Checking your watch, you calculate that you can get to Busters in time to hear him and then go to McCormick's to meet Suzy and Nick.

Turn to page 22.

"Diane Keaton!" squeals Suzy, as she scrambles inelegantly onto the stage, skirt hiked up her thighs.

"Nice try, but no. . . ." The guitarist grins. "Though I wish I could give you some sort of prize just for the view I got when you climbed up here."

The answer, as some guy points out, is Mia Farrow, and he walks off with the mystery prize—a bottle of vodka. Suzy watches him with barely concealed misery in her eyes. "It's Stoli!' she turns to you, distraught. "*Stoli!* Waaaah!"

"Now now, don't get upset. If you work hard and save your pennies, one day you'll be able to afford a bottle of your very own. Let's go check the phone, shall we?"

"Okay." She sniffs.

Hallelujah, there's a message from Nick. "He's going for dinner at the Apollo, he'll be there until ten," Suzy announces as she hangs up.

You breathe a sigh of relief. "See, now we actually know where we're going! It's all going to turn out fine!"

Turn to page 218.

My hero!" Lisa swoons, after you've dragged her back to the front room. She pins you to the bar when someone tries to push past her. You swallow the rest of your drink and put it down just in time to turn back and meet her kiss. You don't even know if you like her, but you go with the kiss anyway and immediately get an erection. It's been way too long. Since you've been with a woman, that is. Certainly not since you've had an erection. Then you feel a strong hand squeezing your shoulder. You pull away from Lisa, dreading facing the asshole from the other room again.

"What's up?" Dave says as you turn.

You heave a sigh of relief.

"You okay, buddy?" he says, giving you a look that says it's way too early in the night to be making out with random women in public.

"Fine," you say. "I'm fine. Boy am I glad to see you."

Lisa elbows you and you introduce the two of them.

"Your friend here just defended my honor against this asshole in the back," Lisa says. "There he is right there. . . ." She starts to talk superloudly and point as the guy comes toward you. "See that guy, right there? *That's* the asshole."

"Hey asshole," Dave says brightly, like it's the guy's name, and you wonder whether everybody has gone insane.

"What's up, Dave," the guy says as he approaches. "You know these two?"

"Yeah," Dave says. "You?"

Everyone gets introduced (sure enough the guy's name is Dick), apologies are exchanged, and Dave gives you the fifty dollars he owes you, ten of which you give to Lisa to cover your burger.

"Come on," you say to her, "we have to catch up with everybody at Spinners."

"Have fun, kids," Dave says. "I'm going to stick around here for a while. The band's playing another set. Leave me a message about where the party is and maybe I'll catch you later."

You're relieved at first, but then you realize Dave's taken off his baseball cap and fixed his hair. Maybe you actually want him to come with you. Lisa's getting a little too close for comfort.

If you just leave with Lisa, thinking Dave will cramp your style, turn to page 191.

If you go after Dave and convince him that he has to come with you, turn to page 194.

You tell Suzy to pick Mia, and in a split second she's clambered onstage and is yelling, "Mia Farrow! *Mia Farrow!*" in the guitarist's ear.

"Mia Farrow, absolutely right," he shouts. "And here's your prize."

"Woohoo!" Suzy is wearing an exultant expression and the reason is clear—the prize is a bottle of Stoli. On the one hand, this is good, because Suzy loves Stoli. On the other hand, it's very, very bad, for exactly the same reason. There is every possibility that the night is going to take a nasty turn.

Before she's even climbed down from the stage, Suzy has opened the bottle and taken a swig. And another swig. Yikes, she's going to have a bruise tomorrow, after knocking into the amplifier like that. And it's a pity she didn't notice that cord—though it's remarkable that she didn't spill a drop of vodka as she fell.

"You okay?" you ask when she finally manages to get down from the stage.

"Peachy! Woohoo, it's gonna be a fun night!"

"Maybe you should slow down? It's still early."

"Nah, don't be so worried. Loosen up a little. Here, hold this while I call and check my voice mail."

You stand beside her while she dials her voice-mail number. "Message from Nick!" she says excitedly. That's a relief. You take a gulp of vodka. Suzy's right; you should just relax.

"He says he's getting dinner at . . . what was that? Polly's restaurant, I think he said, and he'll be there until ten o'clock. Or maybe it was the Apollo . . . why does he always chew gum when he talks? Wait a second and I'll play it again."

She presses a button and then swears.

"Suzy, you didn't, you didn't . . . tell me you didn't hit the wrong number and erase the message by mistake?"

"I didn't hit the wrong number and erase the message by mistake." She winces.

"You did, didn't you?"

"Er, yes."

You groan and down another mouthful of vodka.

"But hey, it's not so bad! At least we have a fifty-fifty chance of picking the right place the first time! And even if we don't, I'm sure we can make it to both before ten!"

You can't shake the feeling that it's not going to be quite as easy as that. In any case, time to pick a restaurant.

If you choose Polly's, turn to page 221.
If you choose the Apollo, turn to page 218.

The guy takes your hand, and you help him up. Only the second he's back on his feet he takes a swing at you. You duck. He misses. You swing at him. He ducks, comes back at you with a right hook, and the next thing you know . . .

You wake up in the emergency room, Lisa calling your name.

"What happened?" you cry out.

"I'm here," she says, trying to sound reassuring. "Everything's going to be okay."

But everything doesn't feel okay. In fact, you're in a good deal of pain. "What happened?"

"You got hit and you went down. Your nose is broken."

Your hand instinctively goes to touch your nose, but all you can feel are copious bandages and pain. "Oh god," you say, closing your eyes hard—like it'll make this whole scene go away.

"He speaks!" A guy wearing a white coat has walked into the room, wielding a chart, which he puts on the foot of the bed as he approaches you.

"Who the hell are you?"

"Not the friendly sort, is he?" He's turning your head from side to side, examining the bandages.

"No, *he's* not," you say. "And *he* still wants to know who the hell you are."

"Dr. Thompson's the name, broken noses the game."

This guy can't be a doctor, you're thinking. He can't be much older than you are. But he's got a white coat and an air of authority, so you go with it. "When can I go home, *Doctor* Thompson?"

"As soon as you're cleared by psych."

"Excuse me?"

"Standard procedure. A psych evaluation."

"I come in here with a broken nose and I have to see a shrink?"

"You came in here with a broken nose that you got in a bar brawl that you no doubt got involved in because you've been systematically abusing alcohol for so long you think it's normal to go out and have ten beers twice a weekend. Or maybe not. We just want to be sure you're not coming in here next week with half of a beer bottle smashed into your head."

"But Lisa here can vouch for me, can't you, Lisa?" Surely the woman who was sucking down her Long Island Iced Tea like it was the first liquid she'd come across after spending two weeks in the desert can see how preposterous this situation is.

"I don't know," she says, eyeing the young doctor, who you suddenly realize is probably considered pretty good-looking by the vast majority of women walking the earth. "You were kind of knocking them back like there was no tomorrow. I don't like who you become when you drink." This, from a woman you've been out with twice, tops!

"Ahem." There's another figure at the door.

"Aha," says Dr. Thompson. "There's the shrink now. Lisa, I'm afraid you'll have to wait outside with me."

"My pleasure," she says, sidling up to him. "By the way, you owe me thirty dollars," she calls back to you.

"Listen, I don't need a shrink," you say to this new doctor as he pulls a chair up to the bed.

"Ah, yes," he says, pulling up a chair next to your bed. " 'Shrink.' " He makes quote marks in the air. "I'm not uncomfortable with the term, you know. In truth, I'm leading a movement within the psychiatrist's community to embrace the term *shrink,* as you say, in much the same way the lesbian community made efforts to make *dyke* their own. I've got this idea for a campaign that would be sponsored by our professional association, ads that play up the *shrink* idea. For example, 'There's a reason they call us shrinks. We shrink your problems away.' I think it could do wonders for the field, what do you think?"

Needless to say, you're not going anywhere for some time.

And when you do, it's going to be home. To bed. Alone.

The End

Outside, Nick leans against the wall and lights a cigarette. Either he does want to make a move but is trying his best to be sophisticated and cool or . . . or he's just strange. Or an idiot. You can't figure him out, though, of course, that's probably the general idea.

"Look, Nick, if you don't have any particular words of wisdom to impart or any real reason why we should be shivering outside the bar, far away from our comfortable seats, then I'm going back in."

"Don't do that. What I wanted to say is this: If you want to end up with Mark tonight, I can't stop you. It's up to you. But there's no law saying we can't do this first." With that he stubs out his cigarette, moves toward you, and, with a flourish that would not be out of the place in a 1940s movie, takes you in his arms—who knew people still did that?—and kisses you.

"Whoa!" You push him off, holding one arm out to keep him at bay. "Down."

"You don't want to?"

But why shouldn't you? No one's going to know. You kiss again, and it's only when you hear Suzy coughing loudly behind you that you break apart.

"This isn't quite what they mean by 'kissing cousins,' is it?"

"Hey, Suze." Nick is grinning, embarrassed.

"You want to go to the party now? Phil and I are ready."

Nick goes back inside to get his jacket, and Suzy grabs you. "What on earth are you doing? What about Mark?"

"It was just a kiss. No big deal. What's the worst that can happen?"

"Well, I dunno," she wavers. "Let's just get out of here."

You, Nick, Phil, and Suzy eventually pile into a taxi and head for Lindy's house. There are already far too many guests crammed into her living room, so you and Suzy find space to stand in the hallway while Nick and Phil go to get drinks.

"So that kiss didn't mean anything?" Suzy asks again.

"I guess not. Kind of childish, huh?" Maybe it *was* stupid.

"Probably harmless. Nick's never been one for serious girlfriends. In fact, those few minutes you spent outside were probably the longest relationship he's had in a while. Hey, will you look who just walked in?"

It's Mark. And miracle of miracles, he is actually approaching. Smiling. At you.

"Hey, good to see you." He's looking intently at you now. "How's things?"

"Great, wonderful." Was that too gushing? Should you sound more apathetic? "Reasonable, anyway."

"Really? Only reasonable?" He leans in a little closer, brushing the hair off your neck. Good lord, you feel like your loins are going to explode. "Judging by the fresh hickey you've got on your neck, I'd say they were pretty good. Who's the lucky guy?" Speechless, you clutch the offending spot with your hand and turn bright red. "Guess I'd better leave you to it." He smiles, more forced this time, and walks away.

You gaze after him, utterly miserable, then sink to the floor, bury your face in your hands, and groan. "I can't believe it! How humiliating was that!"

"Pretty damn humiliating." Suzy pats you on the shoulder. "Should I go see what's happened to those drinks?"

"Just bring me the bottle."

The End

I'd love to." She stands and faces you and Mike squarely. "I'll get my jacket and meet you outside?"

"Great," you say, and she goes.

"Yeah, just great. Sadie'll love that," Mike says.

You explain to Mike that just because you have a huge crush on Sadie doesn't mean she in any way has to reciprocate and that this Elizabeth thing is just too good an opportunity to pass up.

"Well, if young Sadie doesn't reciprocate your feelings, why was she so determined to find out whether or not you were going to the party tonight?"

"You didn't tell me that!"

"It only happened today." Mike watches Elizabeth disappear backstage. "We could split without her."

"I can't, man." You shake your head. "I just apologized for being such a shit to her when we were in camp."

"You know what they say, once a shit, always a shit. Or is it, if it looks like shit, and smells like shit . . . oh, I don't know. You get the point."

If you leave without Elizabeth, turn to page 197.

If you decide to wait for her and worry about Sadie later, turn to page 201.

"I don't want to go outside." You're smiling politely.

"Why not? It'll be fun." He's also smiling politely.

"I don't see any need to go outside. We can talk in here." Still smiling politely, but a trifle forced.

"If we go outside, we can do more than talk."

"I don't want to do more than talk." You've stopped smiling.

"I see." So has he. "Maybe I don't feel like going to the party after all."

"I don't believe this." You slam your drink down and stare at him. "You're sulking? Because I won't go outside and make out with you? How old *are* you?"

"I just don't see why I should go out of my way to bring you and Suzy to some party that I don't even want to go to. It has nothing to do with you not going outside, so don't flatter yourself. Shit, if I wanted I could have any woman in this bar."

"Assuming you brought along a tranquilizer gun and a big net."

"Go fuck yourself, bitch."

"You too, asshole."

"*What* is going on here?" demands Suzy, who's finally dragged herself away from the guy she's been with. "Two minutes ago you were getting along so well!"

"Your dickhead cousin won't go to the party because I won't make out with him."

"Nick? You're kidding. Is that true?"

"Suzy, I don't need this interrogation from you. Or your skanky friends."

Skanky! The nerve! You're holding a nearly full bottle of beer, and even though it's one of those things you swore you'd never do, an utter cliché in fact, you pour it over his head, then jump off your stool and back away before he can retaliate. "Suzy, I'll call you tomorrow. Nick, it's been a pleasure. Don't get up. I'll see myself out."

The End

"No, wait." Elizabeth grabs Mike's arm as he turns to go. She turns back to you. "Go with your friends. Truth is I really wouldn't be great company with the mood I'm in."

"Are you sure?" You can't let this woman slip away again. Not that she was a woman last time and not like you really let her "slip away" per se, but you're feeling kind of arous . . . er, passionate.

"Yeah, really."

"Hey E. B.!" Nat is shouting over at her again. "What did I tell you five minutes ago?"

"You should really go. And I should stay and deal with this"—she nods her head toward Nat—"once and for all. It was great to see you." She takes your hand and squeezes it.

You say the first thing that comes to mind. "I still get an erection every time I'm by a lake."

She laughs and gives your hand another squeeze. "That's the sweetest thing anyone's ever said to me." She plants a wet kiss on your lips, brushes your cheek with her hand, and, suddenly encircled by fans, turns to sell a CD.

"You ready to go, ace?" Mike, who had stepped back to give you some privacy, leans forward again.

"As ready as I'll ever be."

Turn to page 203.

Ah, the Pub. You swing open the door and inhale that familiar scent . . . a combination of smoke, beer, and the old guy who always stands beside the jukebox.

Kate is working tonight, and she gives you a nod and a frazzled smile as she clears two empty martini glasses away.

"Busy?" you ask. "Hey, cute dress, by the way."

"Thanks . . . though I wish I was wearing something else; I can feel at least a dozen eyes boring into me whenever I bend down to get more ice. Two of them belonging to your roommate, incidentally."

"He's here?" It's not often you see him in a social setting.

"He's here," she says, wiping out an ashtray, "and he looks a little weird."

"He always looks a little weird," you point out. "It's those eyebrows. His tweezer skills are somewhat lacking."

"True, but this is weird in a different, nonphysical sense. He looks sad or something. Mopey, y'know."

"I guess he didn't get laid, then. There's a girl he likes, and he was under the impression he's end up fuc . . ." At this point Kate gives a loud cough and you realize he's standing beside you, about to order a drink.

"Another please, Kate, and one for my big-mouthed roommate here."

"Thanks," you say sheepishly. "So I guess things didn't work out with Sophie?"

"Sadie. No, not according to the master plan. And where's Matt?"

"Mark. Long story. I'm giving up for the night."

"Well, stick around for a few minutes at least. I'm bored."

"You smooth-talking devil."

A couple of the regulars are here. Melanie, one of your roommate's former flings, is trading jokes with a friend of hers and laughing idiotically. And there's Ben in the corner. You thought he was cute until you realized that he was congenitally incapable of not flirting with every woman in the bar. Alright, so he's still cute. Too bad he ruins it as soon as he opens his mouth. Your roommate spies you looking at him.

"Ah, the infamous Ben. Easy on the eyes, huh?"

"Not on the stomach."

He takes a sip of beer. "You deserve better anyway."

"You flirting with me?"

A tiny pause, then: "Sure, why not."

He gives you an unmistakable look, and you both put your drinks down on the bar and move toward the dimly lit alcove. Then he's pressing you against the wall and you're making out frantically, so that you hardly hear when Kate walks by and makes one of her customary wisecracks.

"Home, now," you croak.

He just nods and pulls you out the door after him.

The End

"Oh, I'm so glad I caught you."

Elizabeth grabs you by the arm as you go to pay the bartender for your martinis. You see Nat storm past and go out the front door.

"I have to apologize for him," Elizabeth says. "And for me, for having anything to do with him."

"Don't worry about it." This is an interesting turn of events, no?

"I do, though." She calls the bartender back over. "Let me buy you a drink, okay? That way we can really talk and catch up."

You shrug your approval, and the two of you go back to the same table, where Elizabeth left her stuff.

"I honestly can't tell you why I'm still with Nat after all this time. And it looks like I won't be for long. I mean he's such a jerk to most people, but I really believe that he's a musical genius. He wrote this song last week and it's a work of pure brilliance. It's so, like, profound, you know. It's about life, like. And how every little choice you make—no matter how little it is—can have this huge impact on your life, you know . . ."

Two hours later, you know more about Nat's supposed songwriting genius—not to mention his sexual idiosyncrasies (he likes to be spanked with a rolled-up newspaper and called "bad dog")—than you ever wanted to know. You wish, however, you'd had a tape recorder with you. If this Nat guy becomes the pop god Elizabeth thinks he's going to be, you could write the unauthorized biography and make a quick buck.

By night's end you're too drunk and mentally drained to do anything but go home. There, because you've got to see if there's anything to this spanking thing, you retire to your bedroom with a rolled-up section of the Sunday paper. You strip down and begin to experiment, alternately whacking your right butt cheek with your hand and the newspaper to see which—if either—turns you on. Preoccupied by your pursuit, you neglect to lock your bedroom door.

Your roommate's drunken friend Suzy walks in on you midswat.

The End

Within a couple of minutes you're in your apartment, checking messages. One saved message from your old friend Peter, asking you to go see a band he was playing in tonight. Damn—they must be finished by now. Also a new message from Suzy, giving the address of the party and urging you to try to make it. You call a taxi and, on the way there, stop off at an ATM for some cash.

The party is being held by Lindy, who owns a beautiful house and what must be an incredibly powerful music system, judging from the way your ears are already vibrating in time to . . . what the fuck are they playing in there, Chumbawamba? "Very last season," you mutter, just as the door opens and a statuesque blonde peers at you in amusement.

"Yes, isn't it," she smiles. "Some asshole friend of mine has taken over the stereo and is finding all the CDs I'm most ashamed to own. Come on in; I'm Lindy."

You introduce yourself and step inside, hang up your jacket, and gaze around in hopes of seeing someone you know. There's Suzy at least, doing what Suzy does best—drinking a vodka tonic and chatting intimately with some guy who looks familiar.

He ought to look familiar. It's Mark.

You feel your chest tighten and look away again quickly, scanning the room to locate Nick. Aha. Nick is Asshole Stereo Guy.

If you decide to talk to Suzy first, turn to page 225.
If you approach Nick, turn to page 228.

You can't find anyone you know at Spinners. They probably went on to the party. You reach in your pocket for the address Mike gave you, but it's not there. You check your other pockets, then your wallet. Nothing. You know in your heart that your night's a bust, that you'll never hear the liquid joy that is Sadie's laugh. Or maybe, just maybe, they haven't gotten here yet. You find a stool at the far end of the bar and order a drink.

Two hours later, the bartender, John—your new best friend as you see it—cuts you off. Probably the fact that you're slumped on the bar, lovelorn tears barely dry on your cheeks, did the trick. You've spun quite a number of yarns about yourself and Sadie tonight, for the benefit of a group of regular patrons—mostly old men—gathered at your end of the bar. They're convinced yours and Sadie's is the purest love since Romeo and Juliet's. You've even brought a few of them close to tears.

As closing time approaches, there are only about six or seven people left in the bar. Once you're sitting up again, a local named Lloyd convinces John to give you half a shot so you can toast with him. As John pours your drink (barely), Lloyd leans in close, spraying saliva in your face as he talks. "You keep fighting for her, you hear? We'll be here rooting for you, won't we, boys?"

A couple of the other men mutter in agreement.

"A toast." Lloyd gestures to the drink that's been set down in front of you. He clears his throat. "To true love."

"To true love!" the late-night contingent echoes.

You stumble out into the street, John keeping a watchful eye from the door. You're still muttering, "To true love," when you get into the cab.

"To true love."

"To *true* love!"

"To true *love*!"

"Hey, buddy." The driver turns. "This True Love place. It have an address?"

The End

I'd like to go home with you," you blurt. Why not? What have you got to lose? Why wander all around town trying to find someone you like when there's someone you like sitting right beside you? Even if she has considerably more cleavage than the person you thought you were going to end up with.

"You would? I mean, that's great!" She beams, relief written all over her face. "Wasn't sure if I was making a fool of myself there. But I had a feeling about you when you walked in."

You glance at your clothes instinctively.

"No, I'm not saying you look like a stereotypical dyke." She grins. "You looked approachable though. And open. And smart."

"Stop, you're making me blush."

"And you've got great tits."

You burst out laughing. "Funny, I was just thinking the same about you. Let's go."

The End

You stop and reach into your pocket, where you've got a hefty wad of change you've accumulated this evening. Just as you hand it to the homeless man, you see a taxi rounding the corner. From the approaching silhouette you see the backseat's empty. You call ahead to Dave and Lisa, who kept walking, then hail the cab, giving the address of Spinners. . . .

Turn to page 206.

"I'm really flattered, honestly. It just doesn't seem like a very good idea."

"Say no more, I understand. No harm in asking. You want another drink?"

The rest of the evening goes by in a blur of free drinks and increasingly mindless conversation. But it's fun—more fun than you've had in a very long time.

"Guess I should be getting home. I planned to get up early tomorrow and write," Jane says at last. "It was really good meeting you. Here's my number . . . just in case, you know. We can go out for a drink or something?"

You pocket it, and she kisses you on the cheek. "Sweet dreams. See you soon."

"I'll call you," you say, knowing for sure that you will.

The End

The homeless man pursues Lisa, walking mere inches behind her. "Come on, pretty lady, spare a quarter."

Lisa's freaked out and quickens her pace, hurrying toward fluorescent lights and ducking into the first bar she comes to. You and Dave follow, only to find that the oasis Lisa has selected is a karaoke bar called Ditty Bar; from the slight difference in the pink color of the *D* on the sign and the seedy location, it's easy to see that Ditty Bar used to be something else entirely. Damn. Just your luck. Inside, Lisa heads straight for the bar on the assumption you're staying for at least one. Somewhat reluctantly—after all, you're anxious to get to Spinners and the party and get on with your night (and maybe get it on with Sadie!)—you follow, suggesting a round of shots since it'll be quicker.

With three tequilas on the way, Dave looks at you and Lisa pensively. "Which came first as you remember it: the idea of karaoke or Milli Vanilli?"

"Ah yes, the age-old question," Lisa says wistfully. "Which came first: karaoke or Milli Vanilli." She rolls her eyes. "The two have nothing to do with each other, *Dave*."

"I don't know. I always thought Milli Vanilli's would be an awesome name for a karaoke bar."

Lisa considers this a moment. "But the point is that Milli Vanilli didn't sing."

"So?" Dave looks at you for support, but you're not quite ready to give it.

"*Soooo*, it makes no sense." Lisa's pouring salt onto the fleshy pad between her thumb and index finger. "The point of karaoke is that you do sing. The vocal track's missing. Yours would have to be a lip-synch bar. And that doesn't sound like much fun—not enough ways for people to embarrass themselves, because if they suck all you have to do is not look at them and you've still got the song playing intact. So that's just stupid."

"I don't know. I still think it's a good name."

"But it makes no sense."

"Alright you two." You're not sure if this is the old ponytail-pulling routine. Are these two really fighting or just flirting? "Let's agree that at the very least, it's a great name for a karaoke bar with a very ironic owner and clientele. How about that?"

You're quite the peacemaker.

Lisa shrugs and clinks her glass to yours and Dave's, then the three of you do your shots.

Once he's done wincing after sucking on a lemon, Dave proclaims: "Milli Vanilli's: Where Someone Else Is Always Doing the Singing. See, it works."

Lisa raises her eyebrows and tips her head. "I guess so," she concedes. "I mean it's a better name for a karaoke bar than, say, Our Lips Are Sealed."

"How 'bout Sing Out Sister?" you suggest.

"Sounds like a lesbian karaoke bar," Lisa says.

"Mike's."

"Very clever. Probably too clever."

"Big Mouth Strikes Again."

"Too long, and Smiths fans don't go to karaoke bars. Hey, look at this." Lisa picks up a flyer off the bar. "There's a karaoke contest tonight. Grand Prize: a thousand dollars. It's just starting."

You and Dave eye the fluorescent pink announcement as Lisa walks to the far end of the bar. When she comes back, she throws down a song list onto the bar in front of the two of you. "Let's see what you're made of, boys."

If you want to sing, turn to page 208.

If you don't want to sing, turn to page 212.

I'm gonna stay with them," you say.

"Good luck, Mademoiselle." Peter shrugs. "Little Pierre is boarding the first train out of Freaksville. See you later, guys."

Now it's just you and Mark. Oh, and Jay. If there was only some way you could get rid of this guy, you're sure you could be tonsil to tonsil with Mark—at the very least—before the night is over. Maybe you can just get him so drunk that he has to leave.

As if on cue, a girl approaches and hands each of you a piece of paper advertising a promotion for Slaughter, a new brand of vodka, at a bar called Swifty O'Shea's.

"This is the kind of thing I came back to town for!" Jay bellows.

"This is the kind of thing that made you leave town in the first place," says Mark cautiously. "Jay and cheap vodka; I've had nightmares about scenarios like this."

But there's no talking Jay out of it, and with some coaxing from you, Mark is persuaded to give the bar a try. You hail a taxi and make for Swifty's. Deciding it's time to make your intentions clear, you take advantage of the backseat of the cab and put your hand on his leg. Thankfully he takes the hint and you kiss . . . you hardly notice when the taxi comes to a halt, and Jay coughs noisily, your signal to break it up.

Swifty's is swarming with an eclectic mix of college kids, wanna-be bohemian types, and several older men who are pretending not to be married. Jay locates a couple of stools at the bar and orders a round—the vodka is being served straight, in fairly generous quantities, so you vow just to have one to keep the others company, then you'll ease off for the night. Don't want to get so drunk that you won't remember the highlights of later on.

But then Mark orders a round, and it'd be rude to refuse. You realize you're getting a little drunker than planned when you drag him up to dance during a Billie Holiday song, but, you reason, there's nothing wrong with dancing in a bar, is there? Then, of course, it's your turn to buy a round. One more, what the hell. Jay still looks pretty sober. Mark must be drunk though—he's leaning against you for support. Or at least, you thought he was leaning against you, but then you discover that you're clutching his collar. You let go, and . . . ouch, they should get a carpet in this place. Someone falling to the floor could really hurt themselves. It seems imperative that you relay this bit of information to the staff, so you stagger back to your feet and lean over the bar.

"Hey, bartending pershon. You there. Should get carpet. Floor. Hurt knees." Strangely, he seems to be deliberately ignoring you. Oh well. You need to go to the bathroom anyway.

The next thing you know, you're waking up in an unfamiliar room, with sunlight pouring through a slit in the curtains and boring right into your skull. Ow. You have no recollection of what happened after that third drink, although, turning your head warily to the side, you realize that it must have been something pretty good. Because Mark is lying beside you. It's a shame you don't remember what happened, but there's bound to be other nights. Maybe even a little action this morning, if you can quench this hangover.

Mark's eyes open slowly and he turns to you and grins. "Hey, babe," he says softly. "I had a great time last night. Thanks for being so understanding."

"No problem." Understanding? You have no idea what he's talking about. Still, you slink over and run your hand down his body and feel . . . and feel . . . something very familiar. The underwear you were wearing last night. On him.

"Hey, I was wondering," he whispers, "can I borrow that shirt you were wearing last night?"

The End

You and Lisa cross the street to look for a cab going in the right direction. "You know," Lisa says, stepping up behind you as you watch the oncoming traffic. "We don't *have* to meet up with those guys." She kisses the back of your neck and reaches for your crotch just as the feel of her ample breasts pressed against you starts to have an effect again.

"We really should," you say, removing her hand semireluctantly.

"Well, in that case, can we at least stop at my apartment? I need to change out of these shoes. They're new. I shouldn't have worn them. They're killing me."

You hail a cab, get in, and spend most of the ride making out. In front of Lisa's apartment building you contemplate waiting in the cab so you have an excuse not to go in. After all, the point of this evening was to get Sadie, not Lisa.

If you wait in the cab, turn to page 216.
If you go in with Lisa, turn to page 220.

You like Mark. You like him a great deal. Part of you would like to throw him down on one of these pristine new couches and shag him senseless. But let's face it, you never envisaged lazy Sunday mornings spent lying in bed together, both of you choosing your lingerie from the new Victoria's Secret catalog.

"Um, Mark, I think I'll skip the party. I'll see you around," you say.

"Okay," he says. "It was good to see you. I guess this was a little much to dump on someone you hardly know. See you," and he kisses you on the cheek before ambling over to the door. Jay gives a sympathetic shrug and follows him.

Peter puts an arm around your shoulders. "Sorry, baby. I should have seen it coming. Far too much Liza Minnelli on the jukebox. Let's go to McCormick's."

McCormick's is uncomfortably crowded. Huddled around the bar is what looks like the entire Irish rugby squad. Nick and Suzy are nowhere to be seen.

All of a sudden you start to feel queasy. Maybe it's due to the heat in here. Or maybe the Mexican food you just had. Of course, it could, just conceivably, be the variety of alcohol you've been pouring down your throat all night. Funny how that's always the last explanation on the list. You barge your way through the throng and make it to the toilet just as someone is vacating one of the stalls. With a hasty "Scuse me" to the woman waiting in line, you rush in and throw up. It's a spectacular, volatile, and impressively Technicolor burst of vomit, most of which, thankfully, lands in the bowl.

As you're wiping your mouth with toilet paper, there's a polite knock on the door.

"You alright in there?" It's one of the bartenders.

"Nyeargh," you mumble.

"You came in with that guy Peter, didn't you?"

"Uh-hygh," is your affirmative reply.

"Well, he's just poured a pint over someone who complained when he picked fourteen Ramones songs on the jukebox. For his safety's sake, it might be better if you two get the fuck out of here. You don't sound in the best of health either."

Two minutes later you and a contrite-looking Peter, who's trying to shake rum and Coke out of his hair, are standing outside. It's raining. Going to the party is no longer an option, nor is there any point. Peter's suggesting you both go back to his place for coffee. Or maybe you should accept defeat and go for one last drink in the Pub before going home—this night seems to be turning into a catalog of disasters.

If you go with Peter, turn to page 232.
If you go to the Pub, turn to page 179.

"Hold up, guys. I've got to see this."

You back up to the corner, where Dave has stopped to look down the street. "Hey, they're filming a movie. Let's go watch."

You throw a questioning shrug at Lisa, and she shrugs back. You follow Dave down the street, which is lined with huge white trailers. Bright lights are making it seem like midday halfway down the street, where cameras are pointing at the entrance to a beautiful old apartment building.

"Holy shit!" Dave grabs your arm. "It's fucking *Kevin Smith.*"

"*What's* fucking Kevin Smith?"

"Shut up, asshole. It's Kevin Smith. The director."

Uh-oh. You're going to be here awhile. Not only is Dave the kind of film buff who actually asks his video store for a printout of all of his rentals every six months *so that he can double-check his own record book*—but he's practically a disciple of Kevin Smith.

As you're standing there, waiting for something to happen, a guy with a clipboard and a headset comes over. "Hi there, folks. I'm Liam, the extras coordinator, and we've had a few people walk since we're working late. You three would be perfect fill-ins. There's fifty bucks in it for each of you."

"I'll do it." Dave steps toward the crew guy, like he's just been picked for his kickball team.

Lisa shakes her head. "I think I'll pass."

If you want to be an extra, turn to page 223.

If you want to ditch Dave and go to Spinners with Lisa, turn to page 191.

Maybe it'd be better if you went." Perhaps you're being bitchy, but the situation is likely to get complicated if Peter hangs around, looking for innuendo in everything Mark says or does.

"You're not mad?" you add.

"Hell no. You, on the other hand, are possibly deluded, but what do I know? Here, take my jacket; it's raining and I'm not going far."

You initially refuse, but he's right; it is raining pretty heavily and you don't want to arrive at Lindy's looking bedraggled. By the time you get to Lindy's you probably won't even be able to pronounce *bedraggled*.

Jay and Mark are waiting further up the street, and the three of you continue on to McCormick's.

It's so crowded you can barely make your way to the bar. Mark, who's managed to push his way to the back with you, shouts that you should all go somewhere else—at this rate it'll take ages just to get a drink. You're inclined to agree with him.

You leave McCormick's and stand outside in the drizzle, trying to think of a bar where the risk of being trampled isn't so great.

"Ted's house!" says Jay brightly, with the enthusiasm of someone who doesn't have a good idea very often.

"Country Ted's?" Mark looks dubious. As well as gorgeous. You can feel your loins clenching. "Country Ted is another high-school buddy of ours," he says, by way of explanation. "So called because he loves Hank Williams. He still lives with his parents, not far from here."

Mark nips back into McCormick's to call him and appears two minutes later, grinning widely. "Guess what? Country Ted's parents are out of town and he insists we go over for a cocktail. Then he'll come to Lindy's with us."

Country Ted's parents have a beautiful house. Unfortunately, they clearly have an idiot for a son, but those are the breaks. Ted opens the door wearing jeans, cowboy boots, and a Stetson. A Stetson. In his own house. After the guys have done the customary backslapping thing, you all get cozy in the massive living room. Mark nods at a pretty blond girl, about sixteen, curled up on one of the enormous leather chairs. "My sister Alice," says Ted.

"When do Bob and Carol show up?" you quip. A blank stare from Ted. Oh well.

He hangs your coats up in the hallway and returns to blare some Hank from the stereo and invite you all to help yourselves from the bar. "We have everything . . . vodka, whiskey, rum, gin, tequila . . ."

What, no moonshine?

Jay jumps up excitedly and you can tell he thinks he's had another great idea. "Hey, I nearly forgot, I brought a little present for Mark that we could use right now!" He makes exaggerated snorting noises that are obviously meant to imply cocaine. "Everybody up for it?"

If you say yes, turn to page 234.

If you say no, turn to page 236.

You and Mike meet the rest of the crowd out front and divide into taxis to go to Spinners. Just as you're climbing into the second cab you've hailed, Elizabeth comes rushing up behind you.

"Perfect timing," she says, pushing into the cab. "So where's the party, lads?"

Lads? What's up with that?

"It's someplace uptown," Mike answers.

"Who's throwing it? Is he or she cool?" Elizabeth has taken a mirror out of her bag and is reapplying her lipstick. "Hey!" She bangs on the divider separating the front and the backseat when the driver comes to a short stop. "Hey, you prick, would you take it easy on the brakes there." She turns to you. "You believe this?"

You don't know what the hell to believe. Who is this strange woman, and what has she done with that angelic figure you watched on stage for forty minutes? More importantly, why is her vocabulary peppered with English slang?

"So, I'm looking at the lot of you and I'm wondering, is this going to be some lame party filled with people who make their living bullshitting about the people that are really out there doing stuff. Publishing types, that sort?"

"Excuse me?" you ask.

She lights a cigarette, and Mike rolls down his window. Mike works in publishing.

"Oh, lighten up. Has anybody got any speed or anything? I could use a picker-upper if I'm going to be stuck with the likes of you for the next few hours." When no one responds she keeps talking. "Come on, lads, loosen up. It's not every night you get to hang out with a rock star."

"You know one?" Mike says.

"Haaaa. Haaaaa." You can't believe this grating woman was capable of singing such heavenly songs. "For your information, wiseass, we've already had a hit single in the UK and a review of the band compared me to some of the greatest female lead singers of all time. There are over a thousand Web sites devoted just to *moi.*"

"So I guess what they say about the Internet being loaded down with a bunch of crap is true." You've never seen jovial, big-personality Mike turn so harsh so fast. He's usually like the mayor of any room he's in.

Elizabeth elbows you. "Glad to see you've gone on to surround yourself with such sad little bitter people. Then again, you were doing that even back in camp, weren't you? Who was that friend of yours? Oh, I know. Dave Scalza—the one who organized that silly mock drive-in at camp so everyone could watch a movie. I wonder whatever happened to that geek. He probably works in a video store."

It's a good thing Dave went ahead in the other cab. You'd completely forgotten he was at camp that summer, too.

Elizabeth's still on a rant. "I bet he doesn't have shit to show for himself. He sure as hell hasn't had a hit record in England."

If you say, "Alright, that's it!" and tell the cab driver to stop so you can kick Elizabeth out, turn to page 227.

If you say, "Alright, that's it!" and push Mike out of the cab, get out yourself, then direct the driver to take the young lady to the airport and see that she gets on the first flight to London, turn to page 230.

Pierre, how long have we known each other? Too long for you to start getting melodramatic now, right?"

"Cool." He grins. "Just watching out for you, okay?"

You catch up with the others and go into McCormick's, but it's mobbed and none of you feels like staying. Nick is inside though, waiting for Suzy to show—she was last seen at the Upstairs Lounge with her tongue inserted in some guy's ear. You arrange to meet Nick, and hopefully Suzy, later at Lindy's. Meanwhile, Peter wants to go to the Old Red for a quick drink. Mark and Jay are willing to give it a try—in fact, as soon as Peter mentions that the drinks are cheap and strong, Jay's practically running down the street in the direction of the bar.

"He doesn't get out much," explains Mark as you race to catch up with him.

The Old Red is small and musty, but at least there are plenty of seats. Strings of colored lights are dangling from the ceiling and all over the bar.

"It looks like a Christmas tree just threw up in here," Jay comments happily. "Who's up for a shot?"

"What do you think about playing a few rounds of Jukebox Suicide?" suggests Peter.

"What the fuck is that?" asks Mark.

"One of Peter's inventions," you groan.

"Come on, you know it's fun!" Peter insists. "It works like this: everyone in turn goes to the jukebox and picks what they consider to be the worst song. We get someone impartial to judge—that old bartender guy, say, the one who looks like Robert Duvall. Whoever picks the worst song for each round makes the others drink a shot or do something stupid or answer an embarrassing question, whatever takes your fancy. Also, if two people pick the same song in one round, the others win. Very simple."

Jay solicits the services of your bartender, and he agrees to judge if you buy him a beer. You choose the first song. There aren't a lot of truly awful CDs on this jukebox, but you pick a particularly tuneless piece of jazz that you know from experience can ruin anyone's night, and hope that'll do the trick. The others take their turns, and you sip drinks and wait for your songs to come on.

The jazz is a popularly bad choice, but Peter is declared the winner of the first round with an excruciatingly long Bob Marley song that has your adjudicating barman biting the rim of his beer glass in annoyance. "No more reggae, or you're all out of here. That's another rule," he barks.

"Okay, my prize . . ." Peter's rubbing his hands in anticipatory glee. "Something easy to start with. Jay, you can do two shots, one Jaegermeister, one tequila. Mark, the same. You, my precious, have a choice: the same shots, or whatever Robert Duvall here suggests."

Tequila and Jaegermeister will most likely knock you senseless. On the other hand, the bartender, who introduces himself as Joe, is leering at you in a manner that suggests he might have something much more embarrassing in store.

If you do the shots, turn to page 240.

If you do whatever the bartender suggests, turn to page 245.

After an executive decision to bypass Spinners is made, you, Elizabeth, and Mike end up sharing a cab while Dave, Lisa, Tracy, and Will get another. You catch Elizabeth gazing at you longingly a few times during the ride and fear that Mike had it right. You + (Elizabeth + Sadie) = Trouble.

You're only at the party half an hour before the conflict becomes obvious. You're talking to both women and can tell they know they're competing with one another. You wish you had mind-reading powers like that little chess-playing alien kid from *The X-Files* so you could figure out what to do, which one wants you more.

Or maybe you don't need to read minds. . . . When Elizabeth goes to the bathroom, Sadie makes it clear—in no uncertain terms—that she's interested in you. And when Sadie goes to the bathroom, Elizabeth makes that point equally clear. In the state you're in—you're drunk enough that you just promised the women that you'd go and rent *The Mirror Has Two Faces*—this isn't a dilemma you can handle alone.

If you decide to track down Dave, tear him away from Lisa, and ask for advice, turn to page 235.

If you think this situation calls for more heavy-duty advice and you want to call MTV's *Loveline*, turn to page 242.

You tap in *booz* and close your eyes in silent prayer. Please please please let it work.

Yes! It worked! Now you can get money. How much to take out? Fifty bucks should do it. Relieved to have cash again, you wait for a taxi and then direct it back to the Berlin, silently congratulating yourself on your ingenuity.

But Suzy isn't in the Berlin. Nor is Dan. Another bartender has taken over, and he tells you that Dan's shift ended ten minutes ago. The two of them went somewhere together . . . he doesn't know where. They might, conceivably, have gone to Sullivan's to find you. Tired of playing tag across the city, you order a drink and gulp it back, willing yourself to get drunk just so you don't feel so frustrated and angry.

What to do now? Have another quick drink here, then maybe go to Sullivan's again? Or give up on Suzy, the party, and Mark altogether for tonight and just go back to your local bar, the Pub? At least you're sure to see someone you know there.

If you go to the Pub, turn to page 179.

If you have another drink here, turn to page 249.

Everything is going off without a hitch. You met up with whom you needed to meet up with where you needed to meet up with them and when. This is your destiny, to wind your way through a tangle of events to Sadie tonight.

When you step into the apartment where the party is, you feel as if there should be some kind of trumpet fanfare and red carpet. You have arrived!

The only problem is, Sadie never does.

The End

Hayley, there's no point trekking all the way out there if it turns out to be the wrong house. Let's call. How good are you at impersonating AT&T employees?"

She rises gallantly to the challenge, makes her way over to the pay phone, and returns in a couple of minutes with a satisfied grin on her face. "Yes, there is a Ms. or Mrs. Lindy Graham living at that address, and no, she doesn't want to hear about our new cheap rates to the South Pacific. I could hear music in the background—sounds like there's a crowd there already. Better finish these drinks and start walking over, okay?"

Lindy's house is about ten minutes away by foot. As you're walking past a small park, a man runs across your path, knocking against Hayley's elbow. "Hey, scuse you!" she yells, and then, picking up the wallet that he just dropped in the confusion, adds, "You lost this!"

But he's already rushing away, completely ignoring you both.

"Should we chase after him?" you ask.

"What's the matter with you—don't you watch TV?" Hayley says in rebuke. "First we have to look inside and find the secret microfiche files that he's stolen, then David Duchovny will track us down and try and persuade us to part with them, just before Scully turns up and says something like 'Mulder, you can't honestly be suggesting that . . . ' Hold on while I see what's in here." She opens the wallet and starts rifling through it.

"Hmm . . . no credit cards, no address that I can see. Photos . . . probably the guy's mother, or else he's pretty fucking desperate for a girlfriend. A few ticket stubs, couple of receipts . . ."

"Where from?"

"Hold your horses, Nancy Drew, I'm getting to that . . . nah, just grocery stores and shit. A three-leaf clover in a plastic card . . . who the fuck carries around a three-leaf clover?"

"That's a shamrock, asshole." You laugh. "Is there any money in there?"

"Ooh look, a secret compartment. . . ." She giggles, unzipping it. "Hey, forty dollars! You want half? And . . . hello, what's this?"

She unfolds a small white envelope that has been crammed into the pocket. Her eyes gleam . . . that unmistakable Hayley gleam that used to precede stiff talks in the principal's office and days spent in detention.

"Good gravy. Pills," she says softly.

"What are they? Do they have a brand name on them?"

"Nope." She hands them to you. There are two of them . . . large, white, unmarked tablets. "I wonder what they are. You realize we have to try them and find out."

"I dunno, they could be anything . . . ," you demur, though you're starting to feel like it'd be fun to do something reckless and stupid again. Like being a teenager again, only without the bad skin and the geography homework. "Maybe they're harmless. They could be vitamins for all we know. What does it say on the envelope?"

She uncrumples it and squints in the half-light. "All it says is 'For Lance.' Come on, no one stashes pills in their wallet unless they're a little bit naughty. I bet Lancey is a real party boy. You want one? If you don't, I'll take both."

If you take one, turn to page 253.

If you let Hayley take both, turn to page 256.

When you get to Spinners, there's a sign on the door: Closed for Private Party. A man with a clipboard—presumably a guest list—is blocking the entrance.

"We were supposed to meet people here," Lisa says.

"Well, unless they were on this list, they're not in there," the bouncer replies. "Lots of people are going over to the Philosopher's Club." He points to a bar across the street.

You, Dave, and Lisa all look at each other, puzzled.

"You want to check it out?" Lisa asks. "Or maybe they just went to the party. I have the address."

If you want to go to the Philosopher's Club, turn to page 233.

If you want to go right to the party, turn to page 304.

An hour later, you've got a nice buzz going and are rationalizing that everything's going to work out fine. Hayley is deeply immersed in the business of drinking and making scathing remarks about everyone who walks in. Suddenly she flinches and lowers her eyes. "Something wrong?" you ask.

"Don't look."

"Why do people always say that when they know the first thing you're going to do is turn around and look . . . ," you begin, but she grabs your arm.

"No, really, don't look; I don't want him to see us."

Before you can even ask who she's talking about, you catch a sidelong glimpse of the guy who's just walked in. It's Hayley's boyfriend, Cole. "He said he was working late," she mutters.

"But he's by himself," you point out. "It's not like he's with some trashy blonde."

"No, apparently his taste runs to trashy brunettes." She sighs as Cole, oblivious to your presence, approaches a dark-haired girl who has obviously been waiting for him.

"Don't jump to conclusions," you say soothingly. "Maybe it's all harmless. It's not like they're kissing or anything. Wait . . . sorry, scratch that. Can't see any tongues though. Maybe they're just friends?"

"Then how come I've never seen her before? That slimy, weasely little bastard," growls Hayley. "I have to leave . . . if I stay here another minute I won't be able to stop myself going up there and saying something."

Though you don't particularly want a scene, you don't want Hayley to leave yet. She won't want to go to the party in this mood.

If you think she should say something to Cole, turn to page 258.

If you let her leave and resolve to go to the party alone, turn to page 260.

The three of you decide that because there are three of you—and you couldn't look any more different—you're going to sing a Thompson Twins song. After Dave and Lisa have a brief but heated argument about the merits of "Doctor! Doctor!" versus "Hold Me Now"—so now it's obvious they're just arguing as a means of flirting—the decision is made to go with "Hold Me Now."

Lisa fills in the entry form and hands it to a barmaid, from whom you order a round of beers. If you're going to sing, you need to be even more inebriated than you already are. You've secured a table, and what was only ten minutes ago a half-full room has filled up so that there's standing room only. The din of the crowd is loud enough to drown out what Dave and Lisa are saying to each other. Their suddenly intimate, exclusive conversation reminds you of Sadie. You can practically close your eyes and hear her laugh; it's like the echo of frolicking children in a distant valley . . .

"Okay, folks, listen up." An emcee with receding dark hair and a mustache has stepped up on the stage, wearing a tux and sunglasses. "We've got some exciting news for yez tonight. There's a man in the crowd tonight who's got a wad of cash burning a hole in his pockets and he wants to see some good entertainment, so he's doubling tonight's prize money. That's right, folks, *doubling* it. That's times two, folks. That means tonight's grand-prize winner will be taking home two grand."

"Could you imagine?" Lisa's eyes light up.

"So without further ado . . ." The emcee picks up an entry form. "Let's get cracking. Let's get Tracy Q up here. She's going to be singing 'Two of Hearts.' Oh, I get it. *Tracy* Q. *Stacey* Q."

"This is going to be great," Dave says, and the three of you settle in to watch.

Tracy Q proceeds to do a routine she's obviously done before, singing "Two of Hearts" with a tinny, cutesy voice. She's dancing around, her big hair becoming a strange hot pink halo in the stage lights, her moves perfectly in synch with the song. You know she's spent hours in front of the mirror rehearsing, maybe even performed this routine here a few times to work the kinks out of it. She's followed by a man named Jackson

Michaels, who does a rendition of "Thriller" replete with fake fangs, red leather jacket, and yellow contact lenses, and then by Tom Collins, a Tom Jones look-and-sound-alike who sings Phil Collins's "Against All Odds." Clearly, you, Dave, and Lisa are out of your league. When a Celine Dion look-alike takes the stage in a period costume and starts singing a pitch-perfect rendition of "My Heart Will Go On," Dave and Lisa catch your attention.

"We think maybe we should bag it," Dave says, and Lisa nods in agreement.

You can't find the energy to respond.

"Hey, man, come on. Let's get out of here." That's Dave again, and suddenly he and Lisa have you, one by each arm, and they're escorting you out of the bar.

Lisa says something that sounds like, "If you're going to throw up, just don't do it on my new shoes." You're wondering whom she could be talking to. Who's getting sick? Then it suddenly hits you—when the smell of tequila on Lisa's breath makes your stomach churn—that it's you. You're very drunk. No, not just very drunk. Shit-faced. Completely and utterly shit-faced. Or at least you figure that's the reason Dave and Lisa look like they're creatures in some science-fiction movie. What was it? *Blade Runner*?

"Hey, Dave," you say, because Dave'll know. "What's that movie where there's this thing in the forest and it's not quite invisible but—"

"That's it," Dave interrupts. "You've got to go home, buddy. Let's catch a cab."

When you wake up the next morning you don't remember much else. You may have asked the cab to stop so you could get sick. Dave and Lisa might have been all over each other in the backseat next to you. You might have protested going home, insisting you were fine, that you could go to Spinners, the party, wherever Sadie was. But one thing's for certain. You went to bed alone and woke up alone. When, oh when, will Sadie ever be yours?

The End

You can hear Suzy calling after you angrily as you leave, but there's no way you can stomach spending the rest of the evening in her company.

"I'm sorry, Hayley, I really had no idea she'd done that. She never said anything before."

"Yeah, I believe you . . . don't worry. I do know Cole's a jerk, y'know. I'm not stupid. Something told me he'd been screwing around. . . . I just didn't think his taste had sunk as low as that little conniving bitch. Sorry, I forgot, she's a friend of yours."

"Whatever. Don't think any more about it tonight."

"Easier said than done, babe. I guess I've fucked up your night, too? The party, Mark . . . all that? It's not like you can go looking for Suzy's cousin now."

"There'll be other parties. No big deal." Not strictly true, but no point making her feel worse. "Of course . . . we *could* go somewhere else. It's still early."

"*Hey!* I know where we should go! It's perfect; it'll cheer us both up! Swing dancing at Zoë's!"

You look at her skeptically. "I dunno . . . I'm not really in that kind of mood."

"How can you not be in a swing-dancing mood? It's always a perfect time for swing dancing!"

"Funny, I'd never have pegged you as the swing-dancing type."

"*Au contraire*, I am full of natural rhythm!"

"Full of something, certainly."

"Have I ever steered you wrong?"

"Frequently. But what the hell, let's go."

Before long you're lining up at the bar in Zoë's while Hayley tries to squeeze past the impeccably dressed clientele to order drinks. The band, a generic swing outfit with the obligatory "Daddy" in their name, are clearly having a ball up there, and about a dozen couples are dancing, a little too self-consciously to be truly having fun.

"Cool, isn't it? Almost like being in the movie!" says Hayley when she eventually returns with your drink.

"It's not bad. But what the hell is this?" You sniff your glass suspiciously.

"It's my own concoction. Martini à la Hayley. Take a sip. Good, huh? Just don't light any cigarettes for a while."

"It's . . . strong," you gasp. But tasty.

"Hurry up and finish that; I have to dance," she gushes. "Let's go, baby."

"You want us to dance together? Don't you usually have a male partner for this kind of thing?"

"We can ask those two beautiful babies over there." She points. "Not exactly Trent and Mikey, I know. More like Bert and Ernie, to tell the truth, but still . . ."

If you ask them up to dance, turn to page 263.

If you prefer not to dance yet, turn to page 267.

Dave is pumped up by the idea of singing, and he and Lisa start to review the song list, looking for duets. You keep pushing for "Say, Say, Say," and they keep telling you to shut up; it won't work because they're not both men. Dave's not sure he knows the tune to "Up Where We Belong," though he goes off for a time about what a great film *An Officer and a Gentleman* is. When they spot "Don't You Want Me" by the Human League on the list, you think Lisa's going to shit herself she's so excited.

"Oh my god," she keeps saying. "Oh my god. I love that song. Oh my god."

"Okay, folks, my name's Tommy Two-Tune and I'll be your host this evening. A little exciting news before we start. Tonight, folks, someone might get a lucky break. Because right here in the front row is Tony Raymond of the Stars R Us talent agency. Tony's looking for new clients and is going to be keeping a close watch on the performers onstage tonight, so hit 'im with your best shot, folks. So . . . without further ado, on with the show." Tommy Two-Tune, who's wearing black pants, a loud Hawaiian shirt, and several Hawaiian leis, picks up an entry form. "Let's everybody put their hands together for, what's this, oh, I get it—John Mellon Cougarcamp—who's going to be singing 'Jack and Diane.' " A guy in jeans and a white T-shirt with a bad haircut hidden under a cowboy hat gets up there and does a pretty lousy job. Your confidence in Dave and Lisa soars—especially if the little impromptu song they sang while walking here is an indication. You're clearly not prepared for Billy and Joel, the next two contestants, who get up there with sunglasses and black suits and ties and proceed to somehow make it sound like they're singing all four harmonies on that song "The Longest Time." You think the disqualification of a drunken local—entered by his buddies as Kenny Lager, performing "Footloose"—bodes well for Dave and Lisa until the Mock Turtles, a wholesome-looking foursome wearing mock turtlenecks, take the stage and offer up a jovial "Happy Together." Next up, Prints, a guy wearing every kind of plaid and stripe and tropical-print piece of clothing he could find, sings "Little Red Corvette," and you know your friends are doomed to fail.

You tell them you're going to leave.

"Come on," Lisa pleads. "If you stay and cheer us on—they judge by clapping, you know—we'll split the money with you if we win."

If you really do want to leave and go to Spinners by yourself, turn to page 247.

If you can't resist the chance to make a quick buck, turn to page 251.

You watch Hayley leave, unsure whether to follow her but not ready to give up on Suzy yet. "I really can't believe you did that, Suzy. How could you? Is there anyone in the state you haven't slept with? What were you thinking?" You hand her a napkin to wipe the beer off her face.

"What are you talking about? She's the one who threw a drink over me."

"You fucked her boyfriend. I think that ranks a little higher on the scale of bitchiness than getting Heineken in somebody's hair."

"Listen to Mother Teresa. I slept with someone who had a girlfriend. Big deal. Like you've never done something stupid."

"This is beyond stupid! Fine, you and Hayley aren't that close, but I've never known you to do anything vindictive before."

"You're damn right Hayley and I aren't that close. And you want to know why? Because long before he caught sight of Hayley, Cole liked me. And I liked him—I was in *love* with him. Bet you didn't know that. So don't sit there getting moralistic on me when you only know half the story."

"You can't blame me for only knowing half the story when you didn't tell me the rest of it."

"Yeah, well, we don't all go around talking endlessly about our pathetic crushes."

"Are you referring to Mark?" The night is gradually assuming the chirpy, carefree atmosphere of a Jacobean tragedy.

"Of course I'm talking about Mark! My god, have you given a thought to anything else for the last few weeks? Have you ever asked how things are going for me? I do have a life, too, y'know!"

You sit awkwardly in silence for a few seconds.

"I'm sorry if I've been selfish, but my talking about Mark too much doesn't have anything to do with you and Cole."

"You just don't care, do you! You don't even listen to what I'm saying!" Now Suzy is crying drunkenly, actually bawling her eyes out, and what are you supposed to do? Pat her hand comfortingly or tell her she's full of shit? Pat her hand *while* telling her she's full of shit? Who knows? Who cares?

Well, you do, a little bit. In spite of everything, you can't leave her here looking so miserable and forlorn. Now she's started to hiccup in between sobs, and the whole scene is so pathetic that you don't have the heart to ditch her.

"I guess the party's out of the question then?" you say drolly, and laugh when Suzy shoots you a disbelieving look. "It was a joke, Suzy. We'll go home, okay?"

"But . . . what about Dan?" she sniffles.

"Maybe we should come back another time when your mascara and eyeliner aren't smeared all over your cheeks. I don't know how Dan feels about Marilyn Manson."

Suzy nods, sniffs again, and sucks back the last of her drink, and the two of you stand up to leave. "I'm sorry, you know," she adds. "I'll fix things up with Hayley. It wasn't supposed to turn out like this."

"Not exactly the way I pictured it either." You sigh.

The End

When Lisa doesn't return in the time it would take her to change her shoes, you get worried. About the meter. It's adding up, so you pay, get out, and wait on the street.

After another ten minutes—you figure maybe the shoes were an excuse and she really had to take a dump or something—you start to worry, instead, about Lisa. You enter the building and convince the reluctant doorman to escort you upstairs to check on her. Inside, you find Lisa passed out on the bathroom floor. Together, you and the doorman carry her to her bedroom. Once there, she begins to stir.

"What happened?"

"Well, from the looks of it you went out and got sloshed again—and brought home another random loser," the doorman says agitatedly.

"You don't watch many sitcoms, do you?" she asks him, clearly drunk.

"No, as a matter of fact, I don't," he says.

"Didn't think so." Lisa lies down again and puts her hand to her head. "Because if you *did*, you'd know that you doormen are supposed to be *nice* to the people in your building. You know, like right now you should be making me a cup of tea and laughing to yourself about how shocked I'll be when I walk into the surprise birthday party you're planning for me next week. Or maybe you'd ask me how my new novel's coming along."

"You're writing a *novel*?" you ask.

"No," she says disdainfully, not even looking at you. "That's not the point."

"I don't need this shit," the doorman says as he goes for the door. "I'm outta here."

"That's okay," Lisa says, without really looking at you. "Mike'll take care of me."

Mike? You're puzzled.

"Lisa," you say, "it's me."

"Oh, Mike," she says groggily. "What would I do without you? I'm sorry I hit on your friend. I just wanted to make you jealous."

It suddenly hits you that you've been used. Lisa was after Mike all along . . .

"I'm going to change into my pajamas," she says. "You want to wait in the other room . . ." You poke around the living room and find, amid various half-full mugs and empty beer bottles, the current issue of *Glamour*, a bag of grass, and some rolling papers. . . .

If you pick up *Glamour* and flip through it while waiting, turn to page 255.

If you roll a joint and put it in your pocket, turn to page 255.

The Apollo, a cozy Greek restaurant, is doing brisk trade this evening. As soon as you walk in, Suzy waves at two guys sitting at a table.

"He's here!" she trills.

"Great," you say, but there's a vague feeling of unease settling upon you. Why does one of these guys, the one who isn't Nick, look so familiar? You can't place him exactly, but you've definitely met before. And the way he's now glaring at you suggests that he recognizes you, too, and more worrying still, he's having no trouble remembering where and when.

Nick introduces him as James. . . . Somewhere in the distance, a bell is ringing. "We've met before. Didn't think I'd run into you again," James says to you.

You're not sure what to say and just stare blankly.

James has clearly overindulged on the ouzo. "Did you know she was going to be here tonight?" he snaps at Nick, who shakes his head.

"I've never even met her," he says, puzzled.

"This is the girl I told you about, remember? The one who fucked me over last month?" James is staring at you as if you're something he just found lurking on the bottom shelf of his refrigerator. "We met at a party—you were there with some friend of yours; Carina, maybe? You were a little drunk. Anyway, we talked for a long time, we kissed, I told you I thought you were really great and asked for your number, you gave it to me, and I went to the bathroom. When I came back ten minutes later, you were making out with somebody else and when I tried calling you the next day, I realized you'd given me a fake number."

Wow. You did that? You had no idea you could be such a bitch.

"I'm really sorry, James. . . . I must have been completely wasted. I don't even remember. I mean, I remember the party, sort of, but most of the night is a blur. It was Carina's birthday and we'd had way too much to drink and . . ."

"Save it; I don't care. Nick mentioned that a friend of Suzy's wanted to go to Lindy's party tonight to meet some guy. If you think I'm going to watch you walk all over some other poor schmuck, you're sadly mistaken. Sorry, Nick, but I'm not going anywhere with her."

And with that he storms out of the restaurant. After a brief apology and the explanation that James really needs to get out more often, Nick runs after him, taking all your hopes for the evening with him. Suzy is glaring at you. "I can't believe you treated him like that. That poor guy."

"But I don't even remember what happened! Come on, Suzy, you know I wouldn't do something like that unless I was bombed."

"I'll call you tomorrow," she fumes, running out to catch up with Nick and James. Dejected, you sit down and order a glass of ouzo.

The End

You're barely in the door of Lisa's apartment before she pins you up against the wall and starts kissing you and undoing your belt buckle. You're too drunk and horny to be thinking straight; otherwise you might actually resist her advances. Men have been known to do that, you know. In fact, at another time you might actually be slightly annoyed by how easily manipulated you are. She's been brushing up against you all night; standing too close. So close you can smell her. So you've been slightly aroused all evening. This was on the cards whether you wanted it to be or not. Because what it really comes down to is the fact that she wants you and she's done her prep work. You're powerless to refuse.

"There's something I need to tell you," she says, right as you've managed to strip her clothes from the waist up and grab her ample breasts. When you see that her left nipple is pierced, a silver ring jutting out with her hardened nipple, you lower your mouth to flick it with your tongue. You're more aroused than ever, straining against your jeans.

If you say, "The only thing I need to know is where the bedroom is . . ." turn to page 265.

If you say, "What?" but continue flicking, turn to page 269.

A health food restaurant serving only organic food, Polly's' general policy could be summed up with the phrase "We take the fun out of dining out." The hard wooden benches are set too close together. The tables are uncomfortably small. The staff are at best apathetic and at worst downright hostile. The long and complicated menu—most of which seems to consist of seaweed and various types of bean—is written in lilliputian print on a chalkboard out front. The prices are ludicrously high. And yet it's always crowded.

You steer Suzy, who's still clutching her bottle of Stoli like it's made of gold, through the door, and both of you peer around while the guy in charge of reservations gives you a forced semi-smile. "There's a thirty-minute wait, ladies."

"We're looking for someone," you explain. "Suzy, do you see Nick anywhere?"

"Nah . . . Is there a smoking section out back?" she asks.

Your charming host shakes his head disdainfully, as if Suzy is a dim-witted child.

"Can we have a quick look around?" she continues.

"If you leave the bottle here."

"Why can't I take it inside?" Suzy's getting petulant now.

He says nothing, just gives Suzy that look again. What a jerk.

"Well? Why can't I? Hey"—she nudges you—"the host is not responding! Hahahaha!"

"Ladies, I'm going to have to ask you to leave."

"But we haven't done anything!" whines Suzy. "Just give me a second." She barges past him and parades through the restaurant, checking all the diners. "He's not here!" she calls to you. A waiter approaches and takes her firmly by the arm. She tries to shake him off and in doing so, drops the bottle. It shatters instantly, and the look on Suzy's face is almost tragic.

"My Stoli! You bastard!"

"You're leaving now," insists the waiter, escorting her to the door. "Management reserves the right to refuse admission."

"Yeah? Well, customers reserve the right to tell you to go fuck yourself!"

"Come on, Suze, let's try the Apollo."

"My Stoli," she repeats, looking heartbroken.

"I'll buy you one for Christmas. Let's go."

Turn to page 218.

I think I'm going to do it," you say to Lisa.

"Okay, have fun. See you." She takes off down the street.

"Okay, boys, let's get you two prepped."

"How cool is this." Dave elbows you as you follow this Liam person to a trailer where your nose is powdered.

You spend the next hour walking in front of this apartment building as they film a scene with this gorgeous girl, who looks kind of familiar, and three very average-looking guys. Your kind of movie!

When they call a "wrap" Liam approaches with a few papers. "I forgot to get you two to sign these releases. Just sign on the dotted line and we'll set you up with fifty bucks and you can be on your way. We appreciate your help, lads."

"Is this some kind of joke?" Dave has started reading the paper and doesn't look pleased.

"How do you mean?" Liam goes to his side.

"The bit here, about it being an Ed Burns movie."

"Ed Burns." Liam nods his head. "That's the director."

"I thought it was Kevin Smith. I saw Kevin Smith before."

"Oh, you must be thinking of the gaffer John. He gets that all the time."

"No way in hell you're putting me in an Ed Burns movie. I thought you had to date the guy to get a part anyway." Dave rips up his release form.

You go to sign yours, hoping to get your fifty dollars before this gets out of hand.

"*What* are you doing?" Dave rips the form out of your hand and tears it up into tiny pieces, throwing it at Liam like confetti.

"You can't do this." Liam swats at some of the lingering bits of paper.

"Watch me." Dave starts to walk away.

"Do you realize your friend just set us back a whole day's worth of filming?"

"Sorry." You shrug and start to back away in the direction Dave went. "He's a very emotional film buff. Might want to screen your extras a little better next time."

A few minutes later you catch up with Dave.

If you say, "Why do you always have to be such an asshole?" turn to page 273.

If you say, "That was by far the coolest. I'm going to go buy *Variety* for, like, a month to see if we get in there somehow," turn to page 276.

Mustering your courage, you saunter, as nonchalantly as possible given the combination of embarrassment and annoyance you're feeling, over to Suzy and Mark.

"Hey." Good opener.

"Hey!" Suzy seems visibly shocked to see you. "Didn't think you'd make it."

I bet you didn't. "Well, here I am." God, this is scintillating. Not a single bright remark is coming to mind. Fire the scriptwriter! "Hey, Mark." Again, sheer poetry.

"Hi, nice to see you." Well, that's something. "Suzy was just telling me she thought you'd got lucky tonight."

Suzy winces, and the desire to strangle her with her own stockings is almost overpowering.

"How sweet of her. Well no, I was just catching up with an old friend. And what happened to that guy you were with?"

"The English guy? We were just talking," replies Suzy, shooting daggers at you.

"Clearly he has a problem with American accents—it looked like he couldn't understand what you were saying unless you stuck your tongue in his ear." *Miaow!* Perhaps you've both gone a little far, but right now you're pissed and you don't care who bears the brunt of it.

"I thought you two were friends," says Mark, backing away from Suzy and heading for the kitchen. "Maybe I should just leave you to figure out whatever's going on here."

As soon as he's out of earshot Suzy covers her face with her hands and moans. "Oh shit, I'm so sorry. I completely fucked it up."

"Jesus, Suzy, what the fuck *is* going on? You knew I liked him," you blurt.

"I know. But he came over to me and we started talking and I realized . . . fuck, I've really blown it."

"You realized you liked him?"

"Not exactly." She's blushing furiously.

This isn't making sense. "Then what?"

There's a long and painful pause before she speaks. She's staring at you now, and for some reason you're completely immobile. "I realized

. . . that I've been jealous for a while, and thought it was because he liked you rather than me."

She looks so miserable and flustered that any anger you were feeling has drained away. "But . . ." you encourage her.

"But . . . really it was because *you* liked *him*."

Oh my god. "I see." Except you're not exactly sure that you do, until Suzy brushes your cheek gently and an electric shock races right through you.

Instinctively you glance toward Mark. He's looking over, intensely curious.

If you decide to leave Suzy and go over to Mark, turn to page 271.

If you stay with Suzy, turn to page 274.

hat are you doing?"

"Get out," you say.

"What?"

"What's a matter? You don't understand *English*. He said, 'Get out.' " Mike answers.

"You must be joking."

"I'm afraid not," you say.

"You won't get away with this." Elizabeth gets out of the car and you close the door, but the window remains open. "I know people."

"Ooooh, I'm shaking." Mike clutches your arm. "Big bad Elizabeth is going to rally her obscure indie band and call up somebody who works at the NME. Then what'll we do?"

"Fuck you," she says.

"In your dreams, baby," Mike says, then tells the driver to go.

At the corner, the taxi gets into an accident. As you get out of the car to assess the physical damage—thankfully no one's hurt—Elizabeth cruises past in another taxi.

"Suckers!" she shouts out the window, giving you the finger.

You and Mike spend the next hour telling cops what you saw, therefore missing the gang at Spinners. Turns out Mike doesn't know where the party is, and you both check your answering machines. No joy. You find another bar to drink in and end up talking to two girls, one of whom is really cute. Unfortunately, you get stuck with the ugly one. She gets mad when you don't want to take her home.

The End

H*ey!"* Nick's hug of greeting is almost warm enough to make up for what you've just seen. "Any songs you'd like to hear? Special requests?"

"That depends. Do you have 'My best friend is a scheming skanky bitch and she's coming on to the guy I wanted to get lucky with to-night'?"

"Already played it, sorry. Seriously, don't worry about Suzy . . . she's just drunk. There's nothing going on. Go over to them, stick your chest in his face or toss your hair or whatever it is you women do to attract attention. Or"—he pauses—"you could forget about that guy and try the one who's been eyeing you ever since you came over here."

You take a surreptitious glance around. The guy Nick's referring to is smiling at you—he's extremely cute, long-haired, and baby-faced. And he's coming over.

"Hi, I'm Alex." You shake hands, and he holds yours considerably longer than necessary. Alex offers to get you a drink and returns with a nameless concoction that contains a great deal of vodka. Both of you stand around awkwardly for a couple of minutes, while Nick continues battering guests' senses with his choice of party music. Finally some space opens up on a couch and you get comfortable.

Alex is funny, charming, and very easy to talk to. In fact, there's something strangely familiar about him, though you're sure you'd re-member having met someone as attractive as this before. There's a lot of common ground between you—you grew up in the same town and know a lot of the same people, though whenever the conversation is about to get around to exact details of where he lived or went to school, Alex changes the subject. Maybe he's just shy. He seems very sweet . . . perhaps not sweet enough to make up for the loss of Mark, but at least you don't feel like such a loser now that you're talking to someone else instead of glaring bitterly over at Suzy and him.

Speaking of which, they're now dancing to "Crazy for You" by Ma-donna. You could kill Nick for putting this on—not that there's any fooling around going on, but how long will it be before Suzy tries her patented "Sorry, was that your groin that I brushed against?" move.

You can't watch. You need something to hide your eyes with, and what better than Alex's face and hair. He's leaning in close—any second now he's going to try to kiss you. Will you go for it?

If yes, turn to page 278.
If no, turn to page 282.

As the cab pulls away, Elizabeth talks through the open window. "Even when we were twelve I could tell you wouldn't ever be man enough for me."

You're too awestruck to think of a comeback.

"God, what a bitch." Mike is surveying the block you've stranded yourselves on. "Don't let her get to you."

"Ah, don't worry about it." You spy a bar down at the end of the street. "But let's have another before we catch up with the rest of the gang. I need a minute to recover."

"Okay . . ." Mike follows your line of vision to the bar on the corner. "You sure you want to go there?"

"Yeah," you say. "Why not?"

"Well, in that case"—Mike starts walking alongside you—"there's something I've been meaning to talk to you about."

Inside, you find two stools by the bar right near the door and settle into them swiftly. You order a beer, and Mike follows suit.

"So, what's this you want to talk to me about?"

Mike takes a long gulp of his drink. "I'm gay."

You've also taken a fair amount of liquid into your mouth, and you almost spit it out. "What?"

"I'm gay." Mike nods and looks you straight in the eye, waiting for your response.

You examine the crowd and realize that there are absolutely no women in the place.

"This is a gay bar, isn't it?"

"Yup."

"You ever been here before?"

"No." Mike plays with the cocktail straw in his glass. "That's the problem. It's like I know this about myself but I don't really know any other gay people for some reason and I'm really not into going out by myself and checking these kinds of places out. It's kind of exciting just to be here now. I feel like it was a big step, even if it was completely by accident."

You sit in silence for a few minutes, then Mike speaks again.

"I was so scared to tell you. I thought you'd freak out and think I was interested in you or something. It's such a huge relief to have finally told you. God, you wouldn't believe."

You're touched that Mike was so worried about you, but also feel bad that he's been keeping this to himself, and that he's struggling to find his way. "What do you say we stay here and check out the scene here tonight?"

Mike's eyes light up. "You serious?"

You nod.

"I thought you were hoping to get laid tonight."

"You want to stay or not?"

"Of course I do. I'd love to. Maybe *I'll* get laid tonight."

"If I'm giving up a chance with Sadie you'd better. So let's get working. Bartender? Another round."

You're such a good friend.

The End

You've been back to Peter's place after many other nights out, and, as usual, it looks like the bomb squad got there seconds too late.

"Messy, yes, but stylishly so," he insists, striding into the kitchen to make coffee. You slump in a chair underneath his huge framed Ramones poster, close your eyes, and when you wake up, the room is in semidarkness. There's a blanket tucked in around you and a cup of cold coffee by your feet. A note on the arm of the chair that you can just make out in the murky light reads, "Didn't want to wake you. Don't leave without saying good-bye."

You stand up and make your way groggily to the door of Peter's room. He's sound asleep. Maybe you should just go back and crash on the chair for the rest of the night. He looks kind of cute though, all huddled up under the comforter.

Peter mumbles something in his sleep and kicks the covers off. Ah, how sweet. Like a little kid.

Like a little naked kid with a raging hard-on. And it may not be that bright in here, but you have to admit that is a damn impressive display. Who'd have figured?

You're leaning in the doorway staring, unwillingly mesmerized, when you become aware that Peter has woken up and is looking at you.

"I know I should reach for the covers except I'm frozen with embarrassment."

"God, sorry," you start. "Let me." And before you know what you're doing, you're pulling the comforter up over him and giving him an unthinking pat. "Oh fuck . . . sorry, again."

"Hey, don't worry about it. I generally like to at least kiss first, though." He laughs.

If you make a move, turn to page 286.
If you leave, turn to page 288.

You cross the street to the Philosopher's Club and scout around inside for Mike. No joy. Dave, however, discovers that the "Philosopher of the Day," written on a blackboard above the bar, is David Hume, and since he shares the same first name, Dave can drink for free all night. Lisa decides to press on to find Mike and co., but Dave wants to land at least a few free pints and insists he can sneak some in for you. Lisa gives you the address of the party and leaves.

You find a remote corner and wait for Dave to go to the bar. He returns with a pint, from which you both drink for a few minutes. Then he tells you to keep the rest of it and roots around for an empty pint glass. He goes back up to the bar with the empty glass and comes back with a fresh beer. "This is going to be a piece of cake," he says.

"You don't think they'll catch on if you keep going up at this pace?"

"What are they going to do? Kick me out?"

And that's precisely what happens when the two of you are very obviously drunk as skunks about an hour later, still not having paid for one drink. Out on the street, you search your pockets and can't find the address of the party. You won't find it until you do your laundry next week. *C'est la vie!*

The End

Sure," you say, and then realize that Ted is glaring at Jay in a manner that implies he's just committed some terrible faux pas. Mark is gazing at the floor.

"I guess you haven't seen Mark in a while, huh," says Ted. "He doesn't do that anymore."

"Thank you, Ted. No, I don't do *that* anymore." Mark shrugs.

"Because of Meg, you know?" adds Ted. "The girl he just broke up with, the one who spent the last three years coked out of her head and then moved on to every other drug known to mankind before her parents found out she was ripping off money from all her friends, including Marko here, and forced her into detox . . ."

"Can we stop now?" implores Mark. So that's why he and his girlfriend broke up. You had no idea. "You guys do whatever you want. I suddenly don't feel like the party. Maybe I'll go call Meg and see how she's doing."

"If you feel you should, okay," says Ted gently. Oh wonderful, *now* he's being sensitive.

"I'm sorry, I had no idea . . . ," you begin, feeling like the world's biggest asshole.

"Not your problem. You couldn't have known. I'll see you around, okay?"

And with that, he's gone, leaving you, Ted, Jay, and Alice listening to Hank crooning "Long Gone Lonesome Blues."

Appropriately enough.

The End

W*hoa, dude,"* Dave says, once you've explained the situation. "It's like you're Robert Downey Jr. man. How cool is *that*?"

"Yeah," you say. "Only I don't feel like spending the next two hours in a hyperactive dialogue about how I don't see why the three of us can't all live together in perfect harmony. So what do I do?"

"I don't know. Let me think about how I've seen this handled before."

You can only imagine what Dave's going to come up with.

"Well, cloning's out. Though if there were two of you that would solve everything."

What were you *think*ing asking for his advice?

"You don't happen to have an identical twin you've never told me about who's less than an hour away, do you?"

You tell Dave to forget it. You'll make the decision yourself.

At that very moment, Elizabeth comes up to you and says, "Take me home with you now."

If you decide that you're going to stick to the original plan and pursue Sadie, turn to page 238.

If you decide it was fate that Elizabeth Albern came back into your life this very night, turn to page 332.

I'll pass, thanks."

"Me too; I don't really do that anymore," says Mark.

"No problem, more for me later." Jay shrugs.

About half an hour goes by and the conversation has turned, inevitably, to country music. Mark has shifted seats so that he's now beside you, one arm draped loosely on the back of the couch. You're both laughing at Ted, who's lambasting any band he considers "new country" while Jay pleads the case for Wilco and Son Volt, a case weakened by the fact that Jay is on his fourth whiskey and his statements don't extend much beyond "Fuck, yeah!" and "They rock, man!" Suddenly Ted pushes his Stetson back from his head, peers around, and asks "Where's Alice?" No one noticed her leave.

Ted wanders out of the room to look for his sister, and the next thing you hear is an earsplitting "*Alice! You stupid little bitch!*" that drowns out even the godlike strains of Hank.

Out in the hallway, Alice is slumped on the floor amid a pile of coats. Obviously, she went in search of some of Jay's "present" and overdid things a little. Or a lot, judging by the state of her.

"Christ, it was only a little coke . . . it's not even very good shit. What the fuck is wrong with her?" Jay is whimpering. "Hang on though," he adds, wrenching the envelope out of her hand. "This isn't even my stuff. What is this? Who owns it?"

Mark and Ted both plead ignorance—and you're about to do the same when you realize that Alice is sitting on the jacket you borrowed from Peter. Whatever Alice has just shoved up her nose must have been in his pocket. Ohfuckfuckfuckfuckfuck.

"I'm not sure what it is but I know where it came from," you start, but Ted cuts you off with a withering look.

"I don't give a shit where it came from. I'm calling an ambulance and I want you all to get the fuck out of my house. Christ, Mark, couldn't you have found a woman with a brain?"

You're about to argue drunkenly that this is hardly fair coming from someone who wears a Stetson in his living room, but now is evidently not the time. Instead you grab Peter's jacket and make for the door, Jay and Mark following quickly behind.

You could kill Peter. You could hit yourself. Unfortunately neither option is going to be much help right now, with Jay—Jay!—glowering at you as if you're a prize idiot and Mark stonily silent.

A taxi pulls up and you climb in, alone. As the car passes Mark, he deliberately looks the other way.

The End

You completely piss Elizabeth off when you ask her to back off because you've been interested in Sadie for ages and it looks like you finally have a shot at her. She leaves the party in a huff, accusing you of being heartless for bringing her in the first place if this is how things were going to turn out.

It all seems worth it, however, as your conversation with Sadie gets progressively more touchy-feely. You know the way women get when they've had a few; they start leaning in real close, touching your arm—maybe even your leg if you're sitting—to emphasize a point.

When the party starts to break up, you suggest that perhaps you and Sadie could go somewhere else to talk. She invites you back to her place and leads you to the living room. You figure she's just playing a little hard to get, postponing the inevitable; you'll engage in some kissing and groping awkwardly on the couch before moving somewhere more comfortable. But when Sadie doesn't suggest moving to her room by the time you feel the urge to delve below the belt, you make your move, sliding your hand up her skirt to caress her inner thigh. She throws her head back and laughs—imagine the essence of Shirley Temple captured—and you want her more strongly than ever.

"That tickles," she says, her warm mouth pressed against yours.

But when you head for home, she stops your hand with hers. "Not tonight," she says.

You groan.

"I've got my period."

After making out awhile longer, you get up and say, "I guess I should get going."

"You *could* stay." Sadie pulls you back toward her. "I'd like to sleep with you if I can't *sleep* with you."

The two of you go to her room and go to bed, her supple body seemingly molding to fit yours perfectly. This must be love.

Or at least you think so until Sadie starts to snore something fierce. You feel like you're in bed with an eight-year-old who's learning how to play the tuba. You don't get any sleep whatsoever, and when you wake up, Sadie's got the worst morning breath you've ever encountered. You make a swift exit and—because Mike calls and tells you he gave

Sadie your number—you screen your calls for a week. To your relief, Sadie gives up after call number three.

The End

YOU DOWN the Jaegermeister first. Ugh. Jay hands over the tequila, and you're contemplating the glass when, as if by magic, the door opens and Suzy is there, one hand on the wall to support herself, the other pointing in your direction.

"You!" she yells.

"Hi, Suzy."

"Not you. *Him!*" She's pointing at Jay.

"Oh fuck . . ." Jay is wearing the look of a startled bunny rabbit.

"You know him?" you say to Suzy.

"I thought you were still living in Buffalo," mumbles Jay.

"No, asshole," she fumes. "But then I wouldn't expect you to know that—after all, when's the last time we saw each other? Must be, ooh, the day you ran off with my friend Belinda. A week before our wedding. *A fucking week, Jay*. Never thought I'd see your sorry ass again. Then tonight I met a friend who told me you were back in town, and I've spent the last hour combing every bar in town looking for you, you pathetic, slimy, minidicked little . . ."

"Minidicked, really?" interjects Peter. "See, he looks like a big fella. I guess you can never tell."

". . . conniving, back-stabbing, wanky . . ."

"Wanky? Is that a word?" mutters Mark.

"Shut up!" screams Suzy. You have never seen her this mad. Nor had you ever heard of an ex-fiancé, but then Suzy doesn't talk about her past much, understandably if Jay is typical of her ex-boyfriends. She picks up an ashtray from the table and hurls it toward Jay. Who is standing next to Mark. Who gets it smack in the face.

"Don't mess up his face!" you blurt, unthinking.

Mark clutches his head, stunned, then turns angrily to you. "Christ, can you get your insane friend out of here before she kills someone?"

"I'm leaving," says Jay, preparing to scuttle out the door. "Suzy, I'm sorry about everything, but there's no need to get violent."

Suzy is clearly still of the opinion that there's plenty of reason—you can hear her bellowing profanities and threatening grievous bodily harm as she charges out after him.

Mark holds his head and winces. There's a cut over his right eye that's bleeding slightly, and the beginnings of a nasty bruise. You're just about to ask him if he wants to go to the emergency room when he answers the question for you by collapsing onto the floor, banging his head again for good measure.

"Shit," sighs Joe, picking up the phone to dial 911.

Ten minutes later you, Peter, and a barely conscious Mark are in an ambulance bound for the nearest hospital. On the bright side, you're definitely going to be spending the night with Mark; pity it's going to be in the emergency room.

The End

You sneak into the back bedroom and pick up the phone. You dial information and ask for the number for MTV's *Loveline*. If anyone can give you advice about your current dilemma it's Adam Carolla and Dr. Drew—and whatever lame WB Channel "star" they have as their guest.

Once you have the number, you dial it. An operator answers, asks you for your question, your age, and your name; you tell her you'd like to use the pseudonym Oscar. Dr. Drew and Adam, she promises, will be with you shortly.

You're put on hold and get to listen in on the show. The girl on the line is asking whether she should be worried about any of her internal organs if she has one penis in her vagina and another up her butt, both thrusting at the same time. Adam's asked her if she's interviewing candidates, and Dr. Drew is saying something about being worried about her heart; she doesn't get that he doesn't mean that her actual heart is in physical danger. Man, these people are dumb, you think to yourself.

Then there are some commercials and suddenly the volume gets louder.

"Okay, we have Oscar on the line. What's the problem, Oscar?"

You recognize Adam's voice.

"I'm at a party," you explain, "and there are two women who want to go home with me."

"I'll repeat the question," Adam says. "What's the *prob*lem?"

You hear laughter.

"Oscar"—you recognize Dr. Drew's more stern voice—"have you been drinking?"

"Yeah, I've had a few beers—and a coupla shots. That's not the problem."

"I think that may be the problem exactly." Dr. Drew is talking, but not to you. "Can you hear him? He's slurring his words. He's obviously drinking more than he can handle, and I imagine it's a pattern. Oscar, is there a history of alcoholism in your family?"

"No," you say. "But there is a history in my family of getting laid by two women in one night and I'm not sure I want to fall into *that* pattern. Can you help me? Please?" You're pretty proud of your witty comeback.

"Hey, Oscar. Oscar, you there?"—then a pause in which you say,

"Yeah"—"Your parents looking to adopt another kid? 'Cause that sounds like my kind of family."

"You hear the anger here?" Dr. Drew is persisting in spite of Adam, and you envision their guest nodding sympathetically while sitting on the couch beside them. "He's lashing out at us—the very people that are trying to help him. That's because of the alcohol. And he probably isn't aware of it. A lot of people in this situation know they need help on a certain level but fear the vulnerability of admitting that."

"Yoohoo," you say, "remember me?"

"Yeah, Oscar, here's the deal. You know you like one of them more than you like the other one. Am I right?" Adam's trying to get to the root of the problem.

"Well, this might be the only chance I ever get with one of them and she's gorgeous. The other one, though, she's a real catch. More of a long-term interest."

"Oscar, listen to me." Dr. Drew's at it again. "Don't go home with either of these women tonight. You've had too much to drink. You're at a much greater risk of having unprotected sex. And it's just not a wise thing for you or anyone to be doing. This is an explosive situation. Get out of there now. Go home, sleep it off, and get help."

"Come on, Drew. Give the guy a break. I say go home with both of them if you can, go home with the gorgeous one otherwise, and work your apparent charm on the long-term interest next time you see her. And whatever you do, don't be dumb. Use a condom. Alright? And go easy on the bottle. See ya, Oscar."

The line goes dead. You're not any more sure about how to proceed than you were ten minutes ago. You lie back on the floor to try to compose yourself and clear your head. Maybe Dr. Drew had a point. You've had way too much to drink. The room is spinning, so you close your eyes to try to steady things before you get up.

Just then you hear a woman's voice. "Come in here where we can talk in private." Whoever it is obviously can't see you lying down on the far side of the bed.

You lie very still so as not to reveal your presence.

"So what are we going to do?"

You recognize Mike's voice.

"I don't know. I mean, I'll feel bad if we do anything tonight or even let on what's going on."

It's Elizabeth. You're kind of confused.

"Ughhhh." It's Mike again. "Just because you two went to camp together and kissed when you were, like, ten, doesn't mean you owe him anything."

Yes, it finally hits you. They're talking about you.

"I know I don't *owe* him anything." Elizabeth sounds exasperated. "It's just that, well, I don't want to hurt his feelings. Not after he's been so sweet to me tonight."

Ouch, that hurts. You thought you'd really been putting out the vibe and you get *sweet!?*

"You're telling me you're going to deny what's going on between us."

"No, I'm not denying there's something there. It's just, well, maybe we shouldn't act on it. I can let him down easy."

"Screw that. I want you, and I know you want me. This has got nothing to do with him."

If you sit up just then and say, "Well, it does now," turn to page 277.

If you want to hear more, turn to page 280.

Well, little lady," he muses, "seeing as how the last thing I want to do is spend my night mopping up these here toilets, and you already look like you're a couple of sheets to the wind, we won't force you to drink two shots."

Thank god.

"You can just take your shirt off instead."

You're about to protest that he stands more chance of winning an Oscar than of seeing you topless when he holds up his hand, shaking with laughter. "Just kidding! Do one shot, whatever you like."

Seeing as you've been hitting the tequila pretty hard tonight, you go for a shot of that. Mark winks at you, and you take the opportunity to go stand by him and engage in a little subtly flirtatious body language. Nothing too extreme; don't want to scare him off . . .

There's time for another round before you hit the party. Jay goes first this time—he picks an appalling heavy metal song that Joe automatically declares the winner. "That's the worst goddamn song on that thing, hands down. And my word is final."

"Okay, an easy one," says Jay. "Either do a shot of my choosing or get someone in this bar to kiss you."

"C'mon, Jay," moans Mark. "There's only five women in here. One of them has more facial hair than the rest of us put together. Two of them are old enough to be your mother—in fact, there's a definite family resemblance. One is clearly with a guy, and he's big, and I'm scared of him. So that leaves . . ." and he glances at you. Subtle.

"It's your choice," states Jay. He's loving this.

"Fuck, I'll take the shot."

"Joe, could you fix my friend here a Flaming Apocalypse, please?"

Joe's eyes widen and he studies Mark for a moment, like a referee eyeing up a boxer during the big match. "Sure he can handle it? Fella, you don't suffer from a heart condition or anything, do ya?"

Neither you nor Peter have ever seen a Flaming Apocalypse before, and it's likely that, after seeing Mark's reaction, you're never going to try one. He downs it manfully, but you can see the color draining from his cheeks and his eye muscles are starting to twitch.

"Peter? Your call," he gasps.

"Does a peck on the lips count?" he tries, hopefully.

"No," insists Jay. "Tongues must lock."

"Alrighty then, here goes." And with that he grabs you and delivers a huge, wet kiss. Yes, lots of tongue, that's for sure. Actually though, this isn't bad at all. Good technique, not too much saliva. You're about to pull away but his hands slide around your waist, he presses into you, and you, in an automatic gesture, respond in kind. Finally he pulls back, trying to suppress a huge grin.

"That do?" He nods to Jay.

"Looked convincing enough from here. Mark, whadda you think? Mark?"

Mark has landed face first in a bowl of peanuts, a stream of saliva oozing out the side of his mouth. Now is the moment when you should feel disappointed, not to mention embarrassed that you just made out like a slobbering high-school kid with someone else barely two feet away from him, but instead you find yourself licking your lips appreciatively. . . . Jay hauls Mark to his feet and starts dragging him to the door.

"I think now's a good time for us to go," he says. "Been fun."

"See ya," you both chorus.

"So," Peter is looking at you hopefully, "you want a Flaming Apocalypse, too?"

"Nah, they look horrendous. So I guess I have to make out with someone instead."

"Hey, Joe," he calls, "come over here and give the little lady a kiss."

"You bastard." You laugh.

"Yeah well, that's part of Pierre's charm. You coming?"

The End

You wander out into the street in search of a cab. When, many minutes later, you finally see a cab in need of a fare, you hail it. But just as you're about to get in, you hear someone screaming, "Taxi, taxi," and from around the corner this woman appears. She's running for the cab, but her heel breaks and she falls flat on her face right in front of you. She curls up in a ball and starts crying.

"Miss?" You bend down to help her. "Miss? Are you okay?"

She just keeps crying.

"Come on, miss. Get up. I'll help you into the cab."

"But it's *your* cab," she wails.

"Not anymore it isn't. It's *our* cab now."

Wearily, she gets up and climbs into the backseat.

"Where to?" the driver asks.

"I have nowhere to goooooooo," she cries out, and her body starts shaking.

You speak to the driver. "Just drive, okay? I'll figure it out in a minute."

Long story short: the woman's just been dumped by her live-in fiancé. She doesn't want to go home because she doesn't want to face him. You convince her that if she just left him at the restaurant then she'll be home before him so she can get some of her things and call a friend so she can spend the night. She agrees to go home and call a friend only if you come along for moral support, so you oblige. Once you get to her place, you call your answering machine in the hopes of getting a message from one of the gang. Sure enough, Mike's called from Spinners to tell you they're all leaving there. He leaves the address of the party, so you double-check what you have written down. All correct. The only plus about this jilted jezebel you've run into is that she happens to live just a few blocks from the party. When she secures a place to stay for the evening and packs an overnight bag, the two of you part ways. She thanks you for your trouble with a peck on the cheek. You arrive at the party in desperate need of a beer and some fun and see Dave and Lisa, looking ecstatic. You grab a drink and shuffle over.

"What the hell happened to you?" Dave says. "I was just telling everybody about our little adventure." You see that everybody includes

Mike and co. and Sadie—right next to you, thank heavens—and a few people you don't know. Dave speaks: "So like I said, our competition is really, really clever and I'm thinking there's no way we can compete. For starters, we've entered as Dave and Lisa. Not a pun on the Human League in sight. And my supposed best friend in the whole world here"—he raises his beer in your direction—"completely abandoned us." He puts his arm around Lisa. "So anyway, right before we're called to go on, Lisa gets this totally amazing idea. We go into the bathroom—thankfully they were those either/or kinds of bathrooms—and we swap clothes, or at least most of them. Then we fill out another entry form and swap them just in time for the emcee to introduce us as the Who's the Man League. Then Lisa starts singing the male part in this deep voice and I sing the girl part falsetto." He sings a line to give everybody an idea: "The five years we have had have been such good times. I still love you."

Everyone laughs, but it's Sadie's laugh you hear. It's like a rainbow's shooting out of her mouth.

Dave coughs. "God, my throat hurts from doing that. But the crowd absolutely ate it up. I've really got to hand it to Lisa"—he looks at her and smiles—"she was really hamming it up. So we won and we had to perform again, but this time the whole place was singing along, with all the guys singing the girl part and vice versa. It was by far the funniest thing that has *ever* happened in my *entire* life."

"I can't believe you didn't stay to cheer them on," Sadie says to you. Then she shakes her head and walks away.

You spend the rest of the night watching Sadie flirt with another guy. You never have any fun.

The End

Sliding back onto the seat you occupied earlier in the evening, you order another drink. As you pick listlessly at the last of the honey-roasted peanuts on the bar, a voice behind you says softly, "Very careless of you, losing your friend like that."

It's Bryan, one of the guys you were playing Snowball's Chance in Hell with earlier. He looks a little drunker now, but then the same could probably be said of you. In any case, it's a huge relief to see a familiar face. "I'd love to pay for that drink, but you wiped us out earlier," he adds, hopping up on the stool beside you. "Y'mind if I sit down?"

"Where's your friend Graham?"

"Over there." He points. "We tossed a coin to see which one of us would come over first and talk to you."

"You're not going to ruin an already shitty night by saying you lost, are you?"

"Hell, no." He beams. "I would have liked to talk more earlier, but you were busy with your friend. I saw her leave a few minutes ago, by the way; she looked pretty bombed."

"Par for the course."

"She knows that bartender is married, doesn't she?"

You groan. "No. I'm sure she doesn't."

"Wow. Yeah, he's married alright. Graham and I were arguing about it before, so we put a bet on it and asked him."

"Do you two bet on everything?"

"Certain stuff." He laughs. "Just a stupid guy thing, you know. Juvenile. But it usually makes the night more interesting."

You talk for a while longer. Bryan borrows some money from Graham, who's decided to leave, and buys a couple of drinks. You find yourself forgetting about the plan to return to Sullivan's. It's doubtful that Suzy ever turned up anyway—she's probably too busy unwittingly providing Dan with some extramarital frolics.

Bryan is inching his stool ever closer to yours, and it's not a huge surprise when he makes a move, taking your hand in his, and finally leaning over to kiss you. You've no objections. He's laid-back and easy to talk to and, not insignificantly, an incredibly good kisser, even after many drinks. Or maybe the many drinks are helping—at any rate, it takes some willpower to end the kiss, and considerably more effort to remove his hand from your breasts.

"I guess this isn't really the right place, huh?" he asks. "Will you come home with me?"

If you go with him, turn to page 291.

If you think it would be safer to ask him back to your place instead, turn to page 294.

Or you could just leave and go to your local for one last drink. Turn to page 179.

The emcee announces Dave and Lisa and looks as puzzled as everybody else that their name isn't at all punny. They get up on stage, looking ridiculously normal when compared to all the other contestants, and the music kicks in, soulless synthesizer sounds filling the speakers.

Dave's face goes beet red right before he starts to sing. And while he starts with a confident, "You were working as a waitress in a cocktail bar, when I met you . . . ," he mumbles stuff after that, seemingly having forgotten to look at the monitors that supply him with the lyrics. Once he remembers that the monitors are there—that he's not actually expected to know all the words—he tries to catch up but loses his place. Thankfully, Lisa makes her entrance anyway, but in her attempt to sing louder in order to drown Dave out, she's entirely off-key. You can barely resist covering your ears as the two of them struggle through the second verse, Lisa making awkward attempts to turn their performance into some kind of skit by pointing at Dave occasionally. People actually start booing.

Lisa runs off the stage crying before the song is even done, and Dave tells the audience to go fuck themselves.

The three of you are out on the street seconds later. Lisa's crying so hard she's having a hard time breathing, and Dave, who you think might be on the brink of tears himself, pulls her into a hug. "Hey," he says, "come on. It wasn't that bad. You were great. I was the one who fucked up." He looks at you pointedly.

"Dave's right, Lisa. It's really nothing to be upset about. You were fine, really."

Lisa's sniffling and wiping tears from her eyes, now bloodshot. "Really?" God, the woman could break your heart.

"Really," you say. And you make a mental note to remember this moment the next time you get into an argument with a woman about whether or not honesty is always the best policy. "Now, come on. We've got a party to go to."

"I don't know if we feel like it anymore," Dave says. And warning bells go off in your head. They're already a "we."

"What do you say, hon?" Dave asks Lisa, lifting her chin with his index finger.

Yup, your drinking-and-cruising buddy's as good as dead.

Lisa says she wants to go home. Rather, she says to Dave, "I want you to take me home," and writes down the address of the party for you, figuring the rest of the gang has probably left Spinners by now.

They're kind enough to let you take the first taxi that comes along. . . .

Go to page 284.

Okay, I'll take one."

"Atta girl!"

Hayley says. You swallow it . . . not easy given the size.

"What if they're for some old guy's arthritis or something?" you suggest as you resume walking.

"Lance is *not* an old guy's name."

"I suppose that makes some sort of twisted sense. Hey, this must be Lindy's place."

The music is blaring, and you can hear raucous laughter even as you cross the street toward the house. There's about half a dozen people walking up the driveway in front of you, and Lindy—at least, you assume the tall, blond woman who answers the door is Lindy—says hi to two of them. You hear one of the guys say something about having "brought along some friends," so you grab Hayley and tag onto the end of the group, trying to look inconspicuous. Lindy nods politely at you as you walk in and shake her hand, announcing your names.

"Very slick," says Hayley admiringly, once you're far enough away from Lindy. "Hey, this is some place. Where's the booze? We need to find the kitchen."

You scope out the rooms. Eureka: an impressive array of spirits is lined up in the kitchen, and a quick glance inside the refrigerator reveals it to be overflowing with beer.

"Ooh, my favorite!" says Hayley as she pulls out a bottle of cider.

"You sure you should take that?" you ask.

"That's okay, take one; I think I brought too much anyway," says the guy who just came into the kitchen.

"He brings too much deliberately, hoping that someone's going to ask him if they can trade sexual favors for cider," comes another voice close behind him. It's *Mark*! He spots you and gives a little wave. "Oh hey! Nice to see you."

"Hi there. The cider-stealing woman is my friend Hayley," you explain, wishing you'd had the foresight to check yourself in the mirror before you came in here. "The sexual favors might be negotiable."

"And this is my friend Gerard. Haven't seen you in a while. You coming back into the living room?"

Of course you are. You grab a beer, grin at Hayley, who's thoughtfully distracting Gerard, and follow Mark.

There follows a long, fascinating conversation—fascinating from your side at any rate, and at least he's not yawning—in which you and Mark talk about everything from movies to favorite flavor of hummus. He prefers roasted garlic to mild curry flavor, too! What are the odds? Could things be more perfect? Now that the party's getting crowded, the two of you are forced to sit closer together on the couch to make room for other guests. All of a sudden he puts his hand on your thigh and whispers, "Do you want to find somewhere more private upstairs?"

Not exactly the kind of line that fuels romantic fantasies. Maybe you should suggest waiting a while longer? On the other hand, isn't this what you hoped would happen?

If you go upstairs with him now, turn to page 297.

If you want to wait, turn to page 300.

"Mike," Lisa calls, "you can come back in." When you do, you see that she's curled up facing the wall. She can't see you, and she's drunk enough that you probably sound like Mike. Should you have some fun with this and play along as if you really are?

If you say to Lisa, "I'm not Mike," until she understands that, well, you're not Mike, turn to page 259.

If you decide to see how long you can pass for Mike as some twisted kind of revenge, turn to page 262.

"I'll pass," you say.

"Okay, little chicken-licken. All the more for Hayley."

She swallows them both, with some difficulty, and you resume walking toward the party.

Lindy's house is large and elegant, and through the open windows you can hear the strains of Dionne Warwick singing "Walk On By."

"Ooh," squeals Hayley. "Lindy has taste—I'm glad we're crashing this gig now. So when she opens the door, just play it very mellow, okay?"

You knock, and the door is answered not by Lindy but by a middle-aged gnomish man who smiles blearily and stands back to let you in. "Lindy's in the kitchen," he says, slurring a little. "Didn't know she had so many pretty young friends—you are friends of hers, aren't you?"

"We're pretty young friends of friends," you respond, shuffling past him and into the living room, feeling relief wash over you. Not so difficult after all.

Now this is a scene. Lava lamps, beanbags, lurid psychedelic throws covering every modern piece of furniture, girls in miniskirts who seem to have applied their mascara with a trowel, even some guy with a velvet pantsuit.

"Shit, I didn't realize it was a costume party," says Hayley.

"Strictly speaking, it's not," comes a voice nearby, "but some of Lindy's friends decided to go for a Swinging London theme."

You both turn to face the owner of the voice. It belongs to a tall, dark guy in black jeans and a leather jacket. Not strictly gorgeous by classical standards, but his grin is disarmingly friendly. He introduces himself as Tom, and he and Hayley exchange a look that lasts significantly longer than politeness would decree. Then he offers to get you both drinks and disappears into the kitchen in search of punch.

"Madam has seen something she likes?" you whisper.

"Have him washed and brought to my tent. There's something about him, isn't there? Makes me moist."

Then you spot him. Mark. He enters the room and you could swear you hear angels singing. Look at that face. Those eyes. Two of them. And that nose. Right there, in the middle of his face. Those soft lips; again two, the requisite number. Perfect. Lips that are right now taking a drag of a cigarette as he gazes around. What brand is he smoking? Ah, they're roll-ups. Roll-ups that he rolled with his own hands. . . . You become dimly aware that Hayley is pinching your arm in an effort to attract your attention. "Do I even have to ask if that's Mark? Your eyes have glazed over. Look away before you start to drool, girl. Or go over there. Now, before some miniskirted vamp gets her claws into him."

If you choose to approach him right now, turn to page 311.

If you want to wait, turn to page 319.

"Go up and say something to him," you urge. "You know you have to."

"You think it's a good idea?"

"No, actually I think it's a stupid idea, and it'll probably end in tears, but the alternative—leaving here knowing that he's with her—is going to make you feel worse. So go, make an idiot of yourself if it helps any."

"Thanks. Hey, can you believe it's our two-year anniversary tomorrow?" she adds as she puts her drink down and walks toward Cole and his new woman.

To avoid seeming nosy, you study the bottom of your glass thoughtfully and deliberately try not to hear the conversation around you. But there's no missing Hayley's voice yelling, "You expect me to believe that?" Then there's some earnest discussion and Hayley's voice, more subdued this time, saying, "This is incredible. My god . . . and I never had the slightest idea!"

She doesn't sound upset. And when she returns to your table, dragging Cole with her, there's a broad smile on her face . . . and on his, too.

"You'll never believe it . . . Cole just asked me to marry him! It was his anniversary surprise. We're going to Las Vegas, tonight—you know I always wanted an Elvis wedding and he's got the chapel booked for tomorrow and everything! That woman is his sister Jeannette; she lives abroad—I've never met her. They planned the whole thing together! That's why I had to get home by midnight—to pack!"

"This is truly amazing."

"Ain't it the wildest! The flight's in three hours, and you have to come; Jeannette's calling to reserve another ticket. You're my maid of honor. I won't take no for an answer."

"But the party . . . ," you weakly protest, and then realize how lame that sounds. "I guess Mark will have to wait. Vegas, you say?"

"Vegas, baby!" She hugs you. "Vegas!"

The End

"I'm *not* Mike," you say for the twentieth time, and Lisa jumps. Once she recognizes you she calms down again, throwing her head back onto her pillow. "Oh *god*, I'm such an idiot. Ooooh, my head. I need water. Will you get me some? Please?"

Sure enough, you find yourself going to the kitchen and getting Lisa a glass of water. You see a roach in her kitchen, but decide not to kill it. "Go forth and breed," you think to yourself. It's not like you even *like* her all that much, but you're kind of pissed off anyway. Because here you are nursing her when you should be dazzling Sadie with your wit and charm.

"Will you page Mike for me? The number's over there." Lisa nods toward her dresser as she takes the water from you. "He'll come over and stay with me for a while. We've got some stuff to sort out."

"Mike has a *pager*?" If you'd known that, you wouldn't have been busting your ass to make sure you met up with him. You could have paged him and found out where the party was at any time.

But wait a minute, if Mike comes over here, you're stuck going to the party with people you barely know. That is, if you even get there at all. What to do?

If you page Mike and agree to wait for him to call back, turn to page 287.

If you purposely dial the wrong last digit when you page Mike, and leave immediately for Spinners, go to page 290.

Hayley is bent on leaving the bar right now; she's lost any interest in the party, and you can sympathize. Not that it makes it any easier for you, turning up on Lindy's doorstep like a lost puppy, but that can't be helped. Something else is bothering you though—that glint in Hayley's eye as she kisses you good-bye and promises to call, a glint you recognize. An identical glint was there the time Hayley told you about putting half a tab of acid in her little brother's orange juice just to see how funny he'd act.

"Hayley . . . you're okay, aren't you? You won't do anything crazy?"

"Nothing crazy. Promise." She makes a Boy Scouts sign and then creeps out the door.

Cole and his female friend are talking intently and oblivious to anything else, so you order another drink. And a shot, for good measure, to help fix your nerve. A few minutes later you leave the bar and are about to cross the street to start walking to Lindy's when a green Jeep Wrangler pulls up, horn blaring.

"Get in!"

It's Hayley. But of *course* it's Hayley.

"Get in *now*!" she hollers.

There should be a sign on the car door that reads "Abandon hope all ye who enter here!"

You climb in, and Hayley gives a whoop and then takes off.

"Let me guess," you say. "This is Cole's Jeep, isn't it? And he's not going to get it back in one piece, is he?"

"He's not getting it back at all, baby. What does the pretentious little jerk need a Jeep for in this town? The only rugged terrain is in the parking lot near the Seven-Eleven. Man, is he going to regret giving me a spare set of keys."

"So, what are you going to do with it? This isn't turning into a Thelma-and-Louise suicide mission, is it? We'd have to drive pretty far to find an appropriate cliff."

"No, dummy. I'm not crashing it. I'm selling it."

You have to laugh. "At this time of night? Where?"

"Marvin the Maniac, the used-car salesman! Completely untrustworthy, but he's open twenty-four hours a day. My brother's dealt with him; he says he asks no questions."

Sure enough, Marvin is home and open for business. It's clear that he suspects some foul play; it's also clear that he doesn't care how hot the car is if Hayley's asking price is low enough.

When they're through doing business, she calls a cab from Marvin's office and then hands you a wad of notes.

"What's this for?"

"Spending money."

"Hayley . . . where are you suggesting we go?"

"Your place first of all, to pick up some clothes. Then the airport. After that, haven't decided. Don't worry; it's just for a weekend! I'm not crazy or anything. I just need to get away for a few days and I'd love you to come with me. Please. I promise I'll have you back at work on Monday morning."

She's smiling, but you know she really does need this.

"Come on, babe. You're my friend. You're my buddy. You're my galpal. You're all I've got left!" She lets out a wail.

"You're drunk." You laugh. A cab swings into the car lot and pulls up alongside you.

"Absolutely," she answers as you both climb in.

The End

"Oh Lisa, really?"

"Yes, it's you I want. And I honestly think it could work out between us. I know you think you're gay, but I think you're just confused."

"I'm gay?"

She obviously doesn't pick up on the inflection.

"No, you're not. You can't be. I know you were jealous tonight. I just know it. And I know it was low to hit on the very guy you think you're in love with to try to get you to wake up and realize it's me you really want, but I didn't know what else to do."

You sit there in stunned silence. Lisa was hitting on you all night. Mike thinks he's in love with *you!?* This just isn't possible.

"I've got to go, Lisa." You're out the door before she can say another word.

Down at street level, you catch a cab and tell him the address of the Pub. You need the comfort of your local drinking spot to get you through this one; you're certainly in no condition to face Mike tonight, having outted him to yourself under such bizarre circumstances. Your mind is racing, flashes of moments you and Mike have shared over the years running through your mind. Double dates, even. Mike. Gay. Could it be? And could it be he's kept it from you because you're the very object of his affection?

Go to page 299.

Bert and Ernie, or Paul and Robert to give them their proper names, seem like nice enough guys and are more than willing to dance. A little too willing, perhaps; Robert, who's your partner, is soon whirling and twirling and revolving you till you feel like a rag doll in a spin dryer.

"A few lessons and you'd be okay," he shouts over the music. Charming. "You should move your feet more though."

"And I know just where I'd put them, too," you retort.

"Don't be offended . . . just being helpful. Hang on, there's a good part coming up."

The next thing you know, you're being hurled bodily across the floor, colliding with another couple. As you fall, you instinctively grab onto the first thing to hand, which unfortunately turns out to be a table laden with drinks. You don't cut yourself on the glass, which is one blessing, and the table landing on your leg doesn't hurt too much, but you do end up with two bottles of imported beer and a Cosmopolitan down the front of your shirt.

"Okay!" you announce loudly as Hayley helps you to your feet. The band has stopped playing and almost everyone in Zoë's has turned to see what happened. By some fluke, there is actually a spotlight shining right on you. "Listen up, people! This is clearly God's way of telling me that it's time to go home. But first I'd like to thank everyone who helped make this night such a rollicking success. All I wanted to do was go to a party and meet some guy. Not a lot to ask, is it? But no. First, I'd like to thank Suzy, my former best friend, for being a complete bitch. I'd also like to thank Dan the bartender for getting Suzy so drunk that she felt compelled to tell Hayley here all about her cheating boyfriend. And lastly, I'd like to thank Robert, my dance partner, who told me I should take swing lessons just before he threw me across the floor so that I landed on my ass in a pool of alcohol."

"One more thing," adds Hayley. "You must have fallen on a lit cigarette—I think your pants are burning."

"Of course! Of course my pants are burning. That makes sense. Thanks again, everyone." By now you're beyond caring, but you stand patiently while Hayley brushes you off with a wet napkin.

There's a smattering of applause from onlookers as you and Hayley head back through the crowd.

"I thought you handled that well," says Hayley, smirking, when you finally get outside and are taking in gulps of the cool night air. "You want to go somewhere else?"

"I just wanna go home." You sigh.

"Okay, baby. We'll do it again soon though, okay?"

You laugh in spite of yourself. "Oh yeah. Sure."

The End

Lisa smiles and takes your hand, leading you to the bedroom. There, she lights a dim lamp and starts removing stuffed animals from her bed, perching them carefully on a rocking chair in the corner. You step up behind her and unzip her skirt, which drops to the floor and pools around her feet. You see that she's wearing white cotton underwear with hearts and stars on them and curse yourself for the surge of desire that runs through you. You're not a pervert by any stretch!

Lisa sits on the bed, and when you go to take her shoes off she stops you. "The shoes," she says, "stay."

So maybe she's the kinky one!

She pulls you forward so that you're standing in front of her as she sits on the edge of the bed. She undoes your pants and wrestles with them until they're down by your ankles. When you step out of them, you're standing at attention, poking out of your shorts. When she touches you and pulls you down on top of her, you're sure you'll explode before long. As your bodies start to meld together, you're getting unbearably aroused.

"In my jeans," you say as you peel yourself away from her, "I've got a condom."

"Oh, we won't be needing that." She tries to pull you back toward her as you fumble with your jeans.

"I think we should." You're the picture of responsibility.

She keeps pulling at you but you've already got the condom out and open. "I mean that we won't need it because we're not going to be doing that. I'm a virgin."

"Not for long," you say as you roll the condom on.

"I'm serious," she says. "I'm not doing that with you. I think you should go, as a matter of fact." She's reached into her bedside table and slipped on a granny nightgown.

"Oh, come on," you say. "We can still have a little fun, can't we?"

"I'm not comfortable now. I want you to leave."

You get up and get dressed and leave, saying, "Thanks for nothing," on your way out. In the lobby of her building you run into old friends of your parents' who insist you join them for a drink across the street.

You spend the next two hours in a piano bar explaining the Internet to a bunch of sixty-year-olds.

The End

"I think I'll sit this one out. You go dance if you want; I'll wait here."

"Alrighty, if you're sure. Be good now."

She strolls up to the two guys, engages them in chat for a few minutes, then follows Ernie onto the dance floor. You smile as you watch her, sipping your drink, occasionally glancing at the antics of the couples around you.

Then you catch sight of him.

It really is exactly like a movie . . . one minute you're oblivious to his existence; the next, everyone else in the room has faded into insignificance. He's sitting at the far end of the bar, and he must have been looking at you for a while, because he glances away quickly when you first see him, as if embarrassed, and then raises his eyes to meet yours. He smiles. You're tempted to check behind you to see if he might be looking at someone else. But no, now he's standing, picking up his drink, and coming over.

"I thought it was you," he says. Amazing that he looks so much more beautiful close up. You gaze at him blankly, struck dumb both by his physical presence and by the fact that you have absolutely no idea who he is.

"You don't remember me? Jeff Costello? We used to live next door to each other until I was nine; then my dad got a promotion and we moved away. We had that crazy cat, Archie, the one who always used to get into your yard and drive your dog crazy. What was your dog's name again? Holly, Hester, something like that?"

"Heidi." You grin. "I remember now. I can't believe you recognized me after all this time."

"Yeah well, I'm not saying you haven't changed. But I'd still know you anywhere. You don't remember that I used to have a crush on you?"

"No . . . that's not something I'd have forgotten. I have to admit, if I'd known you were going to turn out like this I'd never have let your family leave the neighborhood." Alright, so it's an unbelievably corny line, but at least he's smiling.

"So . . . you're here with someone?"

"My friend Hayley. The one out on the dance floor who's spinning that guy around and lifting him up in the air. She needs to let off a little steam tonight. You're here alone?"

"Yeah . . . I felt completely lame sitting here by myself, but I just moved into the neighborhood and don't really know anyone yet. So it was a choice between staying at home, either watching TV or chatting on-line to other lonely people with no social lives, or taking a chance and going out. And now, well, you're here so I'm glad I did. Even if I've never forgiven you for terrorizing Archie all those years ago." He grins.

Tomorrow you can always blame Hayley for giving you that mysteriously lethal cocktail, but drunk or not, you know that you're going to be going home with Jeff at the end of the night. As great as Mark may be, whenever you're with him you spend most of your time struggling to sound impressive, whereas with Jeff . . . well, Jeff is someone whose main recollection of you is probably the time you dressed his beloved cat up in doll clothes and tied it to the washing line. And he still likes you.

"So, maybe I could persuade you to dance if I stick around long enough?" he asks.

"If you stick around long enough, who knows what you could persuade me to do. . . ."

The End

Lisa throws her head back and thrusts her fingers into your hair, then says, "I've got a boyfriend."

You stop what you're doing and look at her. "You're telling me this now?"

"Yeah." She leans into you to cover her exposed breasts. "I mean I've always had a thing for you and I want to be with you tonight and he lives out of town anyway. But I just thought it wouldn't be fair if you didn't know."

You reach around her and unzip the zipper on her skirt, your mouth resuming its work on the nipple ring.

"So . . . now . . . you . . . know . . . ," she gasps.

"So now I know," you say, lifting your head to kiss her. She stops you by taking your hand and leading you to her bedroom after stepping out of the skirt pooled around her ankles. As you follow, you see she's not wearing any tights and her thong reveals the tightest ass you've seen in years. You can't wait to sink your, well, something into that silky flesh.

In the bedroom, a dim light lit, you go to take Lisa's shoes off, only she squirms away. "The new shoes stay," she says, pulling you toward her so that you're standing in front of her as she sits on the edge of the bed. She undoes your jeans and slides them to the ground. You're standing at attention, poking out of your shorts.

Lisa wastes no time in taking off your shorts, putting a condom on you and laying you back on her bed so she can straddle you. Just as she takes you into her and starts to ride you, the sound of keys in the front door startles you both.

"I didn't think you had a roommate," you say.

"I don't," she says.

"Surprise, babe," says the guy who appears in the doorway. "What the fuck!"

"It's not what it looks like." Lisa scrambles for something to cover herself with, which strikes you as kind of silly; presumably this is her boyfriend, presumably he's seen her naked. Still, this isn't really the time for you to contemplate the way context affects our views of nakedness and exposed skin in general. You pull on your jeans as quickly as you can.

"If I were you, I'd get out of here as fast as I could," Lisa's boyfriend says to you.

"My sentiments exactly," you say as you walk past him and collect the rest of your clothes by the front door.

Downstairs, you hail a cab. But halfway to Spinners you realize you feel like a total asshole. You've sobered up a good deal and know that you wouldn't feel right trying to make anything happen with Sadie to-night. She deserves better. You tell the driver to turn around and take you home. You blew it, you dog.

The End

Look, we'll discuss this later, but I have to talk to Mark, okay?"

"Sure, whatever," Suzy says. "I'll be over with Nick." She looks crushed and disappointed, but this is just getting too weird.

Mark nods at you. "Something going on there that I should know about?" he asks.

"I don't see how it's any of your business," you snap, and then wish you could take it back.

"Hey, I'm not trying to interfere. It's just that I don't need glasses to see that she really likes you."

"It's complicated," you mutter. Fuck, why does everything you say tonight sound like it came straight from *Party of Five*?

"It's okay, you don't owe me any explanations. Want to get a drink? Lindy's husband is mixing killer martinis in the kitchen."

Lindy's husband, Martin, does indeed make a killer martini, and after downing half of yours you start to feel better. Suzy'll get over whatever little phase she's going through. Anyhow, Mark is standing so close that you can practically feel the heat emanating from his body . . . that lovely, manly, taut body . . . god, these martinis are strong. He's gazing at you now, telling some story about his sister, or maybe his aunt—who the hell cares—and all you can think about is when one of you is going to make a move. No time to worry about Suzy. Suzy'll be fine. She's not crazy or anything.

"Hey, some crazy girl is stripping on Lindy's coffee table!"

A red-haired guy bursts into the kitchen and makes this announcement. "You have to see this—she's really going for it," he yells, rushing back out.

"Maybe we should have a look?" Mark prompts—typical guy—and you both join the audience in the living room.

And there is Suzy, perched on a coffee table and performing an elaborate striptease to, of all things, a Bob Dylan song. Who else would try stripping to "Positively 4th Street"? A handful of guys are cheering her on, but she seems oblivious—she's wearing the glassy stare of the utterly inebriated. Then she catches your eye and, with a whoop, unhooks her bra, twirls it over her head, and throws it at you. It lands at your feet.

If you try to talk her down, turn to page 339.

What the hell, you could just get up and join her. Turn to page 346.

W hat did you say?"

"I *said*, 'Why do you always have to be such an asshole?' "

"You're pathetic, man. You'd do anything for a quick buck."

"*Any*thing? I thought being an extra in a movie would be pretty cool and suddenly I 'do anything for a quick buck.' "

"Hel-looo, we're talking about an *Ed Burns* movie?"

"What the fuck do I care whose movie it is? I just wanted to be able to go to a movie theater and see myself up there."

"People like you." Dave shakes his head and spits on the sidewalk. "You make me sick. Have you ever cared about *any*thing in your entire life?"

"What are you *talking* about? Of course I have. That's got nothing to do with this."

"It's got everything to do with this. You just can't see it because you . . . you know what? Forget it." He waves his hands dismissively. "I'll see you, man. Have fun at your little party, chasing after your new little girlfriend tonight."

You're still standing there stunned, wondering what the hell just happened, when Dave disappears around a far corner.

You go home to contemplate the apparent shallowness of your existence.

The End

Somehow, you can't go talk to Mark now. This, whatever *this* is, has to be worked out. Maybe you should have guessed a long time ago that Suzy liked you as more than a friend. There's no denying you spend more time with her than anyone else, that she makes you laugh and supports you and is probably the best friend you've ever had.

And maybe it's more than that.

"Can we go outside and talk about this?" she asks, and you grab your jacket and follow her out the door.

"Look, I know you probably don't feel the same way," Suzy begins, as you lean against the wall in front of Lindy's house. She's standing awkwardly in front of you. "You're being really sweet by not just telling me to fuck off . . ."

"I'm not just being sweet," you hear yourself saying. "Not exactly . . ."

"What then? Hey, didn't we just have this conversation?" Now you're both laughing, and it's your turn to blush.

Who knows whether it's the number of drinks you've had or just because it feels like the only thing to do, but you suddenly lean toward her and kiss her on the lips. She lets out a little whimper of surprise and then deepens the kiss. Instead of feeling weird, it feels perfectly, absolutely right.

You break away after a minute, and Suzy mumbles shyly, "I'm sorry. I'm supposed to be sorry, right?"

"Hey, I'm the one taking advantage." You giggle and pull her toward you again. She's nuzzling your neck when there's a loud cough behind you, and you jump away from each other. It's Nick, with a huge, knowing grin on his face.

"Sorry, girls . . . just wanted to let you know I'm leaving. So, er, have a fun night, okay? By the way, you both look really good in Suzy's lipstick," he adds, hurrying away and stifling a laugh.

Suzy draws you close and kisses you again. "I hoped the sluttish red would work," she says softly. "Come home with me?"

"Well, okay. Only if you promise I don't have to clean your apartment in the morning."

"For you, babe, anything."

The End

"You know what?" Dave is so excited he sounds like he's having a hard time breathing. "Don't tell anyone about this, okay? I'm going to call my friend at *Entertainment Weekly* and tell him about it. Then everyone will be surprised. Cool?"

"Cool," you say.

Turn to page 302.

Once you're on your feet you get in Mike's face, practically bumping chests. "Where do you get off—"

"Boys, really." Elizabeth cuts you off. She steps up to the both of you and takes one of your hands and one of Mike's, squeezing gently. "There's no need to fight. It's always been a fantasy of mine to be with two men, and I can't think of any two—at least not men that I don't have to pay the price of a movie ticket to see and then it's only on celluloid—that I'd rather be with."

You and Mike look at each other, trying to gauge the other's thoughts on the subject.

"I'm game if you are," Mike says steadily.

If you're totally game, turn to page 326.

If you're game as long as you don't have to do anything with Mike, go to page 328.

If you're not interested, turn to page 333.

That's all it takes—soon you're making out with gusto and it's not bad, though Alex's technique suffers from overenthusiasm. The next time you open your eyes, Mark and Suzy are engaged in earnest conversation on the other side of the room, and you sense that you might be the subject matter.

Not to worry, because Alex is dragging you out of the room. "Come upstairs," he urges. You oblige and wind up in a bedroom that must belong to one of Lindy's kids, not that you thought she was old enough to have any. There's baseball paraphernalia hanging on the walls and posters of bands likely to have faded into obscurity by the end of the year. At least there's a comfortable bed, and you take advantage. Just when things are getting heavy and you're debating whether to call a halt now, while you're still wearing a couple of items of clothing, you realize with a shock that Alex is crying.

"Sorry," he's mumbling, "it's just, I've liked you for such a long time."

"Wait, we just met," you point out. "I've never seen you before, have I?"

And then Lindy walks in, sees the two of you, and gasps.

"Allie! Get downstairs this second! What would your mother say? And really," she addresses you, "couldn't you have found someone your own age?"

"Sorry, Aunty Lindy, but I can't go," Alex wails. "*I love her!* I've loved her for years!"

As you gaze at him in amazement, a tiny spark of recognition begins to glow in those parts of your brain not doused with alcohol. It all makes awful, terrible sense. Alex . . . Allie. Little Allie Walsworth, whom you used to babysit back in high school when he was . . . Jesus Christ. That would make him . . .

"You're *sixteen*?!" you shriek.

"In June . . ." he mumbles. "But I love you! I've loved you for years, ever since you let me stay up late to watch TV when you were babysitting! And then I saw you tonight and knew we could be together!"

"I'd like to send God a pillow so he could suffocate me in my sleep," you moan.

Lindy looks less horrified now; in fact she's obviously trying to suppress roars of laughter. "You couldn't have known. He looks older, don't you, Alex? His mother spends a lot of time in Europe so he often stays here with me. It's just an unfortunate coincidence. . . . Alex, you should have told her who you were."

"But then she wouldn't have given me a chance! And now, you'll go out with me, won't you?" he sniffs.

"Sure, Allie. As soon as I've served my time for violating a minor, I'm going to come look for you, babe."

It is definitely time to leave. Who knows where Mark is, and who cares. Lindy is sure to rush back downstairs and tell everyone what just happened, and you can't stand the humiliation. You leave Lindy's house, with Alex still calling after you as you climb into a taxi.

"Maybe in a few years! You'll grow to love me!"

The End

"You're right, fuck him." Elizabeth's voice suddenly sounds raspier. "No, don't. Fuck me."

"I thought you'd never ask." Mike's voice is barely a whisper.

In an instant you're covered in jackets, which you can only assume Mike and Elizabeth have tossed onto the floor in a relatively considerate gesture when you consider the garments' potential fate had they stayed on the bed. Through layers of jackets you hear the muffled noises of Mike and Elizabeth's lovemaking.

Him: "Oh, yeah."
Her: "Ow! No, not there."
Him: "Mmmmn. I'm so hard."
Her: "Where is it?"
Him: "Coming right up, baby."
Her: "Wait. Shit. You're too heavy."
Him: "Better?"
Her: "No, not really."
Him: "Mmmmnn. You're so wet."
Her: "You know what? Forget it."
Him: "What?"
Her: "Forget it. This just doesn't feel right."
Him: "Come on, baby. I know I can make you feel good."
Her: "Quit calling me baby."
Him: "What's a matter, baby?"
Her: "God, you're pathetic. You think women like this kind of shit?"
Him: "What shit?"
Her: "Mmmn baby this. And mmmn baby that. 'Coming right up.' Give me a break."
Him: "Don't talk to me like that, bitch."
Her: "Oh, yeah, that's mature."
Him: "Mature would be to get your ass back over here and finish what you started."
Her: "I don't need to hear any more of this."
Him: "Where do you think you're going?"
Her: "Somewhere where you're not."
Him: "Get over here."

Her: "Let go of me."

Sounds of struggle ensue.

You kick free of the jackets and stand—way too quickly, considering how long you've been lying down. You teeter once you're on your feet, then fall face forward onto the bed, only narrowly avoiding Mike.

"What the hell!" Mike looks over at you.

You get up and steady yourself as quickly as you can.

"What the fuck are *you* doing here?" He is not pleased.

"That's not important. But from the way you've been acting it's a good thing I *was* here." You turn to your damsel in distress. "Are you okay, Elizabeth?"

"She's fine," Mike insists.

"You know what," you say—and remember you've had more drinks than you admitted to Dr. Drew—"Why don't you just whip it out so we can get this over with? You're always trying to prove you can get every girl I want and that you're more of a man, and I'm sick of it." You start undoing your belt.

"Close your eyes, Elizabeth," Mike says. "If you see the pathetic little worm I'm sure this guy's got in his pants you might never be able to look any male specimen—let alone him—straight in the face again."

"I don't know." Elizabeth smiles as you start undoing your button-fly jeans. "It was pretty impressive last time I saw it, and we were only twelve."

"Alright," Mike says. "You're on, ace." He starts undoing his own pants.

"I didn't realize guys actually did this," Elizabeth says. "I mean, girls are always saying that—'Those two should just whip 'em out and get it over with'—but we didn't think guys actually *did* it."

"We don't," you say.

"First time for everything," Mike says.

If you really don't want to go through with this, turn to page 329.

If, in your drunken state, you feel compelled to see this ridiculous display of male competitiveness to its conclusion, turn to page 330.

You back away slightly just as Alex is preparing for the Lunge. "Maybe we shouldn't." You smile politely.

"Why not? What's wrong with you?"

"What's wrong with *me*? Nothing."

"So why back out now?"

"I don't want to kiss you, that's all."

"You could have fooled me."

"A goldfish with a learning disorder could fool you."

"Why are you being such a bitch all of a sudden?"

"Sorry." You sigh. "You're right; I'm being a bitch. It's just that I'm having a really weird night and things haven't turned out as I hoped, that's all."

"That's okay. Look, you wanna go smoke a joint? My brother has some stuff."

"Sure." You shrug.

"Wait here and I'll go ask him." Alex gets up and walks over to . . . Mark. Alex is Mark's brother. No wonder Alex seemed familiar—they do look alike, now that you see them together. With a sickening lurch you remember that Mark has mentioned having one brother, but he told you his brother was sixteen. *Sixteen.* My god, what you almost did . . . it doesn't bear thinking about.

When Alex returns, you look him in the eye and say, "You're sixteen, aren't you?"

He blushes furiously. "Who told you?"

"I know your brother. You look a lot older than sixteen, but then you knew that."

"Okay, so I'm sixteen. We can still go out and smoke, can't we? Mark said he's gonna come, too."

Lindy has specified that she doesn't want anyone smoking dope inside, so there's a cluster of people congregated in her backyard. You and Alex traipse out, closely followed by Suzy and Mark.

"Hey," Suzy catches up with you, tugging your sleeve, "are you ignoring me?"

"Should I be?"

"There's nothing going on," she says quietly, gesturing toward Mark.

"We talked, we danced, end of story. I wasn't flirting with him, and vice versa. He asked about you."

"He did?" Oh, to be wearing a school uniform and braids.

"He was wondering why you were talking to his little brother. I kept waiting for you to come over and say hi." She nudges you and passes the joint to you. "So go talk to him."

"In a second." You inhale deeply. "Wait till I get my nerve."

"No, do it now. Come on. Before somebody else . . ." Even as she's saying the words, a girl you recognize as Meg, Mark's ex, comes over, locks him in a bear hug, and squeals. "Oh Maaark! It's so good to see you! I hoped you'd be here!"

"Meg, I thought we agreed to avoid each other for a while?" Mark looks embarrassed and annoyed.

"I don't wanna." She pouts. "It's stupid, us splitting up like this. Come over here and talk to me." She tries dragging him away, but he firmly removes her arm from his jacket, then whispers something to Suzy, smiles at you, and tells Alex he's going home.

"He's *going*?" You stare after him, aghast. Meg is trailing him back into the house, but he hasn't even turned to look at her.

"Hey it's okay, don't worry!" Suzy beams. "He just told me he'd be in the International tomorrow night at nine and that he hoped he'd see us there!"

"Really? Oh, that's great!" The relief!

"Wait, did he say the International or the Continental?" She furrows her brow in concentration.

"Suzy, which one was it?"

"The International! I'm sure! Though it might be the Continental. We can try both!"

"Not again, Suzy . . . I need another drink."

The End

You walk into a party in an overcrowded, pitch-dark loft and are convinced you'll never find any of your friends. Instead, you decide to seek out the alcohol supply. There, at a folding table covered with bottles of booze and mixers, you make yourself the stiffest gin and tonic you've ever had.

"Had a rough night?"

You turn and see it's Sadie standing next to you. She looks flushed, like she's been fucking—or, and admittedly more likely, just dancing. There's loud house music pounding through the room.

"Not the best night I've ever had. But getting better by the minute."

She smiles at what you meant to be an offhanded compliment. Did it come out right? Did it make sense?

"Did you come alone?" She reaches for the gin, and her bare arm brushes against yours.

You nod somberly. "That wasn't the idea, but the two people I was with decided they wanted to partake in activities with one another of which I couldn't really be a part."

She laughs that laugh you love so. It's like caged-up glee suddenly set free.

"Oh my god," she says. "The same exact thing happened to me. Well, sort of. I brought my friend Elaine with me, and she's off making out with some guy on the dance floor."

"What do you say we join them?"

Her mouth drops open.

"I mean, on the dance floor. Do you want to dance?" God, you can be such an idiot sometimes. You'd swear you were at a high-school dance or something.

"I don't know. I was kind of thinking I'd had enough of this music. I was thinking of leaving."

"Oh."

The two of you stand there in silence watching people dance. This is your so-called life. You know you should say something, but what?

"You want to go somewhere? Someplace quieter and where the drinks aren't lukewarm?"

That would have done the job, but Sadie beat you to it.

"That'd be great."

You and Sadie find a cozy spot around the corner and talk until closing time. You offer to walk her home at night's end, and when she slips her hand in yours, it's confirmed. You feel like you've known this woman forever. And want to be with her forever. You also want to be with her, in the more primal sense, tonight, and you're thinking it's on the cards.

Back at her place, candles on the bedside table lit, all's going well. She's everything you imagined she would be in bed; a great mix of vulnerability, aggression, and know-how. Right as you're about to go for the gold, she whispers your name.

"Yes?"

"Do you have a condom?"

You don't.

Sadie sends you out to the twenty-four-hour drug store, only when you try to come back you realize you don't know her last name, her apartment number, or her phone number. You wait for an hour, but when she doesn't come looking for you, you have no choice but to go home.

The End

Taking this as your cue, you reach over and give him a tentative kiss. Nothing too heavy . . . if he objects you can pretend it was just a friendly peck. But no, he doesn't seem to be objecting, not unless shoving his hand up your shirt could be interpreted as rejection.

He pulls you down onto the bed and starts grappling with buttons and fasteners, as you both giggle and fumble. You're relieved now that you didn't get together with Mark. Maybe there is something to be said for starting off as friends first and then getting into a relationship. And let's face it, you and Peter are definitely really, really good friends. . . .

It's just as well, because when Peter turns to you the next morning and ruefully explains that he feels like he's just had sex with his sister, only the fact that you and he are really, really good friends stops you from cracking an alarm clock over his head.

"Wasn't it weird for you, too?" he asks.

"I guess so," you lie.

"Thank god, I was afraid it was just me."

"Actually," you add cattily, "my little brother might have lasted longer."

"Yeah, sorry about that; my concentration got thrown off when you made that noise that sounded like a horse."

You both lie there fuming for a couple of minutes. Finally Peter suggests getting breakfast, but with the pounding in your head and the way your stomach is churning, you know you'll never be able to hold down food. You scramble around, getting dressed, while Peter ignores you. Pulling on your jacket, you give him a peck on the forehead.

"We're still friends, aren't we?"

"Of course," he answers, not very convincingly. "I'm going to be pretty busy with the band over the next while, but I'll call you, okay?"

What an asshole, you think. "Whatever." You smile. "See you around, little bro."

The End

When the phone rings, you pick up. You explain the situation to Mike, who's confused as to a number of the evening's details—like how the hell you ended up at Lisa's apartment in the first place. Then again, you're not too clear on that yourself.

"Let me talk to him," Lisa blurts, and you go out of the room to give her some privacy.

In a few minutes, Lisa calls you from the other room. "He wants to talk to you again," she says, holding out the phone and looking away.

"Hey," you say to Mike.

"Get your ass down here. Everybody wants to leave for the party any minute now."

"Aren't you coming here?"

"No fucking way, man. Let her sleep it off. I don't feel like dealing with her shit tonight."

You notice that Lisa's got her head buried in her pillow, crying.

"Alright," you say. "Don't leave without me."

You get out of Lisa's as quickly as you can and practically run the rest of the way to Spinners because you can't find a taxi. Mike, Will, Tracy, and some people you're sure you've seen at a happy hour once or twice before are waiting for you. You all walk to the party, a few short blocks away.

Sadie's arriving with a female friend just as you are. She's all dolled up, with a short skirt and knee-high boots. If Dave were here, he'd call them fuck-me boots, and you're suddenly grateful he's not. Nobody to babysit. You can concentrate on the task at hand. Namely, taming the raging hard-on in your pants.

If you hang back so that you're climbing the stairs with Sadie, turn to page 335.

If you play it cool (act like you don't see Sadie yet) and keep talking to Mike, turn to page 337.

You start to back out the door, banging into a lampshade as you go, incoherently mumbling that you should get going now.

"You're leaving me in a very compromising position—lonely, clearly aroused, and lying under a comforter that's covered with pictures of little lambs. My mother bought it, honest. She thought it was cute."

"I like it, makes you seem harmless."

"Eh, this might sound tasteless, but are you sure you want to go? It's early, or late, or whatever. Let me at least make you more coffee. Or maybe you'd like to make it and bring me some?" he says brightly.

"And then you can come back in and pleasure me, okay?" he calls after you as you give an exasperated snort and head for the kitchen.

What the hell, may as well make some coffee.

"The sugar's in the microwave," Peter shouts.

Naturally. You potter around looking for clean mugs—no luck—and ponder what to do. You're a little too groggy to be horny, but on the other hand, Peter's bed looks damn comfortable and maybe it's time you just got it over with and threw yourself at him. What's the worst that can happen?

Maybe the clean mugs are under the sink. You open the cupboard and see a sheaf of papers. Idly you pick them up and just then Peter rushes in, the comforter wrapped around his waist. "I meant to tell you, don't look in there."

You're about to say "Why not?" but one look at the top page of the bundle you're holding makes it abundantly clear. It's a stack of pictures downloaded from the Internet, and this one, at least, features a middle-aged woman doing something extraordinary with a ferret.

"Fuck," is all you can think of saying.

"It's not as bad as it looks," Peter says as he tries to grab the pile from you, causing some of the pages to spill to the floor.

"You mean the ferret gave his consent?" you say incredulously. "My god, Peter . . . your mother . . ."

"She doesn't look anything like my mother!" he shrieks.

"No, I mean, what would she think!" you say, picking up pages from the floor. "Jesus, is this a *canary*?"

"Oh hell . . . don't freak out. It's just a load of harmless pictures. Lots of people enjoy this stuff. No one gets hurt. See, even the canary looks happy."

"Peter, I think I'll take a raincheck on the coffee. I'm gonna go."

"This would be the wrong time to hit on you, wouldn't it?"

"I'm just worried you'd want me to make koala noises or something."

"No, of course not . . . Maybe a couple of ferret squeaks would have been good though. Hey, seriously, we're still friends, aren't we, sweetie? You don't think I'm a pervert?"

"Sure, we're still friends."

"Well, okay then, I'll call you tomorrow," he says as you slink toward the door. "Hope you had a good night anyway?"

" 'Good' might be overstating it."

Memorable though. Definitely memorable.

The End

The second you get to Spinners— a huge bar decorated mostly with fluorescent beer signs and a collection of bras donated by drunken female patrons over the years—Mike rushes to your side.

"I just answered a page from Lisa." He looks terribly anxious and practically pushes you back toward the door. "She said you must have dialed the wrong number when you tried to page me because five minutes later the cops were at her door saying that that pager belongs to a drug dealer they've been tracking. Come on, we've got to go straighten things out."

Then you hear it—that laugh—and you turn and search the crowd frantically for the source of that audio honey. Sadie's in the house!

"Is Sadie here?" you ask, stopping your movement as Mike holds the door open.

"Lisa's about to go to jail because of you and you're still thinking about Sadie?"

Well, duh. Of course you are.

Reluctantly, you follow Mike back to Lisa's. There, a swarm of cops in blue uniforms are posted in the hallway, others standing around Lisa in her living room. She looks absolutely petrified.

The cops approach you and Mike.

If you took a joint from Lisa's place earlier, turn to page 293.

If you didn't, turn to page 296.

Bryan has a great apartment. A *great* apartment. Everything's color-coordinated and impeccably tasteful. When you see his collection of CDs and vinyl you gasp audibly.

"Big, isn't it?" he grins.

"Enormous. I've never seen one so huge. Can I . . . can I touch it?"

"Sure. Be gentle though."

You run your fingers over the shelves full of CDs. "What is it you do, exactly?"

"I'm a music journalist, freelance mostly; I do a lot of writing for magazines overseas. Also I'm writing a book about the development of singer-songwriters over the last thirty years . . . from Tim Buckley and Nick Drake to Mark Eitzel and Elliott Smith, y'know?"

"Sounds upbeat."

"Yeah, not exactly a festival of laughs, but interesting. Anyway, want to see the rest of the place?"

The tour starts in the kitchen and ends, inevitably, in the bedroom, which is where Bryan stops pretending to care what you think about his taste in furnishings and suggests you take off your jacket. Maybe the boots, too. And your shirt, while you're at it. Though he is, as you've discovered, an excellent kisser, he obviously hasn't put as much thought into the rest of his technique as he has into, say, choosing the right color cushions for the couch.

"Ouch."

"Sorry, am I hurting you?" he asks.

"Yes, that's what the 'ouch' meant. Your hip bone is boring a hole in my leg."

"You should have said."

"I just did." You smile sweetly. "I've got to go to the bathroom; back in a second." In the bathroom you lean your head against the cool mirror. Is this really what you want to be doing? He seems nice, and you wouldn't mind borrowing some of those CDs sometime, but something's not right. Then you hear Bryan's voice, barely audible, probably from the living room; he must be talking on the phone.

Instinctively you put your ear to the door and listen. Is he talking to a girlfriend? No, doesn't sound like it, too jovial and too much swearing.

You open the door slightly and hear something that sounds like ". . . no, not yet, but any minute now. Yeah well, I told you I would, man, and she's kind of fun anyway, so it's not a bad way to earn fifty bucks. Might see her again. Can you drop the money off tomorrow? I'm strapped till that check clears."

It's as if somebody turned a lightbulb on over your head. Sleeping with you must be part of a bet. That has to be Graham on the phone. You flush the toilet for effect to give him time to hang up. Bryan is still in the other room, ostensibly putting on music.

"Everything okay?" he calls.

"Great." You pull your clothes back on.

"You want something to drink? Wine, maybe?"

"Wine would be great, thanks," you shout.

You hear him padding into the kitchen, so you slink into the living room and grab your bag and jacket. In the living room you stop by the CD racks, pulling out certain ones that caught your eye and shoving them quickly into your bag, then closing the apartment door quietly behind you.

Just as you're reaching the bottom of the stairs, you hear Bryan's voice above you. He's leaning over the stair rail, naked, holding two glasses of wine. "What's going on?" he wails.

"Tell Graham I said hi," you call back.

The End

As the cops approach, you take your hands out of your pockets, so as not to appear as if you're taking this situation lightly. But when you pull your hands out, the joint you rolled earlier in the evening falls onto the floor. One of the cops immediately bends down to pick it up and slide it into a plastic bag marked Evidence. Mike looks at you like you've got to be the dumbest person in the entire world, and Lisa starts bawling.

"You have the right to remain silent." The cop turns you around and cuffs you. "Anything you say can and will be used against you in a court of law . . ."

You spend the night in jail with Lisa because neither one of you wants to call your parents (not that they could even do anything at this hour) and all your lawyer friends—hell, all your friends period—are out getting drunk. You pass the hours tracking the progress of a lazy cockroach across the floor.

The End

I'd prefer to go back to my place."

"Sure, whatever you like. I'm hardly going to argue, am I?" He grins.

You take a taxi back to your place and after the standard guy foreplay of admiring your apartment and complimenting your CD collection, Bryan leads you to the couch and you pick up from the Berlin. He may not be Mark, true, but at this stage of the evening you're willing to make do with what's available, and, to be honest, Bryan is damn good fun. You've finally moved the action to the bedroom and are deeply engrossed in what Bryan's doing with his right hand when there's a noise in the front room and he sits up suddenly.

"Who's that?"

"Just my roommate," you whisper. "It's cool, don't worry."

"I didn't know you had a roommate."

"Well, now you know. Will you get back here now?"

"Hey." He nuzzles your neck for a second and murmurs, "Do you think your roommate would come in here and join us?"

"You want my roommate to get in bed with us?" You're trying so hard not to laugh that you might choke at any moment.

"Sure . . . it's a standard guy fantasy. Every woman knows that. Come on, babe, it'd be fun. Have you guys ever fooled around before?"

"No, we haven't, though I suppose I've always found my roommate quite attractive. I mean, I have considered the fact that something might happen between us one day."

"Really?" If Bryan gets any more excited he's liable to erupt before you've got any use out of him. "Wow, that's really hot. Go on, ask. Please." Sad to see a grown man beg.

"Okay. Be right back."

Pulling on a robe, you slip out of the room and close the door behind you. Your roommate is in the bathroom brushing his teeth. "What the fugh?" he asks, his mouth full of toothpaste.

"Ssssh! Listen, I've got a guy in my room and he thinks my roommate's a girl and he's been begging me to bring you in so you can, y'know, join us."

He creases up with laughter and you shove your hand over his toothpasty mouth in an effort to keep him quiet. "You're kidding, right? Wow, that's funny," he gasps. "Well, I guess I have to do it, don't I? Just give me a second and I'll be right with you."

You go back to your room, where Bryan is sprawled across the bed, trying to look debonair and sexy. "Well?"

"The answer's yes." You climb back into bed, and a few seconds later your roommate opens the door. Standing in the door frame, wearing only his shorts and backlit by the living-room light, he flexes his arms, pouts, and rasps, "Well, are we ready?"

Unable to control yourself any longer, you screech with laughter as Bryan turns bright red and shouts, "Oh haha, very adult of you." He leaps out of bed and starts pulling his clothes back on.

"I'm sorry!" you gasp as he bolts out the door. "It was just too funny!"

Your roommate flops down on the bed, giggling hysterically. "Oh, baby, that was the best. It even makes up for not getting together with Sadie tonight. And I assume that loser wasn't Mark?"

"No . . . things didn't quite work out there either." You reach over to ruffle his hair and he grabs your hand. He's still smiling, but clearly an idea has struck him. One that has, coincidentally, just occurred to you.

"The night doesn't have to be over yet though, does it?" he says, edging closer. "I mean, now that we are, technically, in bed together, for the first time in roommate history, it seems a shame to, y'know . . ."

"Will you shut up and turn off the light?"

"Sorry. I was just . . . well, I guess you know what I was . . ."

"Get over here!"

The End

As the cops approach, Mike produces his beeper as evidence that this was all a mix-up. You explain you must have misdialed the pager number when you were at Lisa's apartment earlier. Still, the cops aren't thrilled they've come all the way here for nothing. They take the three of you down to the station, question you all separately, and give each of you a drug test. Since the alcohol level in your blood is so high, they insist on escorting you all home separately.

At home, you find that your roommate and her friend Suzy have brought home two guys. Suzy and hers are having sex in your bed, and you freak out on them. They scuttle away, muttering apologies, and you fall into bed, wishing you'd done laundry so you had clean sheets to put on. Exhausted, you fall asleep anyway, only to wake up a few hours later in extreme discomfort. What's that awful itch? And why won't it go away?

The End

You nod and follow him up the stairs, feeling a mixture of embarrassment and excitement, and luckily the alcohol has gone a long way to counteract the former. Mark's approach might not have been the most seductive in the world, but what's the point in playing hard to get when this is, after all, what you came for. Finally, after months of wondering what he feels like, tastes like, kisses like, you're going to get the chance to find out.

He pushes open a bedroom door and, finding it empty, ushers you inside. Dragging you over to the double bed, he murmurs, "C'mere," and then pulls you on top of him. Mark turns out to be one of the few men who has mastered the art of unhooking someone's bra in one swift and professional movement; in fact, it has to be said that Mark's whole technique is a little *too* polished. And god, would he ever stop with the running commentary?

"Your skin's so soft. You're really turning me on. Can you feel that? You're pretty hot. You like this, don't you? What about that—do you like that, too? You do, don't you? I can tell."

"Mark." You finally sit up and adjust your shirt. "I like you, really, but could you shut up for a couple of minutes? Someone's going to hear us."

"Okay, sorry," he says, not thrown off his stride in the slightest. Now he's undoing his zipper. "Maybe you could do something to keep me quiet."

Even as you bend your head and start going to work you realize this night is not going to work out as magically as you might have liked. There are two reasons for this. One: there is an unmistakable feeling in your gut, telling you that though you might have been attracted to Mark for months, now that you're actually here with him, the chemistry just isn't right . . . and it would help if he quit acting like he's starring in a low-budget porn flick. Two: there is another unmistakable feeling in your gut, one that has been building since a few minutes after you took that pill . . . whatever the hell it was. You're about to throw up.

You lift your head and hold still for a second, hoping the nausea will subside.

"Hey . . . you forgotten about me?" Mark says, prodding you.

"Can you excuse me for a minute?" You stand, shivering slightly, and you can feel the color draining out of your face.

"Get back here," Mark says, feigning jokiness, but it's clear that the only thing he's interested in is getting off. He tries to pull you down again, and you struggle to get free. All the jostling is only making you feel more queasy, but Mark just won't get the message.

"Look, asshole, let me go," you shout.

"What the hell is all this about?" he snaps. "You say you want to come up here and then you freak out on me? What's your fucking problem?"

For a moment you think you'll be able to hold it in till you get to the bathroom. But this is a force that won't be denied—nanoseconds later your stomach is heaving and you can feel the vomit rising in your throat. The look on Mark's face as you finally give into the inevitable and throw up—all over the bed, the carpet, and him—is something you'll never forget.

"That," you say, as you leave a dazed, horrified Mark and go to clean yourself up, "is the fucking problem."

The End

You enter the Pub and go straight to the bar and order a shot of whiskey. "Your roommate's here," Kate says. "Make sure you take her home, will you?"

Why hadn't you thought of that?! You down your whiskey, then start to work your way through the crowd like a hunter seeking his prey. You find your roommate by the pool table, handing the pool cue off to someone and shaking hands with her opponent. She smiles at him, but you can tell from the expression on her face that she lost. She hates to lose.

"Hey," she says to you. "What are you doing here?" She looks behind you. "Where's your little chickie?"

"Listen," you say, pinning her against the wall opposite the bathrooms. "If I don't have sex with a woman tonight, I'm going to go crazy. I've already seen you naked, so—"

"You *have*?"

"I live with you. I'm a guy. Of course I have. So my point is . . . well the rest is just a technicality, really."

"Okay."

"Okay?" You were coming on superconfident sure, but you hardly thought she'd go for it.

"Okay."

"Really?" You're going to blow it if you're not careful.

"Yes."

"Just sex?"

"Just sex." She rolls her eyes. "I could really use a good lay and you're at least a little more fun than my vibrator, providing you have a tongue and know how to use it. Is that what you wanted to hear?"

"Exactly what I wanted to hear."

The two of you head for the door, and you nod at Kate as if you're being so caring, responsible, and *gentlemanly* as you leave. Your roommate's trailing behind you, her warm palm touching yours.

The End

Not just yet," you murmur. "Okay?"

"I guess," he answers, sitting back on the couch and crossing his arms.

"You're not mad, are you? You want another drink?" Or maybe a treehouse you can sulk in? Men.

"I'm not mad, no. I just thought you'd want to, is all. But fine . . . it can wait. I'll go get us both a drink."

He wanders off toward the kitchen and you sit there patiently. And sit there. He's taking an inordinately long time to find that drink, and, meanwhile, there seems to be something weird going on in the region of your stomach. A queasy feeling has been building for the last thirty minutes. At first you attributed it to Mark's proximity, but now that a little clarity has set in, it seems more likely to be related to whatever was in that pill you took. The only way to check out this theory is to find Hayley and see how she's feeling.

She's not in the kitchen. Nor, for that matter, is Mark. You climb the stairs, pushing past couples in various stages of intimacy. There seems to be some sort of instinctive hierarchy at work—the further up the stairs you get, the more intense the making out. The bathroom door is straight in front of you, pushed open a crack, and you can hear the distinctive sound of retching closely followed by the even more distinctive sound of Hayley swearing. You're about to call her name when there's another voice—and no mistaking that one either. It's Mark.

"You okay now?"

"Yeah, I think so," comes Hayley's muffled response. She must be talking through a towel. "Must have been something I ate. Thanks for helping me find the bathroom."

"No problem."

Pause. Sound of flushing toilet and running faucet.

"So," Mark continues. "Do you want to find somewhere more private?"

This can't be happening. In the course of an evening Mark has been transformed from Object of Your Affections to Something You Stepped In. Even though you can't see her, you can imagine the look on Hayley's face. She is the master of the withering stare. "I don't believe I heard you correctly," she says very softly.

"Come on, it'd be fun."

"But you're with my friend," she says, as calmly as a nun. There is something positively intimidating about Hayley's composure in situations like this, even after losing the contents of her stomach in a stranger's bathroom.

"I'm not really with her. Nothing happened."

Oh Mark, Mark, why have you forsaken me!

"Thank you for the offer, Mark, but I would rather sit on my finger." With that, Hayley opens the door and stops short when she sees you. "Hey . . . ," she begins, but you shrug and motion for her to follow you downstairs. Mark doesn't even see you—he's busy admiring himself in the mirror and getting prepped for victim number three.

"I'm sorry, babe; that guy's an asshole," she says when you get downstairs. "But I guess you figured that out by now. We can go home if you want."

True, you could go home. Still, this is a party, and your stomach is feeling a little better, and why let some lecherous scumbag with the morals of a weasel ruin your whole night?

"I vote we stay, Hayley. You know my motto: If at first you don't succeed . . ."

"Give up, get drunk, and throw yourself at the next available guy?" she suggests.

"That sounds like a plan."

The End

When you and Dave show up at Spinners—a bar that basically looks like a big decorated barn—Sadie, to your extreme pleasure, is the first person to greet you.

"You two look like you've been up to no good," she says.

"What on earth do you mean?" you reply, as innocently as you can.

"Yeah." Dave shrugs. "What do you mean?"

She looks back and forth between the two of you, then puts a hand on her hip. "Whadaya think I yam, dumb a somethin?" You know it's a line from a classic movie, perfectly delivered, and the look on Dave's face says he could be in love. This could be trouble. Time to make a move. . . .

"Can I get you a drink?"

The problem is that these words, directed at Sadie, came out of Dave's mouth. He beat you to the punch. Maybe you should have made your intentions toward Sadie more clear to Dave; you imagined there might be some cock blocking going on tonight—Sadie's a desirable girl—but you hardly imagined it coming from Dave.

"Dave, do you know *Sadie? Sadie*, Dave?" Surely he's heard you sing her praises a million times. Surely he knows she's the very reason you've come here. You *told* him that. Something will click in his brain.

They say hi to each other and it's obvious Dave hasn't caught on. They go to the bar together—Sadie turns and says, "Mike's over there," and points—so you make your way over to Mike, making a quick stop at the bar along the way.

"There you are." Mike pulls you into a circle formed by him, Lisa, Will, and Tracy. "Maybe you can help us out, ace. You know how 'Mony Mony' had that thing where everyone always shouted out, 'Get laid, get fucked,' in the middle of the song? We're trying to think of a nineties equivalent of that."

You confess that nothing strikes you right away, then set your mind to thinking. In the meantime Tracy speaks: "You're not going to think of one, Mike. None of us are. We're too old. All those things had to do with adolescent sex. Like people used to add 'sex' to that Depeche Mode song any time they said 'I just can't get enough.' "

"Sex," you say.

"Thanks for the demonstration," Tracy says wryly. "My point is all of those things were started by sex-deprived teenagers. Even if there's a new one that kids everywhere are dancing like crazy to at their proms, you're not going to know what it is."

"Well, then," Mike says. "What are we sex-starved twentysomethings supposed to do? If we're not letting our frustrations out on the dance floor, what are we doing with them?"

"I don't know." Tracy takes a swig of her beer. "You can always make up some ridiculous story about a threesome you were involved in and how amazed the women were by your good eight and a half inches and post it on the Web."

Mike turns beet red and you wonder whether he's already done that.

"Or," Lisa cuts in, "you can just whip out 'Mony Mony' once in a while and play it really loud and scream the 'get laid, get fucked' part yourself. Whenever I'm really horny and I know I'm not getting any I'll put on that old Liz Phair album and sing that bit 'I'll fuck you till your dick is blue' really loudly."

If you suddenly feel like Lisa's the most appealing person in the room, turn to page 309.

If your sudden erection prompts you to go find Sadie and Dave, turn to page 313.

You go to the address Lisa has and find it suspiciously quiet. Still, you ring the bell, are buzzed in, and proceed upstairs. There, you find that the word *party* has been used loosely; no doubt the host, Kelly, also calls those five discs near the stereo her "CD collection." The gathering consists entirely of Mike, Tracy, Will, Sadie, her friend Alyssa, and Kelly. They're all sitting around looking more bored than a bunch of lesbians at Chippendales. You, Dave, and Lisa get drinks and join the quiet circle.

Before long, Mike proposes a game—X-rated charades—and everyone acts like it's the best idea they've ever heard. Kelly seems reluctant—woohoo! the girl knows how to throw a party!—but eventually succumbs and digs out some paper and pencils. You all write five words on little pieces of paper and throw them into a pot. By a miracle of the musical-chairs game that goes on while people replenish their drinks and empty their bladders, you end up beside Sadie on the couch. Can you help it if your arm occasionally brushes against hers?

Volunteering to go first, Mike gets up and picks a word out of the pot. "Okay, you ready?"

He gets down on all fours and you quickly shout out, "Doggie style." He shakes his head.

"Humping," you say. He shakes his head again and proceeds to slink around the room and then act like he's grooming his claws.

"You're a cat?" Sadie says, and Mike nods and points at her. "What has a cat got to do with . . . Ewww. Who wrote that word down?"

You're hardly going to admit to it now.

"Alright," Kelly says, snatching up the piece of paper on the floor beside Mike. "Next word."

"Why do women hate that word so much?" Mike's laughing.

No one answers, so he shrugs. "Guess you're up, Sadie?"

"Alright." She reaches for the pot. "But if it's gross I'm not doing it." She looks at the paper, deliberates, and decides to go ahead.

She holds up six fingers and someone says, "Six." Then she holds up nine. You shout out, "Sixty-nine."

"That's no fun," Dave says. "You're supposed to get down on the floor and try to act it out."

"In your dreams," she replies, taking her seat next to you. Is it your imagination she's sitting closer than before?

Unfortunately, you have to get up to take your turn. You pick out a piece of paper and find that other word women hate so much—the *c* word—written on it. You recognize your own handwriting. Maybe you should act out something else? Perhaps *cock ring*?

If you go with the word you have, turn to page 306.
If you go for *cock ring* turn to page 307.

You make the sign for "sounds like" by cupping your ear. Then you proceed to mime the act of bunting. Dave catches on immediately and shouts out, "Bunt," followed by—

"You know what?" Kelly gets up and picks up the pot. "This isn't really what I envisioned when I planned this party."

"What? You envisioned people not having fun?" You can't believe you just said that, but this girl's just way too uptight.

"I think maybe you should go," Kelly says. "All of you. Well, except you, Sadie, since you're crashing here."

You look at Sadie and she shrugs.

The End

You hold up two fingers, and Tracy says, "Two words." You nod.

You hold up one finger and she answers, "Yeah, yeah, first word, get on with it."

You point at your crotch as people start throwing out words.

"Penis."

"Dick."

"Balls."

"Testicles."

You shake your head and cup your ear.

"Sounds like," Sadie says.

You put your thumbs up by your armpits and strut around the room, flapping your arms.

"Cock!" Mike shouts.

You nod and move on to the second word by pointing at your finger. The responses—"Cock finger?" "Cock blocking?" and "Cock hand?"—are less than inspired. Then an idea hits you. You turn to the couch where Sadie's sitting and get down on one knee. Then you act like you're pulling something out of your pocket and hold it forward in the palm of your hand. You pretend to be opening a small box. She's laughing the whole time, and it's all you can do to keep from putting your mouth to hers to capture some of that sweetness.

"Cock ring?" she says, once she's stopped laughing. And you shout out, "Yes!"

"Only you, ace, could make a cock ring romantic," Mike says.

"I haven't laughed that hard in a while," Sadie says, once you're sitting beside her again.

You haven't *been* this hard in a while.

"I like to make you laugh," you say.

"I'm ticklish, you know." Sadie smiles at you.

"See now, I would have liked to find that out firsthand."

"You still can," she says, with a glimmer in her eye. "I suddenly don't feel well. Could you see me home?"

The End

There's a message from Mike telling you that they're going on to the party, but you can't hear it because Dave's blabbing on about Elizabeth Albern. You tell him to shush and play the message again, memorizing the address.

"C'mon." You hang up. "Let's go."

You pick up some beers on the way to the party and, because you suddenly have the urge, you throw in a pack of smokes.

At the party, you see Sadie across the room, but decide to play it cool. You and Dave crack open some beers, and you light up. Mike comes over and joins you.

"Boys," he says. "Glad you made it. Can I get one of those?"

The cigarette bumming has begun.

Dave, too, decides to light up, and the three of you start talking (at Mike's suggestion) about what character from another sitcom, if added to the cast of *Friends,* would have the greatest impact on the group's dynamics. Dave's making an argument for the fat woman from *The Drew Carey Show,* but Mike's insisting that both Niles and Frasier Crane are better bets.

Sadie comes over just as you're about to offer a suggestion—maybe someone from *Third Rock from the Sun.*

"I didn't know you smoked." She looks at you as if she's terribly disappointed, and you want nothing more than to make your cigarette vanish. You're not even enjoying it all that much. In your discomfort, you find yourself saying, "Well, you do now," and laughing awkwardly. Sadie walks away.

"What was that all about?" Dave asks.

"Sadie's training for a marathon," Mike explains. "And her father just got diagnosed with lung cancer. I've never met a woman who hates smoking more."

Nice one, ashtray breath!

The End

You act like you've got to get out of the flow of the crowd, and step over to Lisa's side. But just as you're about to engage her in conversation, Mike finishes his drink. "Come on. Drink up." He gesticulates for you, in particular, to hurry. "We should hit this party. I'll go find Sadie and meet you outside in a few minutes."

The mere mention of Sadie makes you agitated, and you quickly down your drink.

"Wow." Lisa turns to you. "That was fast. You want to help me with mine? I've had too much already." She sways slightly, her breast brushing against your arm.

"Whoa." You take her drink from her, before she can spill it. "You okay?"

"Yeah, I'll be fine. Can I walk with you?"

"Sure." That'll show Sadie!

You finish Lisa's drink for her, then follow Will and Tracy out to meet Mike on the street. Sadie and Dave are there, talking excitedly about some Australian film about a picnic. You pretend not to care and let Lisa loop her arm through yours.

At the party, in a really cool duplex apartment that makes you insanely jealous, you have another quick drink to tame your anger. When Lisa asks you to dance, you accept; what better way to prove how much fun you're having to Dave and Sadie? Things are going fine until Chumbawamba comes on and Lisa gets a little too into it. She's jumping up and down shouting, "I get knocked down, but I get up again, and you're never going to keep me down," and proceeds to topple backward and land flat on her butt. Her *bare* butt. That's right, during the fall her skirt gets thrown up and she's not wearing any underwear. When she lands, she's flashing her whole kit and caboodle—carefully trimmed, it should be noted—to everyone who happens to be looking, and because she's so drunk, the reflex response to cover herself is delayed. You're too stunned to approach and help her up, and besides you don't want to call any unnecessary attention to yourself lest someone notices the bulge in your pants.

"You see that?" Mike steps up to you shaking his head in disbelief just as Lisa is ushered away by some girlfriends. "Man, I bet there's not a limp dick in the room."

You turn to say something witty—a wry smile on your face in anticipation of your clever retort—when you see Sadie glaring at you. Apparently she overheard Mike.

If you go ahead with your clever retort because you're mad at Sadie for liking Dave, turn to page 314.

If you decide to hold your tongue, turn to page 316.

Okay, I'm going in. How do I look; is my makeup okay?" Running a hand through your hair, you turn to her for a quick assessment.

"Gorgeous. I'm barely controlling my urge to jump you right here. Go *on.*" She pushes you toward him. "Move! There's an eager redhead at four o'clock."

You walk toward him, every step feeling as if it's in slow motion. Sure enough, there's a redhead nearby who's eyeing Mark with interest. Not fast enough, honey.

"Hey, Mark." You flash your most winning smile.

"Oh, hey!" He grins in recognition. "Good to see you. I don't recognize many people here. How do you know Lindy?"

"Oh, you know, friend of a friend," you mutter, inhaling the scent of him. There is nothing about this man that isn't infinitely adorable.

"Cool. Got a cold? You seem to be sniffing."

"Me? No . . . perfect health." You can see the redhead skirting around, doing the hair toss, looking for a chance to move in. No time for subtlety! Think Hayley! "So, Mark, I was wondering if maybe you'd like to . . ."

"Shh, sorry to interrupt, but is someone calling your name?" Mark asks.

He's right. Hayley is. From upstairs. She sounds desperate.

"You want to go see what she wants? I'll wait here."

You nod and run upstairs, shooting the redhead a withering look as you leave. Hayley is peering out the bathroom door. "Get in here!" she squeals.

"What's wrong? What the . . . did somebody die in here?" The smell is foul.

"Me! I'm dying! I don't know what the hell those pills were, but everything I've eaten over the last two weeks is pouring out of my ass. You have to help!" She looks pale and worried.

"Hayley, what do you want me to do? Buy an economy-sized air freshener?"

"No, smart-ass, call a taxi! Take me home! I don't think I can make it alone; I'm scared I'm going to collapse."

If there's one thing you haven't missed about Hayley, it's her talent for hypochondria.

"You're not dying. Look, I can call a taxi, but can't you get home by yourself?"

"No!" She's screaming. "Please! You wouldn't even be here if it wasn't for me."

"Stop yelling! I'll take you home! But you owe me big time!"

"Fine." She sulks. "Just get me out of here."

You stomp downstairs with her. "Wait here. I'm saying good-bye to Mark."

There he is, standing just where you left him, every ounce as beautiful. And there, inevitably, is the redhead, closing in like a vulture. You stride right up to them. "Mark, my friend's sick and I've got to take her home. But it was great seeing you."

"You, too," he says, with apparent sincerity. "Listen, can I have your number?"

"Sure." You smile and dig around in your bag for a pen and scrap of paper. "Here. Talk to you soon?"

"Great. Take care."

"Don't worry, he'll call," says Hayley as you leave the room.

"You think?"

"Well sure," she declares. "Why wouldn't he?" You turn around for one last look. Mark's little carroty-haired friend catches your eye and gives you a smug smile.

The End

You excuse yourself and find Dave at the bar. He's sitting on a bar stool with an empty one next to him.

"Where's Sadie?" You take the seat beside him.

"Bathroom. She's coming back, though." He looks at you like you shouldn't be sitting.

"Jeez, man. I'll get up when she comes back."

"What's gotten into you?"

"What's gotten *in*to me? You know I've been after Sadie for, like, ever."

"*What?*"

"You had to know."

"I'm not a fucking mind reader, man. I didn't know. You're always talking about loads of different girls. I'd need a diagram to keep track. I always thought that if I wanted to, I could put together a videotape for your bachelor party like they did for Tom Cruise in *Jerry Magui—*"

"Will you cut the movie crap for once! She's the girl. So back off."

"No way, man. She's awesome. And she's into me. She already invited me to go to a movie screening with her next week. Sorry."

You catch the bartender's eye and order a shot.

"What are you doing a shot for?" Dave is constantly looking over your shoulder to see when Sadie's coming back.

Instead of responding, you simply hand the bartender your money, down the whiskey, and walk away, you drama queen, you.

You leave without saying good-bye to anyone else and head for home. When you get there, you find your apartment's been broken into. Everything you owned of any value is gone.

The End

You got that right. But ten bucks says it's this very unlimp dick right here"—you indicate your groin—"that's in *her* by the end of the night."

Mike starts laughing, but Sadie approaches swiftly and slaps you. She glares at Mike, too.

"You know, sometimes I really envy lesbians." She's so mad her voice is shaking. "If you have to give up actual dicks in order to avoid dicks like you, it's something I might want to try."

"Can I watch?" Now Mike gets the slap.

You'd probably feel the need to apologize if you weren't so turned on. You can see Sadie's nipples through her top and can't get the image of a spread-eagled Lisa out of your mind. When Sadie turns tail and goes upstairs, you set out to find Lisa.

She's in a downstairs bedroom at the end of the hall, being consoled by a bunch of girls. When she sees you she tells them it's okay if they go. You sit down beside her.

"I am *so* totally mortified." She's holding her head in her hands.

"It's really no big deal." You'll never get that image of her out of your mind, as long as you live. "Everybody falls down once in a while."

"You *know* what I'm talking about." She looks up at you defiantly.

"Sooo?" You can tell she's not convinced by your carefully articulated argument. You guess you should say something else. "So what if a couple of people know how incredibly beautiful and sexy you are."

"A couple?" She laughs, wiping the last of her tears away.

"Okay, so what if an entire roomful of people, some of whom are no doubt writers who will use this as material at some point in the future, saw, um, a side of you they've never seen before." You're happy when you see she's laughing.

"Do you think you could sneak me out of here?" she says. "I can't face anybody."

You offer to shepherd her away as quickly as possible—and proceed to do so, taking her hand and leading her to the door while she hangs her head low. Once outside, she invites you back to her place and you go. There, because you've both had way too much to drink, you proceed to get naked and have unprotected sex. You fall asleep right after, then wake up when you feel a woman's body stir next to you. For a second, you think it's Sadie, then your splitting headache reminds you it's not. Not by a long shot.

An arm stretches around you and rests on your stomach. Instinctively, you tighten your gut.

"That was amazing." Lisa sighs contentedly. "Wouldn't it be great if we've already made a baby?"

The End

You maintain eye contact with Sadie and raise your voice slightly. "Give the girl a break, will you, Mike?"

He shrugs and walks off, and Sadie approaches. "I feel so bad for her."

"I know." You're willing your erection to go away, but with Sadie this close to you, her nipples just slightly jutting out under her shirt, it's a losing battle. "I do, too."

She takes a sip of her beer. "Your friend Dave's nice."

You're reminded again that you're mad at her. "Well, it doesn't take a brain surgeon to figure out *you* think so."

"What's that supposed to mean?"

You take a swig of your beer. "Nothing. I don't mean anything. You two look great together."

"What are you talking about? Just because I said he's a nice guy doesn't mean there's anything going on."

"It doesn't?" There's not?

"No."

"But you asked him to a movie screening."

"Yeah, well, he's the only person I know who doesn't balk at the idea of subtitles."

"Oh." This could be good.

"Why?" A smile creeps across her face. "Were you getting jealous?"

You take another sip of beer for cover. "Maybe a little."

"There's really no need." She looks around the room for Dave, who's talking to Will and Mike. "I guess I should make sure he knows that, huh?"

"Probably a good idea."

"You'll be here awhile?"

"You bet."

Before long you see Sadie and Dave start talking to each other in a far corner of the room. You're halfheartedly listening to a conversation Mike, Tracy, and Will and a few other people are having about the stupidest things they've ever done. You're thinking of contributing a stupid thing you did last week until Tracy tells her story; last Christmas, she spent all day before a party she was having making this mulled wine, which basically involved letting all this fruit and stuff sit in it all day. When she went to strain the fruit out so the wine would be ready to serve, she poured the mixture through a strainer and proceeded to pour the wine right down the sink, leaving herself with a mushy pile of fruit. Everybody seems to agree it's a tough story to beat.

You look at your watch and see that at least an hour has passed since Sadie and Dave started talking. You look over just in time to see Dave—could he be crying?—go for the door. Sadie looks after him, stunned.

If you go after Dave, turn to page 318.

If you go to Sadie, turn to page 321.

You exchange a brief, mutually concerned look with Sadie before going out into the hall after Dave. You call his name and he stops and turns on the stairs. "Dave, where you going?"

"Home."

"Why?"

"It's like in *Dumb and Dumber*, man. When the two guys are after the same girl. Or maybe more like *Kissing a Fool*. Oh, I don't know. She likes you is the bottom line. Once again, I'm the idiot."

"You're *not* an idiot."

"Yeah, whatever. I'm going to go, though." He looks down at his shoes.

"You gonna be okay?"

"Me? Ha!" He waves a hand. "You kidding? I'll be fine. I'll pick up some Chinese, stop in the video store on the way, or maybe just pop in *The Sound of Music*, and life will be wonderful again. Now get back in there."

If you decide to leave with Dave since he's so down, turn to page 322.

If you go back in to the party, turn to page 324.

I can't, not yet. I need another drink first. And to fix my makeup."

"And to grow a spine, apparently." Hayley shrugs. "Hey, I think those pills are beginning to kick in. I'm starting to feel sort of weird. . . . I'm gonna go find the bathroom. Look after Tom while I'm gone and make sure he doesn't get away."

She passes Tom as she makes her way out, mouthing, "Be right back," and giving her most winning smile. You take your glass of punch from him, keeping a close eye on Mark all the while. So far he hasn't seen you—he's talking to two guys over by the stereo.

"Yeah, you missed the excitement earlier," says Tom. "Someone crashed the party and then rifled through a couple of jackets, trying to find stuff to steal. By the time we realized, it was too late to catch him. Bastard didn't get much, just a purse and my wallet. Not that I had anything in there; I keep most of my money and credit cards on me. But there were little things; photos and souvenirs and stuff. Lindy should be careful—anyone could walk in here tonight. She's too bombed to notice."

You listen to this speech with amazement. Could it be his wallet that you picked up? Except that this guy's name isn't Lance. "What kind of souvenirs did you lose?"

"Just sentimental junk, I suppose. . . . A shamrock that my mother sent me from her trip to the Blarney stone. And, oh shit, Lance's pills, too! I forgot I had those."

"Lance?"

"Yeah, my dog, Lance. Big German shepherd. Great dog."

"What does he need pills for?" you venture, trying to sound as flippant as someone with a desperate need to know can sound.

"The vet said he was constipated. Been like that for a few weeks now, so he gave me these big ol' laxatives to put in his food. I'll have to go back tomorrow and get more. Just hope Lance doesn't make a mess around the house . . . hey, you going somewhere?"

"Just to check on Hayley. Back in a second."

Those words about making a mess around the house are still resonating in your ears as you gallop up the stairs to find the bathroom.

There's no line, thank god. You knock at the door. "Hayley? It's me. You okay?"

There's a rustling sound and eventually the door opens a crack. Hayley peeks out. At the same moment, a noxious odor hits you full in the face. "I think I'm dying. I haven't felt this bad since the night Cole took me to the Garden of India and persuaded me to try his lamb vindaloo. Oh no, here we go again . . . get in here quick."

You kneel down beside the bath, holding a towel in front of your mouth and nose, while she straddles the toilet. "Hayley, those pills you took. They're laxatives."

"No fucking kidding," she deadpans. "Excellent diagnosis, Dr. Carter."

"Hey, don't take it out on me! They're for Tom's German shepherd, Lance."

Hayley starts laughing in spite of herself, inducing another gush of whatever it is to pour out of her. "Oh my god . . . *shit!* I think that might have stemmed the flow for a few minutes. I'm gonna go call Cole and get him to pick me up; he should be finished work by now. Will you be okay? You wanna ride home?"

"I'll be fine. Go on."

She fixes her clothes and rushes out of the bathroom, clutching her stomach. You stay behind and open a window, but there's no escaping the smell . . . it's unbelievably putrid. You open the door and run right into Mark, who's been waiting his turn. "Thanks." He smiles and walks in, and the next thing you hear is a loud "Holy *fuck!*" and the sound of gagging. He staggers back out, gasping for air. "No offense, but I think you should see a doctor . . . *soon*," he mutters, running downstairs.

"It wasn't me!" is your weak response. What's the use?

Hayley is just walking out the door as you get downstairs. "Cole'll be here in a minute. You changed your mind about that ride?" she asks.

You nod glumly. "Someone kind of changed it for me."

The End

"Is he okay?" you ask.

"Yeah." Sadie wipes her brow. "I think so. Ego's a little bruised is all."

"What about you, you okay?"

"Yeah." She doesn't sound convinced. "But you know what: that whole thing really drained me. I think I'm going to go."

"But I thought. . . ."

"I'm just beat. I'd love to do something sometime, though. Give me a call, okay?" She reaches into her bag and takes out a piece of paper and a pen, then writes down a number.

"I *will* call." You look at her very seriously as you take the number.

"Okay, I'll talk to you soon then." She kisses you on the cheek and leaves.

You stride over to Mike and Will and brag that you got Sadie's digits. You hold up the piece of paper to show them.

"Hang on a minute." Will takes the paper from your hand. "This is the number Tracy gave me when I first met her; I'll never forget it. It's one of those joke lines that some radio station set up. The idea is to lure men into leaving dumb messages for women who have no interest in them. I called and left a message for Tracy, and when she heard it being played on the radio the following week she felt so bad about how badly the DJs were making fun of me that she decided to track me down. You've just had a fast one pulled on you, buddy."

Mortified, you make your excuses, then leave. You spend the entire cab ride home composing the message you'll leave on the fake line. By the time you fall asleep that night you know it'll have something to do with Sadie's overwhelming desire to have you defecate on her—oh yeah, and it'll definitely include her last name. You'll have to find that out in the morning. . . .

The End

"Screw this," you say. "I'm coming with you."

After securing way more food than you need and more movies than you can watch in a night, you and Dave head back to his place and settle in, Sadie the farthest thing from your mind. Well, maybe the quadratic formula or the gross national product of any number of South American countries is farther from your mind. But, to your surprise, after a couple of dumplings, an egg roll, some moo goo gai pan, and the first movie Dave put on, you're hankering for true love again. Or at the very least, a Dewars on the rocks. Dave made you watch *Swingers* for the umpteenth time.

Not prepared to sit through *Clerks* again, you decide to take off.

When you get out of a cab in front of your apartment you find your roommate sitting on the front stoop in tears.

"What's wrong?" You rush to her and scoop her up in your arms.

"Nothing." She's sniffling and trying to hide her tears. "Everything. I'm locked out."

"Come on." You take her by the hand and open the front door, then the door leading to your apartment. The two of you fall onto the couch and you put your arm around her. "Now tell me everything that happened."

She looks up at you, her chin trembling. "I don't want to. Will you just sit here for a while and hold me?"

"Of course I will. As long as you like." And we all know what that means! You're going to get lucky after all!

Sure enough, before long she starts caressing your hand. You can smell the alcohol on her and know she's had too much to drink. Maybe you shouldn't take advantage of the circumstances this way.

Just then she leans her head on your shoulder and you can feel her breath on your neck. You're not sure whether she's doing this intentionally, but when her fingers link with yours, you think maybe she is. From where you're sitting—and because of the strange position she's in—you can see right down her top, her breasts pushed together by a black lace bra. Something in your pants stirs, and she notices. She must. Because she gets up, still holding your hand, and says, "My room or yours?"

You shake your head, and she looks as if she's going to start crying all over again.

Then you get up and pull her toward you. "Right here on the living-room floor."

She laughs as the two of you topple to the ground.

The End

You go back inside, grab another beer, and find Sadie, who's looking troubled.

"He okay?"

"Yeah." You wince as you nearly rip your hand open on a beer bottle that's not a twist-off.

"Here," Sadie offers her key chain. How cool is *that*?!

"Thanks." You open the beer and hand it back. "He's gonna be fine. How about you, you heartbreaker?"

"Oh, stop it." She hits you gently on the chest. "I'm not a heart-breaker."

"Oh come on. A girl like you . . ." You take a swig of your beer and let her complete the sentence herself . . .

You spend the next half an hour flirting, and then the party starts to break up. Out on the sidewalk, you ask Sadie for her number. "I'm so embarrassed," she says, with a smile. "We just got a new number and I don't know it. But I'm just around the corner if you want to walk me home. I can give it to you then."

"Ooooh," you say, not buying it for a second. "That's goooood."

"You think?" Sadie starts walking, and you follow. "I've been working on that one for the last half hour."

You walk in comfortable silence to her apartment. She shushes you when you get inside—she must have a roommate—and leads the way to her bedroom in the dark. You start kissing awkwardly, hitting teeth and getting your tongue bitten. Then Sadie undoes your belt and your pants and goes to touch you, poking your most sensitive part with her nails.

"Ow," you practically scream, grabbing her hand. "Careful," you whisper.

"Sorry," she says, but then she does it again, her fingernails digging into your balls.

The next five minutes prove that Sadie is by far the worst lover you've ever encountered. Unable to proceed any further for fear of accidental castration, you tell her you should go, that you really like her and want to take things slow. You get ready to leave and purposely don't ask for her phone number. The next time you see her she throws a drink in your face and laughs the wickedest laugh you've ever heard.

The End

Let's do it," you say.

"Not here, though." Elizabeth starts to ferret around for her jacket. "There's a hotel a few blocks away."

You walk to the hotel in silence; this all seems so surreal. You think about starting a conversation to fill the silence, but what do you say to two people you know you're about to get naked with? "Seen any good movies lately?" just won't cut it.

At the hotel—a bare-bones establishment, no surprise—the desk clerk gives you all a funny look. You feel terribly self-conscious, but the momentum of the event has swept you up. There's no way you're not going through with this now that you've come this far.

Inside the room, Mike and Elizabeth start kissing, and she strips his shirt off. You're looking for an in, but you're not quite sure how these things work. Then, when Elizabeth drops to her knees, undoes Mike's pants, and goes to work, you step up to the plate. You grab Mike and plant a deep, wet kiss on his mouth as he starts to take your shirt off. When he manages to undo your pants, Elizabeth starts to pump you both. Unsatisfied with manual stimulation, Mike pulls her up.

"Where do you want us?" he asks.

"Where *don't* I want you?" she counters with a sultry smile. "But for starters, I want both of you in me at the same time. Then I want to watch you two."

As if by magic, Mike produces two condoms, hands one to you, and throws the rest of a pack on the bed. The two of you get to work on Elizabeth, taking turns in front and back. After the next few hours, you're sure that when Mike and Elizabeth were kids and played with that toy where you're supposed to fit different-sized blocks into differently shaped holes they were the types of kids who just jammed things in wherever they saw fit.

When you wake up with a pounding headache at 6 A.M. and see Mike and Elizabeth in the king-sized bed with you, you decide to leave and avoid an awkward morning scene times two.

Out on the street, squinting in the daylight and searching for a cab, you're a sight to behold. Your hair's a mess, your clothes bear a strong resemblance to an elephant's hide, and your face is chaffed from Mike's

out to pull her toward you. “And thank god for that.”

The End

You take Elizabeth's hand and head for the door. She's just too gorgeous to refuse; you're going to see that luscious black hair cascading over her bare breasts tonight if it's the last thing you do. And you've got a feeling it won't be the *last* thing you do, wink wink.

As you leave, you walk right past Sadie, who's talking to a few girls, all of whom give you dirty looks. Yes, this is a terrible risk, but you're taking it!

Back at your place you and Elizabeth waste no time getting down to it. It is by far the best sex you've ever had in your life. She's insatiable, in the best of all possible ways; she's more interested in your satisfaction than in hers, perhaps because hers comes so easily, at least when with a master such as yourself. She basically tells you as much.

In the middle of round four or five—you stud, you—Elizabeth is screaming in ecstasy. Your roommate pounds on the door and yells, "People are trying to get some sleep around here."

You and Elizabeth finish off more loudly and elaborately than before, getting off on the fact that someone's listening. Then you collapse into a sweaty heap of giggles and fall asleep. Could it be you've met your match?

The End

You tell Elizabeth and Mike that you want no part of such depravity, then head out to join the party and look for Sadie. You start talking to her, and when she asks about your friend Elizabeth, you're drunk enough that you tell her about the offer Elizabeth and Mike made earlier. You go on at some length about how completely offensive the idea is to you and how sex is supposed to be a cherished act between two people who really care for each other. You figure a girl like Sadie's going to lap that stuff up.

Well, think again.

"God, you're uptight," she says, before disappearing down the hall—no, could it really be? In search of Elizabeth and Mike?

The End

Elizabeth's entire body tenses. "Oh, and you think I'm that kind of *girl*?"

You immediately feel the need to back off lest your chances be ruined. "Actually, I was hoping you were."

"Well, good. Because I am."

"You want to be that kind of girl at my place?"

"Let's go to mine. I only live a few blocks away." She brushes her lips against your neck. "I think you'll like it there, bad boy."

You don't know what that's all about, but you're going anyway.

Not half an hour later, you find yourself in handcuffs with a hood over your head. You're being tickled with a feather, and while at first you were nervous, you're starting to get into it. Then you suddenly realize that there's got to be more than one person doing what's being done to you. There are now too many hands and tools involved.

"Elizabeth?"

"Yes?"

"Is there someone else here?"

"Oh, no, Eliza"—you don't recognize that voice—"he's onto us."

"You know what that means . . . ," Elizabeth says.

"I certainly do," the other woman says.

"What? What does it mean?" You nervously try to move so you can take off your hood or at least protect your privates. Somehow. You don't quite know how. No approach seems to work.

"It means you need to be punished for being such a nosy boy and having to know who else is here."

"How? How are you going to punish me?"

"What do you think, Eliza?" You struggle as two unbelievably strong women manage to tie cuff your ankles, your legs spread. "The whip?"

"To start with, sure. But hold on a minute while I reload the camcorder. And take that hood off him, will you?"

The End

"Hey," you say. Great opener.

"Hey," Sadie says back. See how well-suited you are for one another! "I didn't know you were going to be here," she says, and you think you sense she's pleasantly surprised.

"Yeah, well," you begin, playing it supercool, "I ran into Mike and those guys and they asked if I wanted to tag along." Ha! If she only knew the lengths you'd gone to, she'd, well, if she had any sense at all, she'd run away and hide.

You step into the apartment where the party is and it's unbearably loud. You want to continue talking—you feel like you're on a roll—so you devise a plan. Only Sadie beats you to it. . . .

"You want to check out the roof?" she says. "There's supposed to be an amazing view, and it's kind of loud in here."

"Sure," you say. "Let me grab a beer. You want one?"

"Sure," she says.

You return with two Rolling Rocks and follow Sadie to the door.

"I'm not really in a party mood tonight," she confesses.

"Why? What's wrong?" You're such the sensitive man of the nineties!

"It's stupid," she says as she opens the door to the roof, where a few other partygoers are spread out in small clusters. "I'd be embarrassed to tell you."

"Don't be silly."

"You promise you won't laugh?"

"Promise."

"Well, I went out on a date last night with this guy I met on-line. We'd been talking to each other for months and I really liked him. But it was a total disaster last night. It makes me want to just become a hermit or something."

"But if you did that," you say, having just noticed the spectacular view, "you wouldn't be able to appreciate places like this." You nod in the direction of the sparkling lights of the city, and Sadie seems to be as taken with the scene as you are.

"You're right," she says. "It's really incredible, isn't it?"

You can't believe how smooth you've been so far and decide to push it further. "I wouldn't let it get you down," you say, after taking a sip of your beer. "A girl like you? Forget about it. There's tons of guys who'd want to go out with you."

She pulls her beer from her mouth and wipes a lingering drop away with the back of her hand. "It's really sweet of you to say so."

The two of you settle into a comfortable silence. "God," she finally says, "I'd really love a joint right now."

If you didn't roll a joint at Lisa's, turn to page 344.
If you did, turn to page 343.

You enter a crowded apartment and make your way to the kitchen, where you help yourself to a beer. As you linger by the fridge, expecting Sadie to follow since she was just behind you coming in, you hear "Dancing Queen" go on in the other room. After a minute you decide Sadie must have bypassed the kitchen.

You go back into the living room and see that she is dancing with a bunch of people you don't know. Worse yet, there are two girls—a long-haired brunette and a short-haired blonde—doing what they think are really impressive, choreographed ABBA moves. They're singing along and pointing at each other whenever they get to the word *you*—as in "*You* can dance, *you* can jive, having the time of your life" (though to their credit they alternate hands on each *you*). They're very obviously drunk.

To your surprise, their routine becomes more complicated when track 2—"Knowing Me, Knowing You"—comes on, what with different pointing movements for both *me* and *you*. Pretty tricky stuff, indeed. It dawns on you that these girls have probably done this before. Many other times. Perhaps whenever drunk and in the presence of ABBA and one another. And that there are more girls like this all over the city—probably doing very similar things at this very moment. Scarily enough, no one's going for the stereo; on the contrary, everyone seems to be taking a lesson from this drunken dynamic duo and choreographing little routines of their own.

Before you know it, half the room is singing, "If you change your mind, I'm the first in line, honey I'm still free, take a chance on me," while the other half is rapidly repeating, "Take-a-chance, take-a-chance, take-a-take-a-chance-chance." People are dancing side by side while facing an imaginary audience all through "Super Trouper," many of them marching in place. Drunken people start slow dancing—just holding on to each other and swaying, really—when "The Winner Takes It All" comes on, and so it goes. . . . At the peak of this ridiculous ABBA fest, "Waterloo" is on full volume, the crowd providing definitive proof that the art of social dancing is lost for good. There's a misguided group in the corner trying to do the Macarena and realizing that "Waterloo" is either way too fast or way too slow—and either way the dance still doesn't work. And for lack of grace and women, a bunch of guys have started moshing and jumping into the air and banging chests. The CD ends, and in the silence that follows, you hear Sadie's laugh.

That laugh! Now *that's* what you call music!

You've been distracted. You must and shall make contact.

As you start across the room, there's a loud rapping on the door, and since you're passing by, you answer it.

"We'd like to speak to whoever lives here."

The fuzz. Busted.

The host appears at your side and exchanges words with the cops, who then come into the room and clear out the party. In the confusion, you completely lose sight of Sadie. The woman of your dreams is gone before you get a word in edgewise.

The End

"Alright, Demi, time to go home!" you yell, and reach her just as she's about to take off what little clothing is left. There are boos and hisses from some of the guys, but you drag her off the table, picking up the various garments strewn around the room.

A few minutes later you're in Lindy's bedroom, fuming as you watch Suzy struggle to get dressed, feeling like a mother reprimanding a naughty child. "There's a perfectly rational explanation for all this, isn't there?"

"I was hoping to get an audition for *Showgirls Two*," says Suzy, vainly trying to put her head through the armhole of her sweater.

"You'd have better luck with *Godzilla Returns*," you retort. Suzy giggles in spite of herself, and soon both of you are overcome by the stupidity of the situation and start rolling around on Lindy's bed, laughing hysterically. "What a night," Suzy gasps. "What a fucking night."

"Baby, you have no idea," you wheeze. "And now—woohoo!—I get to put you in a taxi home and make sure you don't collapse in a pool of vomit somewhere."

"Never let it be said that I don't know how to show a girl a good time."

Nick pokes his head around the door and eyes you both curiously. "I met Mark on his way out the door. He said he just peeked in here and saw you rolling around with a half-naked Suzy. So he figured his services were no longer required."

"Oh, shit. Doubleshit. I'm sorry, again . . . ," begins Suzy.

"Oh, forget it." You sigh, too tired and too drunk to contemplate missed opportunities. "Big deal. Any normal guy would have at least offered to join in."

"You said it," says Nick, gazing at you both sprawled on Lindy's bed. He has a definite twinkle in his eye. "Suze, why don't you and your lovely friend come back to my place for a drink? We could play a game of Captives, like when we were kids, remember?"

Suzy giggles again, and you nudge her and ask, "How do you play Captives?"

"Oh, we'll teach you." She grins. "You'll love it, trust us."

The End

It's funny you should ask." Amanda smirks as she puts down a mug in front of you and pours it full of coffee. "The time when Sadie pointed you out in that picture at Mike's . . ."

"Yeah . . . ?"

"She was wondering what I thought of you for that very reason."

You scald your tongue on your first sip of coffee.

"Be careful." Amanda's laughing. That laugh! It's the same as Sadie's, lord god in heaven!

Once the pain has subsided in your mouth, you look at her. "You're joking."

Surely she must be joking. Things like this just don't happen to you.

Amanda shakes her head and tightens the waist tie on her robe again. But not before you see the start of the shadow of her cleavage. "I'm dead serious. We talk about it all the time. I could page her in a while if you're up for it. We have a code word."

"You have a *code* word?"

"Yeah." Amanda takes a sip of the coffee she's poured for herself. Then, looking dissatisfied, she goes to the cupboard and pulls out a bottle of whiskey. She pours a shot's worth into her mug. You push your mug toward her, but she shakes her head. "Not yet. You look like you've had too much already." She screws the cap back on. "But yeah, there are a few guys we've agreed upon, and we made up a code word in case any of them ever brought it up."

"What's the code word?"

"Bosco."

"Bosco?"

"What do you want? We were watching *Seinfeld* reruns when we were thinking of it."

"Who are the other guys?"

"You don't want to know."

"Come on!"

"They're silly."

You stare her down until she caves.

"Steve Buscemi."

"Holy shit. I saw him at a keg party tonight!"

"Get out!"

"I swear." But you know she's never going to believe you. "Who else?"

"Our UPS man."

"No shit!"

"Yup. He's hot. And he's sooooo nice. And he brings us J. Crew packages all the time. What's not to like?" She smiles easily, and you decide you might actually like her. Part of you doesn't want to. Because we all know what a sap you become when you actually like someone. It'll ruin everything.

"So what do you say?" She leans in so close you can smell the whiskey and coffee on her breath. "You *up* for it?"

If you say, "You bet," turn to page 351.

If you say, "I don't know. I think it might be kind of weird," turn to page 352.

You and Sadie find a cozy corner to settle into on the roof and—sheltered from the wind—share the joint you took from Lisa's earlier. The lights of the buildings around you blur as the pot goes to your head, and you feel all of your muscles relax. You slide your arm around Sadie's shoulder and she lets you. Minutes pass, maybe hours, in quiet contentment.

"I'm dizzy." Sadie leans her head on your shoulder.

You think she must be referring to the wonderful sensation of lightness you're feeling—like your brain's wrapped in cotton candy. "I know; isn't it great?"

"I think I'm going to be sick."

"Deep breaths," you say. You're not really registering her discomfort since you yourself are feeling like every breath you take is filling your lungs with sweet air, numbing your teeth and everything else.

Even when Sadie coughs up a tidy clump of puke and it lands on your lap, you're slow on the uptake. You feel a warm sensation through your pants and the effect it has on your groin is not entirely unpleasant.

"I'm sorry." Sadie gets up, wiping chunks from her lips with the back of her hand. In the light, you see a wet streak on her skin. "I've got to go home."

By the time you come down enough to want to deal with Sadie's puke, it's practically encrusted on your pants. Too embarrassed to go back to the party to clean up, you make a swift exit, holding your coat in front of you. Out front, you get a cab.

"Man," the cab driver says as he uses his master controls to open all the car's electric windows, "you stink."

The End

"I'm sure that could be arranged," you say, anxious to indulge this woman's every whim, particularly if it'll eventually involve a little bumping and grinding. "My friend Kurt lives right near here. He's always got stuff around. I bet he can hook us up."

Sadie produces a cellular phone from her bag. "Give it your best shot, superman. I'd be forever indebted to you." You *really* like the sound of that!

Kurt picks up after four rings. "Yo."

You explain your predicament to Kurt. "Get your ass over here if you want some of my Lemon*grass* Chicken so badly." Kurt hangs up. He's paranoid about talking about drugs on the phone.

"Well?" Sadie says.

"Well, if we want it, I have to go get it."

"Let's go," she says, putting the phone back into her bag.

But you're not sure you want to expose her to Kurt this early on in your relationship. This is the kind of guy who was lining up *The Wizard of Oz* with *Dark Side of the Moon* years before any of the reports about the freaky coincidences. If you're not careful, you and Sadie could end up sitting through *Withnail and I* with a Smiths album as the sound track.

If you say, "Let's go," turn to page 345.

If you say, "Don't move; I'll be back in twenty minutes, tops," turn to page 347.

You and Sadie get to Kurt's place without incident. He answers the door and lets you in. "Hey, man," he says, "how's it hanging?" Then he sees Sadie. "Or maybe it's not hanging at all, if you catch my drift."

Sadie, luckily, started coughing and didn't hear him. "Jeez," she whispers to you, "did we just miss the Bob Marley gig?"

The air is so dense with smoke you could carve your initials in it.

"So, once again, you're looking for the Kurtmeister to hook you up, huh?"

"Yeah, well . . ."

"What about you, pretty lady? Our secret safe with you?" Kurt always acts like he's selling every hard drug on the market instead of just grass. Like the DEA has a post in his hallway.

"Absolutely," Sadie says.

"Just enough for a couple of joints, Kurt," you say, "then we'll be on our way. We didn't mean to bother you."

"Bother me? No bother, man. Have a seat and we'll have a smoke together. The bong's the way to go, you know."

Sadie shrugs.

If you say, "I'd love to, but we've really got to get back to this party," turn to page 360.

If you take a seat and encourage Sadie to do the same, turn to page 349.

"More over," you shout, clambering up on the table alongside Suzy.

The audience cheers even louder as you start taking off your shirt.

"Why are you doing this?" demands Suzy, half-annoyed and half-laughing, as you grapple with the zipper on your pants.

"No idea. Hey, Mark, *Mark*!"

Unbelievably, or perhaps inevitably, given the turn the night is taking, he strides up to you both, stands in front, and begins to take off his own shirt, doing a little dance routine straight out of *The Full Monty*. Within a couple of minutes at least half the guests are seminaked, whooping it up, while Lindy and her husband, clearly stoned out of their minds, smile indulgently at everything. The coffee table gives way under the weight of five stripping women, and still nobody flinches. Now Nick is hurtling CDs around the room like Frisbees, and for some reason another guy takes this as a cue to wrench the fire extinguisher off the wall in the kitchen and spray everyone with foam. No wonder it takes ten minutes before anyone hears the cops banging at the door.

Sensing impending doom, Mark drags you and Suzy, and whatever clothes you can pick up off the floor, out the back door and through the neighbors' garden to safety. A taxi pulls up nearby, delivering a posse of unsuspecting guests to the party, and you, Mark, and Suzy hover awkwardly around it.

"Well, I guess you should take Suzy home; she's pretty bombed," says Mark at last. Suzy takes this as her cue to climb in and sprawl out on the backseat. Damn.

"But, ah, I was hoping you'd call me?" He gives you his card, and you hug good night. "It was fun. Wild, but fun."

"Okay, I'll call. Can't guarantee that the police are going to show next time."

"See what you can do." He grins. "Good night."

The End

You practically sprint to your stoner friend Kurt's apartment and quickly get hooked up with a bag of grass and some rolling papers. On the way back to the party, you stop in a deli to pick up a lighter so you've got everything you need. It takes ages for someone to buzz you into the building where the party is, and you're getting more anxious by the minute. You take the stairs to the fifth floor two at a time, stopping for a second before you open the door to the party to catch your breath. You scan the room for Sadie and spy her in a far corner. Boldly, you approach.

She nods an acknowledgment at you as you reach her, and the guy she's talking to pauses briefly midsentence. He continues as she turns her eyes back to him. "So the groom gets up and says he'd like to make a toast, alright? So the whole room is listening, and he tells everyone to look under their seats. So it turns out there are all these envelopes taped under everyone's seats and just as they're opening them and figuring out what they are, the groom says, 'Here's to my best man and my beautiful bride, who've been, excuse my French, fucking each other behind my back.' Only he didn't say, 'Excuse my French,' that was just me trying to be polite in the presence of a lady. So anyway, then he walks out, leaving the bride and the best man there with everyone in the room holding a picture of the two of them in bed together."

"No way!" Sadie says excitedly. "There's no way that happened."

"I swear," her male buddy says. "My friend's cousin was at the wedding."

"Oh, please!" You can't stand to listen to any more of this guy's bullshit, particularly not with Sadie standing there eating it up. "That's just one of those urban legends. I've heard it a thousand times. I've even told it a few times. And the picture's not supposed to be under the chair, it's taped to the bottom of everyone's dinner plate. And he turns to the best man and says, 'Fuck you,' and then to the bride and says, 'Fuck you,' then drinks his champagne, *then* walks out."

"Oh yeah?" The two of you guys, admittedly, might as well have a big colorful splay of feathers sticking out of your butts at this stage. "Well, if you're such a star storyteller let's hear another one of these so-called urban legends of yours."

Sadie crosses her arms across her chest and looks at you.

If you want to tell the urban legend about the two girls who are vacationing together but come home one night to their hotel room at different times, turn to page 356.

If you want to tell the urban legend about the guy flashing his headlights at the car in front of him on a deserted highway, turn to page 357.

If you want to tell the urban legend about the ransacked hotel room and the mysteriously used-up film in the camera, turn to page 358.

You and Sadie settle in on the couch as Kurt readies the bong. The three of you start taking hits from it and, increasingly, you realize that the program on the TV—some PBS kind of special featuring loads of time-lapse photography—is, how do you say, fucking with your head. Then suddenly, Jenna, Kurt's girlfriend, appears, wearing nothing but a black lace bra and thong. You look over at Sadie, half-worried about her reaction, but she's engrossed in the TV show, which is now showing an orange rotting—a few days' time condensed by photography into a few seconds. "Holy shit," you hear her whisper under her breath.

"Enough of this," Kurt says. "*Dazed and Confused* is on pay-per-view." He fumbles with the remote and goes to the schedule for pay-per-view stations. *Dazed and Confused* is in fact on—on channel fifty-nine—with an adult film called *Backdoor Fantasy*, you happen to notice, starting on channel sixty-one. Kurt changes stations numerous times before hitting the AUTH button. Suddenly, the screen is filled with images of a man and a woman having sex doggie-style, another couple up to their own antics in the distance.

"Whoa, dude," Kurt says. "I hit the button on the wrong fucking channel. Jenna, pass me the cordless. I'll call up and change—"

"No, leave it." Jenna sits down next to Kurt and puts her hand down the front of his sweats.

You're afraid to look at Sadie. Afraid of what she thinks of you and your friends. You're also reluctant to turn your attention from the TV, however, because you're totally engrossed by *Backdoor Fantasy*.

Still, this is Sadie. You have to check whether she's uncomfortable. She *has* to be uncomfortable.

Finally, you get up the courage to turn to her. And when you do, she looks at you pointedly, grabs you by the head, and starts to kiss you. Then she straddles you on the couch and starts to unbutton her blouse as she looks over her shoulder to see the TV. You can see her chest rising and falling, her breathing deepening and quickening as her shirt slips off her shoulders to reveal a sheer black bra. Beside you, Kurt and Jenna are touching themselves, and each other, and—hang on a minute here!—Sadie.

What follows is a blur of limbs and orifices, moans and groans, that seems to last for an eternity. Then the next thing you know, you wake up on the couch with Sadie in your arms. Under the blanket you can tell you're naked—both of you—and your mind rushes to re-create last night's activities. But with being high, and *Backdoor Fantasy* and three other people involved, you're not even really sure what actually happened.

Sadie suddenly stirs.

"Morning, sunshine," you say, because it can't have been bad if you ended up in each other's arms on the couch at night's end.

"Oh my god," she says, moving away from you. She lifts her head and looks around the room, then buries it in the pillow. "Find my clothes."

You're no more excited at facing the naked walk across the room than Sadie is, but she keeps her face hidden in the pillow as you get up. You pick up your shorts and slip them on, then gather Sadie's things.

"Do you mind?" she says, when you give her her clothes but don't look away. So you turn.

"Are you okay?" you ask.

"Why wouldn't I be okay?" We all know what that means.

By the time you turn again, Sadie is on her way to the door fully dressed.

"Sadie, wait," you cry out. "What's wrong? Where are you going?"

She turns abruptly at the door. "I'm only going to say this once." She's talking through clenched teeth, and you think she might cry. "I never ever—ever—want to see you again. And if I do see you, I don't want to talk to you or have anything at all to do with you." She slams the door behind her, leaving you standing there in Kurt's apartment—a long way from home—feeling heartbroken, confused, and, well, really really sore. What exactly *did* you do last night?

The End

Amanda pages Sadie and waits for a page in return. Apparently there are code words for the response, too. So when Amanda's beeper starts vibrating and gyrating all over the kitchen table, you're as curious as she is.

"Shit," she says.

"What?"

"It says Drano."

"What does Drano mean?"

"She's got her period. You know, Drano, clogged . . ."

"Okay, okay, I get it." Women can be a little too graphic sometimes.

"Sorry."

"But hey . . ." You take a minute to double-check what you know about menstruation, then decide you can proceed. "You two live together, right, and you're twins. Shouldn't you have yours, too?"

Amanda gets up and looks at the calendar on the front of the refrigerator. "Oh, god, no."

"What?"

"I'm late." She starts pacing. "I'm never late."

"I'm sure it's nothing."

"No, me and John, when we first got back together. We didn't use . . ." She trails off. "Oh, my god. What am I going to do? We've only been together again a few weeks and this'll, god, *this'll freak him out*."

"I should go," you say. "You probably want to be alone, or call somebody."

"Yeah, sorry," Amanda answers, so you head for the door. Preoccupied, she doesn't offer the address of the party, and you can hardly ask her for it! Not that it even matters. You're not going to get lucky with Sadie tonight, her having her period and all. Not that that's the point, you dog. In fact, a part of you is even relieved. Pregnancy stories always freak you out. You end up going home for lack of anything else to do.

The End

"You men are all the same."

You always prickle at statements like that, and this is no exception. "And just what in the hell is that supposed to mean?"

"You're all talk." She writes something on a pad of paper on the table, then rips it off and hands it to you. "Here, that's where my sister is."

"But—"

"Oh, just go on and get out of here and try whatever little seduction routine you think you've perfected over the years on Sadie. *That'll* work."

"Wait," you say. "Maybe I want to reconsider . . ."

"Get out of here." Amanda's already pushing you toward the door and opening it. "I wouldn't even want you now." She closes the door in your face.

Dejected, fuming mad, and unbelievably horny all at once, you crumple the piece of paper up in your hand once you're out on the street and hurl it at the sidewalk; the gesture is an unsatisfactory outlet for your emotions. You go to the store on the corner and buy a pack of cigarettes and wander the streets aimlessly, chain-smoking. You smoke yourself sick, then go home.

No matter what you do, no matter where you go—and whether or not the opportunity for twins arises again—you will regret this night for the rest of your life.

The End

Say anything about you?" Amanda puts a mug on the table in front of you and pours it full of coffee. "To hear her talk, you two are practically married. Milk and sugar's right there."

You dump two spoonfuls of sugar into your coffee and regard Amanda suspiciously. "Really?"

"My god, yeah." Amanda gets up. "Follow me."

She walks down a long narrow hall and opens up a door. You follow her into a dark room. "I hope you're prepared for this," she says, then she switches on a light.

You're standing right in front of what amounts to a shrine to you, covering about half of the largest wall in what must be Sadie's bedroom. You look at Amanda, and you're clearly horrified.

"I know." She nods her head solemnly. "I've never been sure what to do about it. Maybe there's something you can do to put an end to it."

You step up to examine the wall more closely and find everything from joke E-mails you've sent out to people who then forwarded them to Sadie, to pictures of you from your high-school yearbook. You didn't even know Sadie then. There's a ticket stub from *Starship Troopers*, which you saw with a huge group of people including Sadie, and a lock of hair that's frighteningly like yours in color and texture. There's a bottle of your cologne, a small jar that looks like it's holding fingernail clippings, and—if you're not mistaken—a pair of your underwear. How on earth!

"You didn't know . . ." Amanda speaks softly as she steps up beside you.

"I had no idea." You don't know whether you feel like crying or running for your life. You're thoroughly creeped out. "What do I do?"

"I don't know. But you can't let her find out I showed you. She'll kill me."

"You don't really mean—"

"No, I don't think so. But I'm worried about her . . ."

You just stare at the shrine, your mouth agape.

"I didn't mean to freak you out." Amanda switches off the light. "Come on. You should get out of here." On the way to the front door she picks up her wallet and takes out her card and hands it to you. "Call me at work and we can maybe think of what to do, okay?"

You find your way home and make sure all doors lock behind you. You don't turn on any lights in your apartment, and you look out all of your windows—standing several steps back, of course—before fumbling to undress in the dark and falling into bed, wide-eyed. Hours later, you fall into a troubled sleep and have a dream that you're a Latino pop singer.

The End

You tap in *buze,* then close your eyes and offer up a silent prayer. But the omnipotent being is not on your side right now—a message flashes about third consecutive incorrect password, and Suzy's card is swallowed by the ATM. Damn. Before reconciling yourself to going home, you check Suzy's wallet one more time to see if there's anything else of use in there.

And there, stuck between her driver's license and seldom-used library card, is five bucks. Not enough to get you a taxi anywhere, but enough, you reason, for one last drink in your local bar, the Pub, a short walk away.

Turn to page 179.

"Alright," you begin, shooting a challenging look at Sadie's companion. "*This happened to a friend of mine's cousin.* She was on vacation in some resort in the Caribbean with a friend and they were out drinking in one of the hotel bars one night, but her friend got tired and decided to go up and go to bed. But since she'd met a few people, this girl felt like staying awhile longer and having another drink. So her friend goes up to go to bed, and she follows maybe two hours later. She doesn't want to wake up her friend, so she just feels her way around in the dark, slips off her shoes and shorts, and falls into bed. She's had a few so she falls asleep really quickly and sleeps pretty heavily. So in the morning she wakes up, and she looks over at her friend's bed and there's blood everywhere and her friend is obviously dead—stabbed like a hundred times. And written in blood on the wall of the room, it says, 'Aren't you glad you didn't turn the lights on.' "

"Woah," Sadie's friend says. "That is pretty cool. I'll give you that much."

"I think it's just awful," Sadie says. "I can't believe you go around telling such a horrible story. I'm going to have nightmares tonight, thanks to you."

Sadie storms off in a huff and you never talk to her again.

The End

O kay," you begin, shooting a challenging look at Sadie's companion. "*This happened to my cousin's friend.* She was driving cross-country, on her way out to grad school—alone—and she's on this deserted highway at night."

"I don't like it already," Sadie says. "I don't want to hear it. I'll see you later."

You watch, stunned, as she walks off and joins another group.

"Well, are you going to tell the story or not?"

"No offense, but I don't really see the point now."

"Trying to woo Sadie, are we?"

"Kind of." Are you that easily read?

"Well then you should do your research, man. Sadie's sister's car once broke down on a highway and she was basically kidnapped and brutalized for days. Besides, she's got the hots for Leo over there. They've already been out a few times."

You spend the rest of the night composing an apology to Sadie in your head, but you never get to deliver it. She's engulfed in conversation with this Leo person, and they leave together before long.

You find the rest of your group and somehow—you're sketchy on the details because you started pounding beers after your Sadie fuck-up—you end up escorting a puking girl home. By the time you get to your own place, you're stone-cold sober and reek of beer, cigarettes, and puke. You decide to take a shower and find out you've got no hot water. Then again, that cold water could come in handy.

The End

"Alright," you begin, shooting a challenging look at Sadie's companion. "*This happened to a friend of mine's cousin*. He was on vacation and spent a long day on the beach. So when he gets back to his hotel room, everything's been thrown all over the place and he figures he's been robbed. But as he goes through everything, he realizes nothing's missing. Strangely, however, he notices that the roll of film in his camera has been used up. He rewinds it, throws it in with other used-up rolls of film, and reloads the camera. So he finishes his vacation without incident and goes home and gets the film developed. He's obviously a little curious to see what's on the mystery roll of film. So he gets all his pictures back and he's flipping through them and sure enough, he gets to the mystery pictures, all of which contain a naked man, in various positions, with this guy's toothbrush up his ass."

"Oh, my *god*," Sadie shrieks. "That is dis*gus*ting. Will you tell it again? There's someone I want to gross out."

"Sure, I guess." This worked better than you expected.

"Come with me."

Sadie says good-bye to her male companion, then pulls you across the room. She introduces you to her friend Alyssa. "He just told me a story I want you to hear." Sadie urges you along with her eyes, and you launch into the toothbrush tale again. Only this time you decide to spruce it up a little. You say it happened to your brother. And end with the fact that he ended up getting hepatitis, but only hepatitis A, so it wasn't fatal.

"That's it," Alyssa says. "I've had it with so-called civilization. I'm going to find some remote house in the woods where I grow my own food and everything. Either that or I'm going to start wearing a gas mask and rubber gloves and carrying my own utensils and toilet paper and everything everywhere."

"See, I knew I'd get a rise out of her," Sadie says good-naturedly, turning to you.

"Glad to be able to entertain you," Alyssa says. "Just don't come crying to me in my cabin in the woods when some psycho gets a hold of *your* toothbrush."

"Oh, it's not even a true story." Sadie shoves her friend with her hip in an unbelievably endearing girlish gesture. God, she's gorgeous. And the way those hips can *move*!

"Tell her," she says, nudging you. "It's just a stupid urban legend."

"Yup," you say. "It is."

"You two are quite a pair," Alyssa says, and you and Sadie look at each other.

You say, "We are, aren't we?" and smile.

"You think?" She laughs that laugh that makes you want to curl up to her like she's a hot-water bottle.

"I think." You step toward her and place a gentle kiss on her forehead. She looks up at you and says, "We're going to get married, you know. I've just had that feeling everyone always talks about. The knowing."

"Good," you say, because you feel it, too. "Because I feel it, too. You want another beer?"

"Sure."

The End

"Wow, that was a great escape," Sadie says. "But I don't want to wait to smoke this back at the party. Where can we go?"

"Follow me," you say, remembering the roof on Josh's building. A few floors up, you prop the roof door open so you don't get stuck up there. You sit down on a low ledge.

"Shit," Sadie says, searching through her bag as you roll a joint. "I thought I had matches."

"That's okay," you say. "I've got a lighter."

She smiles, then cuddles up next to you. It's starting to get chilly out. Huddled together, you smoke a joint, and Sadie's body seems to mold into yours. After a while—when an amazing sense of peace has overtaken you—she says, "Let's go."

"I'm feeling pretty mellow now. You think the party's still going strong?" you ask.

"I was thinking of just going back to my place."

"Oh," you say, and you apparently sound dejected. Have you come all this way for nothing?

"Hey," she says, lifting your chin and stepping up to you. "I thought maybe you'd come with me."

"I'd like that," you say, and the two of you head back downstairs.

"Let's just walk," Sadie says. "It's only five blocks."

"Here," you say. "Take my shirt." You strip off your long-sleeved shirt, braving the crisp air with just a T-shirt.

"You think of everything," she says.

"I try," you say.

"No, it was kind of a question," she says, nodding in the direction of a twenty-four-hour drugstore. "Did you *think of everything*?"

The two of you duck in to buy condoms arm in arm.

The End